The Rescue

S L ROSEWARNE

The Rescue

Copyright © S L Rosewarne 2022

ISBN 978-1-912009-34-3
First published 2022 by Compass-Publishing UK

Typeset by The Book Refinery Ltd
www.TheBookRefinery.com
Cover artwork by © Tammy Barrett

A CIP catalogue record for this book is available from the British Library.

To Pip and Moll. Of course.

1

'She's very bright you know,' Pip said to everyone when I was little. He may have been biased, but it was still gratifying to have my intelligence acknowledged.

He still said it now, five years on; most recently on their wedding anniversary, when we had a day out to our favourite beach. A little boy mis-hit a tennis ball which landed nearby and bounced over to me. I stood guard over it, my eyes fixed on the boy as he ran over.

'He looks like he's talking!' The boy laughed. 'He's saying it's mine now.'

Pip smiled, reached over and threw the ball back to him. 'She speaks great English. She just pretends she doesn't. She's very bright, you know.'

The little boy rushed off but that day has stayed with me since, because it was a perfect reminder of how happy we were. You know those pictures of a couple wandering along a beach, where the sky is blue and the sea is calm and it's sunny and everything's perfect? Well, that's how it was, on that unseasonably warm day in May.

Pip never liked walking far, so he drove to the car park nearest the sea, while Suki and I took the longer route, along the clifftop, and met him on the beach. The cove was long and narrow and when the tide was out there was a vast expanse of smooth, unmarked sand that was perfect for running and chasing on. No one else there; no paw prints or footprints, just a few seagulls waddling along the shoreline.

Suki and I ran along the edge of the sea, chasing the wavelets that chattered to us as we splashed in the shallows. I barked and barked, and ran in circles, I loved it so much and I was so happy to have a whole day with the three of us. It was like old times, when I was little and Pip wasn't poorly.

When we'd tired ourselves out, we ran up the beach to where Pip was sitting on a blanket. We collapsed, scattering sand everywhere, and lay listening to the sound of the waves lapping the sand, saying, "Welcome, Moll. Happy anniversary, Pip and Suki."

Pip and Suki held hands and laughed as they ate their sandwiches. Creamy egg mayonnaise that got caught in my whiskers, and tangy cheese and pickle. I got the crusts and a bit more and Pip produced a little bottle of wine which they shared. I had a bit of wine on the end of Pip's finger but it tasted sour and I didn't like it much.

After lunch, we lay on the blanket and looked up at the clear sky above, listened to a curlew crying on the rocks, to the distant roar of the sea. The tide had gone out a long way since we arrived and I could hear the voices of the little boy's family who'd set up camp the other end of the beach. They'd lit a barbecue and the tantalising smell of beef burgers and sausages wafted over, but I knew I must stick with Pip and Suki today, so we stretched out in the sunshine and my nose twitched while we had a snooze. I loved hearing about how they met. I had heard this story many a time, but I never grew tired of it, as it changed slightly with every telling.

'I'll never forget the first time I met you,' Pip said with a deep chuckle.

Her laugh was musical and high. 'How could I forget?' she said, snuggling closer. 'It was your eyes that got me; those pale blue eyes that turned dark blue when you looked at me.'

He wrapped an arm around her, pulled her close. 'I was living on White Heather, my oyster fishing boat, and I was content, or thought I was. I'd go to work, go to the pub, go to bed – and do it all again the next day.' He paused to sip his wine. 'And then one day, I called in to see a friend, and who should be sitting in his cottage but a girl with a headful of dark curls.'

She giggled. 'We got talking and Becky asked you to give me a lift to the Celtic village the next day.'

'That's right. And I went to pick you up and you were running round doing all the chores so we were late getting there.'

'And we talked and talked and went for a drink...'

'And then we had supper in the pub the next day. And I took you to see the workshop where I made our jewellery.'

'And I took Becky's dog for protection!'

'Then you had to go home but I wrote to you and asked you down the next weekend.'

Suki laughed. 'That's right. I was very touched to get that letter. You said, "Don't worry about being cold on the boat. I have a hot water bottle and it's called Pip". I remember telling a friend and said, "isn't that sweet?" And she looked at me and said, "Suki. He doesn't *have* a hot water bottle!"'

Pip kissed her nose. 'It got you down here, though, didn't it?'

'It certainly did,' Suki said.

'I never thought you'd come,' Pip continued. 'But you did and we stayed up all night on the boat, talking and drinking.' His voice faded away and I waited. The next bit was great.

'I never realised how much you would change my life,' Pip said, sounding dreamy. He smelt of ripe camembert. Delicious and happy and creamy. 'I was fifty and I'd never been in love before.'

'I never thought I'd get married,' said Suki, and love bounced off her like spring sunlight.

Pip laughed. 'I didn't either, but I decided to propose to you that Good Friday...'

'And I was in a bad mood because I thought we were going to work on the boat again but you insisted we went, and we climbed inside the frames of the boat, and then you went down on one knee and asked me to marry you!'

'And you burst into tears and I thought, oh no, I've blown it!'

'But I said yes and we went to the pub and met Michael and he took us back to their place for a drink. And then we went out on the punt for a trip down the river to celebrate,' Suki said. 'We ran away to get married in Gibraltar, and never looked back.' She sighed contentedly. I could always sense emotions. I could smell their togetherness, which was like a beef-scented casserole of happiness: I could taste and touch their joy in the air around me. I felt warm and secure in their love, for I knew it led to me coming into their lives.

Suki sat up and reached for the wine, took a sip. 'Do you remember, that first weekend on the boat, you said you'd teach me how to make toast in return for sex?'

He nodded, his eyes crinkling as blue as the spring sky.

'Your toaster was an old wire coat hanger, bent in a diamond shape,' she said, stroking his beard. 'You put a piece of bread on it, balanced it over the the single flame burner and singed your fingers.' She smiled. 'It worked though, didn't it?'

He laughed. 'And then you went on to write about it for that boating magazine. The editor must have had a laugh!'

'I think that's why he commissioned it,' she said. 'We've had some wonderful times, darling. Just think, we've been married twelve years.'

Pip raised his glass. 'And here's to many more.' He caressed my ears, silky and soft. 'With this one too.'

'Of course. How could we ever forget the day Moll came into our lives?' She tickled my tummy. 'You came over from Ireland, Moll,' she said proudly. I knew this of course, but I still liked hearing it. 'The farmer had gone over there to buy some ponies, but he brought you back too, and we found you at a farm near Chacewater.' She paused. 'I wonder if you remember, Moll?'

Of course I remembered, though it was five years ago, so it was a bit hazy. I dimly recalled the constant movement, the sharp smell of frightened horses neighing and whimpering, stamping on the wooden floor next door while we lay in a big cage in a tangled, frightened heap, feeling sick as we tried to take comfort from each other's uncertain warmth.

Finally we stopped and were emptied out into a huge container with high wooden walls and sweet prickly straw on the floor – the relief of seeing daylight, of rolling in that loose box! We tumbled and fought, ecstatic at our release, not thinking about what lay ahead.

My brothers gradually disappeared, then one day, two people came in; an older man and a young woman. I could smell their hesitation. The man crouched down in front of us. He smelt kind and gentle. He picked me up, very carefully, and I fitted perfectly into the warm palm of his huge hand. He stroked my belly tenderly with a large finger and looked up at the woman and his uncertain smell vanished. 'If you want a dog, you should get this one,' he said, in a deep voice that made me feel safe.

'Are you sure?' Her voice was higher, and she smelt powdery. They played with us a bit, and she picked me up but her hands smelt nervous, as if she was afraid she'd drop me. She held me very carefully, against the soft warmth of her jumper and I could smell hope oozing from her.

They came back the next day, to take me with them. When I saw their car my ears and tail drooped and I weed because it was all so strange and confusing, but we got in and I sat cradled in his big warm hands that smelt of sun-baked wood and metal.

When we finally stopped, through the open window I could smell salt blown in on a warm wind. They carried me into a house and he placed me gently on the carpet. I staggered forward, my legs unsure all of a sudden, and she bent down, picked me up.

'Hello Mollie,' she said, gazing into my eyes. She stroked my tummy very carefully, and I wasn't sure what she meant. Mollie? Was this my name?

'Mollie McGinty,' he said with a warm rumble of laughter. 'You're going to live here now.'

Well, I'd kind of gathered that: I wasn't stupid. But they were looking at me with such a blast of warmth and joy that I didn't know what to do. So I had another wee.

They laughed and took me outside, exclaiming, 'Look at her fat little tummy!'

'Isn't she gorgeous?'

'Her coat's so white, and her ears so black.'

'And her beautiful dark eyes – look at those eyelashes!'

'She's just perfect,' he said, and it brought tears to my nose the way he said it.

And that was the beginning of five years of getting to know each other. We went to school, where Pip and Suki learned how to be responsible dog owners. I learned silly tricks like Stay, Wait, Sit and Come (when I felt like it).

From the start, Pip realised that I understood. 'She knows what we're saying, have you noticed?' he said. 'Every single word.'

Everyone we met, out walking, would admire me. I am good looking, though I say it myself, and he would say, "she's very bright you know. She speaks very good English." And because I was such a quick learner, I heard him say one night, "You know Suki, I reckon Moll is up to A Level standard now." He said it very seriously, and I preened, though I had no idea what an A Level was. Suki laughed and said, "Darling, I know she's clever, but she's not even three months old yet. It's a bit early for A levels!"

We had so many firsts together. My first trip to the beach, where the sand was fine and pale and didn't get stuck in between my pads. My first swim, when the waves were small and pretty and whispered to me. I was so excited I did a little wee.

Our first long walk, along the cliffs where the sea rumbled far below us. My first trip to the pub and a sip of beer which was acrid and horrible. But the salty sharpness of a packet of crisps made up for it. My first rabbit leg, discovered on a walk at Trelissick. I carried it the whole way round, chewing as we went: I would *not* drop it for anyone. I got terrible guts ache, but it was worth it. The first time I met my beloved Titch (more of him later), the first (and only) time I had sex – so many wonderful firsts.....

From talking to other dogs, I learned that their owners could be quite soppy with them, but often weren't very soppy with each other. Pip was different. He wasn't shy about telling Suki he loved her, even though he was older than her. Or perhaps because he was older. And he didn't just tell her, he drew little pictures and put them in her lunch box when she went to work. He cooked for her. He was always thinking of things that would make her laugh, and he said how much he loved her, every day.

After we'd all had tea, the three of us sat on the sofa watching TV while they held hands. Every night.

She bought cards and wrote little messages for him, which she left on his pillow, or at work. When he got cancer, I was only a tiny pup, and she read up on his illness and talked to a nurse on the phone when he was out. She never made a fuss, but she was always quietly on his case. Doing everything she could to make his life better. Showing how much she loved him.

Sometimes he looked up from whatever he was doing and said, 'I love you Suki,' and she grinned and said, 'how much?' and he held his arms out wide and said, 'this much,' and then she held out her arms even wider, and said, 'but I love you this much!' and they laughed and hugged and had this game trying to outdo the other one about how much they loved each other.

And I was always part of it. Every day, they told me how much they loved me too. Pip even drew some pictures of me. He called them cartoons, and my favourite one was of me running along with my ears flying out behind me. Suki put them in frames and hung them in the living room so whenever people came in, they saw the real me, and the cartoon me on the walls. He also took a photograph of me in her arms when

I was a tiny pup, and called it "my darling girls' and said it was his favourite. I kind of liked being famous.

I never thought I would love people like I loved these two. It was quite a nostril opener. It made me feel vulnerable in case anything happened to them, but at the same time love gave me this incredible strength and joy. I felt I could run from here to anywhere, if one of them needed me, and I would save them.

The trouble was, when Pip became so poorly, so quickly, I soon learned that saving him wasn't that easy. It was out of my paws.

Not long after I arrived, Pip was diagnosed with cancer, and he was very ill and had to have injections which hurt him and he smelt of chemicals and fear, but then the smell gradually went, and he started coming out for walks and stuff. He was much better, apparently, which called for lots of beer.

But about two months ago he started smelling sour and damp again, and that smell got worse until it invaded the whole house and I could hardly breathe. He couldn't eat which was most unlike him, and he got very weak and couldn't get out of bed, and eventually Suki cried and made a phone call, and shut me in the kitchen while two big men came and they were very kind and jolly from what I could hear, but they took Pip away with them.

She went too, but came back very late that night and she smelt so desperate, and sounded so unhappy, I licked and licked her hand to take away all that nastiness. Then when she bent down, tears dripping on my fur, I licked her face. She seemed to like that, for she said, 'Oh, Moll, what are we going to do? Thank God I've got you.'

I didn't understand, but I knew something bad had happened, and fear crept down my spine and into my fur. My whiskers twitched while I thought, fast. I might not have known what was going on, but I knew I had to look after Suki. And that was quite a responsibility. Not every dog could rise to the challenge, but I would be an example to other dogs. Show them how to do it.

But as the days and weeks passed, I realised, with a sinking feeling that smelt like rotten eggs, that loving someone and being brave wasn't enough to save them, no matter how hard I tried. Suki visited Pip every afternoon and came back smelling of chemicals and something that wasn't Pip but smelt faintly of him. He got a bit better, and her footsteps were lighter as she came round the corner. Then the next week, her footsteps were heavy with dread and I began to fear the worst.

'Pip looks awful, hooked up to all these machines,' she said as we walked round the block one night. 'We saw his consultant, and he said that Pip's got pneumonia on top of everything else.' She gulped. 'His lungs are filling up with water.' She carried on walking, so I trotted beside her, wishing I could take away her pain.

'And he's being so brave, but I can't bear to see him like this, and I bet he's really frightened.' She paused. 'They said they could put him on a ventilator or life support but he'd hate that. So they said he's only got a couple of days left, poor darling.'

I didn't understand what she was saying. Lungs? Water? Days left? But we walked on and after a little while she smelt a bit calmer. She gave a big sigh as we got to the beach where the tide was coming in with small, hesitant waves. 'In a way it's a relief, to think he won't suffer any more,' she said. 'And just think, I've had fourteen years with him. You've had five. Aren't we lucky?'

We didn't feel lucky now. It was Christmas Day and Pip had come home but he wasn't like the man I used to know. There was no flesh on him, and he smelt of decay; a sharp smell mixed with rotten chicken. I was really worried and I nipped the nurse who came in and gave him an injection. She yelped, which I thought served her right, but Suki told me off. 'She's here to help, Moll,' she said, and she sounded so upset that I had to back off.

Perhaps she was right, for the nurse smelt kind, like warm milk, and propped Pip up in bed, making him comfortable

While Suki and the nurse went to the kitchen to make some drinks, Pip turned to me. 'I'm frightened, Moll,' he whispered. 'I don't want to leave you.'

Leave us? Where was he going?

'Suki's too young to be a widow. After I've gone, promise me you'll look after her, make sure she's happy.'

What was he talking about? How could he go? Where? All these thoughts spun around my head, down to my whiskers that twitched frantically. I could smell how ill he was, but surely he'd get better? That was what the nurse was for, wasn't it? I'd never felt helpless before but now I panicked. There must be something, *anything* I could do to help him.

I nudged him with my nose, gave a yip to say, 'Of course,' and my ears flattened as I thought about what he'd said. How would we manage without him? This big strong man was so much a part of my life, even though he had faded to a skeleton. This gentle giant who always smelt so kind and loving until he smelt of chemicals and sickness. I burrowed my nose underneath his hand, trying to compose myself, then I heard his voice, growing fainter now.

'You'll look after her, won't you? Promise?'

I licked and licked his hands, then his face, as if I could lick him back to life, for I could see he was fading fast.

He looked up as Suki arrived in the doorway holding a package. 'Your Christmas present, darling.'

He tried to smile, but I could smell the effort.

'Shall I unwrap it?'

He nodded, and she kissed him, sat down on the bed and tore the package open. Inside was a mobile phone: one of the newest ones, that she'd ordered ages ago. Before he'd become so poorly. Gently, she handed it over. 'Happy Christmas, my darling.' Her voice cracked.

He took it with a look of awe, turned it over, and whispered, 'Thank you.' He held it and closed his eyes and lay there with this phone on his chest. What could he do with it now? Why hadn't it arrived earlier so he could have used it? I nuzzled him with my nose. Already his spirit was going. It wouldn't be long now.

We lay on the bed together, me and Suki and Pip. She held him, and said, 'I'll always love you, darling, and wherever you go, Moll and I will always be with you. I promise.' And I nudged her and licked his hand which held the phone that he'd never use. And it was just the three of us, as it always had been. Until his breathing stopped, ever so gently.

And then it was just the two of us.

2

I'd thought that once someone died, life would be like falling off a cliff: there'd be nothing. But after Pip died, Suki was incredibly busy. Friends were always ringing up, or arriving with potfuls of stew or bowlfuls of curry. Plates of chocolate brownies (yum) and biscuits. Bunches of flowers.

Then this small fellow with a long white beard came but he smelt kind and he sat on the sofa and talked in a very calm, soft voice. He said he'd known Pip for a very long time, and he was going to Conduct the Wake, whatever that meant.

Suki rang all the people who'd been in the same jazz band as Pip, and they said they'd like to play for him. Then one day, a few weeks later, she parked outside a building, went in and emerged with a big green cardboard box. 'Here's Pip,' she said, putting the box on the passenger seat.

I sniffed the box curiously, but it didn't smell of him. It looked heavy, from the way she carried it and I wondered how they'd managed to fit him in there? A small box for such a big man. Still, it was nice to think he was back with us, even though we couldn't see him. Or smell him. Or taste him.

Later we went to this big room and all Suki's family were there: her mum and her brothers and their wives, and lots and lots of people I'd never met, and they all wore really bright colours and there were lots of my dog friends there too. That was fun – we had a chase around the room but Suki said "No," sharply so we stopped and sat by our People and listened.

The man with the long white beard talked about Pip, and Suki cried so I jumped on her lap and she held me and the tears dripped onto my back and drenched my fur but I was brave and put up with it.

Then five people stood up on a stage and played this really loud music that hurt my ears, but Suki clapped and cried and so did lots of others and then they started singing and that was a bit much, but it made her happy, so I shut my ears and thought of biscuits.

And then it was over and they clapped again and Suki stood up and said, 'Everyone's welcome to come to the Star and Garter for refreshments.' And she picked up the big green box and said, 'Come on darling, mustn't be late for your party.'

We all went to the pub and stayed for ages and there were sandwiches and pasties and cream teas and everyone drank and ate and I had some pasty crumbs and bits of scone and crisps and I was having a great time until someone went up to Suki and said, 'Your dog's just eaten a whole bowlful of pate, is that all right?' And she came and took me for a walk round the block and I was a bit sick.

Finally we went home and it was very late and we fell into bed but I knew that tomorrow I had to start thinking about how to fulfil my promise to Pip.

Suki had many talents but, unlike me, she had never been overly interested in food. I mean, she enjoyed eating, but as Pip once said, 'you eat to live rather than live to eat, don't you, darling?'

She told me that she used to do the cooking, before I came along, but after five days of eating mince every night, Pip gently suggested they eat something else, and she said, 'Like what?'

After that, she said, he took over the cooking, though they did go shopping together and she did the washing up, so it suited them both well.

Now, with no one to cook for her, it was just as well that people were leaving her food, or she would have forgotten to eat. But I could foresee trouble ahead. She would have to learn to cook, or – I had a sudden brainwave – perhaps this was what Pip meant! I had to find another man who could cook for her.

Congratulating myself on my forethought, every time we went to the fields where we met lots of other dog walkers, I kept my nose and whiskers primed. There were more women than men, but I zoomed in on the men to check them out. If they smelt of food, that was good. If not there was no chance.

Trouble was, the men usually had partners, so I had to sniff them very carefully. I ran over to them, so Suki had to call me (I would play deaf) and then come over so they could meet. But when anyone saw her reddened face, her sunken eyes and her unbrushed hair, they headed off in the opposite direction faster than you could say 'biscuit'.

After a week or so, I realised it wasn't going to be as easy as I'd thought. To start with, there weren't many men, and none of them smelt of food. But more to the point, how on earth could I replace someone like Pip? Let alone anyone who could cook. Then there was the added problem of Suki. All she did was cry.

She cried in bed, and that exhausted her so much that getting her out of bed was difficult. More often than not, I had to pull the duvet off her with my teeth. She cried when she got up, when she looked at that phone of his, when she tried to eat something and when she listened to music on the radio. In short, she cried all the time. Endless tears that fell in a ceaseless river at all times of day and night. She was blotchy faced and her eyes almost disappeared from so much crying. Luckily she remembered to feed me, but it seemed that she couldn't eat more than a few mouthfuls herself before she pushed the plate aside.

I overheard friends whisper behind her back, concerned about her. 'She's too young to be a widow,' said one. 'She's only forty-two.'

'Poor lass. That's what comes of marrying someone so much older. I mean, he was over sixty, wasn't he?'

I tuned out after that. I mean, what did it matter how old they were? The important thing was how much they loved each other.

'Come on, Suki,' a friend said when we went round there for supper one night. 'Try to eat a bit more.'

'My throat just tightens up,' she replied. 'The food won't go down.'

'Poor thing. Never mind. Have a glass of wine.' Anne poured her a glass of red wine and we sat and listened to the murmur of the radio in the background. 'What about work?' Anne said.

Suki shook her head. 'I can't concentrate. Honestly, Anne, it's awful. My editor's given me a few weeks off but I can't *afford* to have time off. I need the money. I can't just *not* work. Pip was broke so it's not like I'm going to inherit anything. I've decided I'm going back next week. I have to.'

Anne opened her mouth and shut it again. She got up to clear the table and Suki helped while I hung around, hoping I could eat the leftovers. No chance. 'Shall we play a game?' Anne said. We usually did when we went round there.

Suki shook her head. 'Sorry, Anne. I'm not really very good company. I'd better go home.'

'No,' said Anne quickly. 'We'll watch a film. Something cheery,' she added.

We stayed and watched a film but halfway through someone had an accident and had to go to hospital and Suki wept on Anne's shoulder. Great wracking sobs that sounded as if she was splitting apart. I cuddled close, but I felt powerless. How could anyone cope with so much grief?

At first I could still smell a bit of Pip on the sofa. On his clothes, but they were hanging up, so I had to stand on my back legs and sniff hard. His shoes still smelt faintly of him: there was a pair in the hall and I would lie on them sometimes. He was everywhere and then gradually nowhere. But his presence hovered. I would turn round in the kitchen expecting to see him. Or wait by the door for him to come in.

Suki talked to me a lot, particularly when we were out walking. I think it helped her deal with missing him. I missed him too, of course, but I think dogs are more pragmatic than humans. I learned that word the other day and I really liked it. I am a Pragmatic Dog. It sounded important, and it was.

It meant, basically, that although we dogs mourned just as much, and it was really painful, we knew that it was part of life, and we just had to get on with things. Sniffing, eating, weeing, pooing, chasing, treats, walks: the essentials of life.

I did miss Pip terribly, especially first thing in the morning. I always had my breakfast while he had his first cup of tea and we watched breakfast news on the telly together. It was how we first bonded, and how we cemented our bond. It was our way of starting the day together, just us two, and made me feel very special and content.

Although I felt his loss like a great ache in my stomach, of course I still had Suki. She wasn't as cuddly as he was (and she was getting thinner by the day which didn't suit her) but she did her best, and I knew how much she loved me.

But it emphasised, now that one half of my People were gone, that I had to look after Suki all the more. No way had I wanted to lose Pip, but what would happen if I lost Suki as well? It didn't bear thinking about. I wouldn't say I was anxious, but it did make me realise that I must be wary, and plan ahead. I had to look after her, as I'd promised, for she clearly wasn't coping on her own. I had to find her another partner. The pressure was on.

One morning the telly in the kitchen stopped working. This was the one that Pip and I always watched, so it was extra special. He liked watching it while he cooked, and I hung around getting little scraps of carrot, or bacon or cheese while he made their tea, and I gave him tips about herbs and spices and so on. Us dogs have a much finer sense of smell than humans.

When this television stopped working, Suki howled as if the end of the world had come. I knew how she felt. It was yet another link with Pip that had been unfairly severed.

But after I'd licked and licked her to calm down, it got me thinking: scrub the cooking idea, what she needed was a practical man. Someone who could repair broken televisions, chop wood and mend locks: all the essential things that Pip used to do.

The trouble was, Suki was still weeping and blotchy faced, and I hadn't had any luck finding a man, let alone one that could cook. How on earth could I find one that could mend things?

I would seek advice in the local community, I decided, while I waited for Suki to recover. Surely one of my friends would know of some man who wanted a lovely partner like Suki? And surely, most men could mend things, couldn't they?

So I laid my plans. I left messages sprayed on all the local notice boards: by the post box, at the junction at the end of our road, on the corner by the shop, all of which I knew were visited by many dogs every day.

Of course, when we went to the fields or somewhere with other people dog walking, I would run ahead and sniff everyone out just in case. There was one tall fellow who smelt gorgeously of bacon, but he was very fat and so was his pug. In fact, they were so big they could hardly walk, so that wouldn't have been much good for me and Suki, for we loved our walks.

Another fellow turned up with his lurcher in a van that had MJ Handyman written on the outside. I couldn't read it, but a friend of Suki's did and said, 'he might be useful for you, Suki. What about the dripping tap in your bathroom? And your telly?'

My spirits rose and I thought yes! But at the mention of the telly, her face smelt all sad and hot and she started crying again. I went up to sniff the man. He was called Martin, and his lurcher was Bingo, and he smelt of metal and wire and wood and cheese and pickle sarnies. An interesting mixture. Good for fixing stuff.

Suki's friend spoke to him about a job she needed doing, and he gave her his card, and I thought, well, you never know, he could be useful. But I had a feeling he wouldn't be. Still, I was determined to keep trying.

Those next few months were very hard for us both. I dragged Suki out to the pub to meet her friends as I didn't want her staying in all the time. At least she'd *got* friends. She also went back to work and I went with her. I had my own bed in the office which was a short walk away, in Falmouth, but most of the time she sat staring at her screen, doing nothing, and then she'd go to the loo and cry there, and when she came back her editor usually said, 'Take the rest of the day off, Suki. Don't worry.'

But she did worry. She couldn't work and we needed the money.

The weather didn't help, of course, because it was very wet and that made everyone miserable. This was winter, and it rained a lot in Cornwall. Neither of us liked getting wet, but we went out anyway, and one day she shouted at the sky, 'I've proved I can manage on my own. Can he come back now. Please?' That sort of thing was terrible to hear, but I knew how she felt.

I learned that her needs varied from day to day, hour to hour, minute to minute. I noticed she became careful about who she spent time with. Some people couldn't cope with all her crying. Some people wanted to hug her, and as she told me, 'The trouble is, they're not Pip, and he's the only one I really want to hug.'

The other day she turned to me and said, 'Moll, how can he be *dead*? Have I just mislaid him, like my car keys? I can still feel his presence here, and I worry because I don't want him to go.' She mopped her eyes and added, 'I keep thinking he's going to come in the door and I'll jump into his arms and you'll run up to him too, and I'll say, "Where have you *been*?" and life will go back to being as it was.' She stroked my back, and tickled under my chin, where I like it. 'But that's not going to happen, is it?'

Well, what could I say? I'd imagined the same thing, so many times. I *had* to find another man for her. If only she'd stop crying.

A few weeks later, we were driving back from a walk with Anne when she said, 'You look a bit better. How do you feel?'

I was interested to hear what Suki would say. She sighed. 'Some days I feel so normal I get worried, and then it hits me like an avalanche. What does dead mean? It's such a small word with such a massive meaning. Too much for me to understand. I'm getting used to Pip's absence, but I can't get my head around the thought of life without him.'

Anne didn't say anything, but I saw her squeeze Suki's hand.

'The strange thing is,' Suki continued, 'When we go out for walks, it's almost like he's walking with us. As you know, he was never much of a walker when he was alive, but now he's with us all the time.' She turned to Anne and her face was streaked with tears. 'And I don't know if that's a good thing or not.'

In fact, I thought this was progress. And the following week, she was actually able to do some work, which was a real breakthrough.

'Well done, Suki, this is great!' her editor said, reading what she'd written.

Suki smiled, even though I could see her eyes were shiny with tears, but she brushed them away and said, 'About time, eh?'

A few days later, she agreed to go for coffee with a few of the others. OK, she still cried, but only a bit. That was another breakthrough. So I decided it was time to try again with my Find a Man Plan.

Suki had lots of girlfriends and quite a few male friends. I knew that she would only want the sort of relationship that she'd had with Pip. And why not? If you've had something good, you want to repeat it. She deserved to be with someone kind and loving. So I devised a checklist of what we needed:

* He had to be able to cook and/or be practical.

* Have a good sense of humour.

* Someone who liked walking with us, sniffing out good adventures.

* It would be good if they liked going to the pub, because I LOVED cheese and onion crisps.
  They always finished off a walk nicely.

* Preferably no cats.

* Of course, no other woman. I wasn't sure about other dogs or children, but I could be flexible about them. What else?

The next morning, we were up at Boscawen Fields, overlooking the sea, and I smelt a really tasty fellow with a greyhound. I'm not all that sure about greyhounds. They have such long legs and they're skinny and so *fast* but this one seemed quite good natured, so I sniffed his owner and yes, he smelt kind. I could smell a bit of bacon which was promising. He didn't smell of Other Woman or Cat, and his boots were well worn so he obviously walked a lot. I decided he might be worth a go.

Suki was on the other side of the field talking to a friend: they were deep in conversation, so I had to bark, twice, which was a bit obvious, as I was sniffing round this fellow's feet all the time. Eventually she saw me and called. Of course, I ignored her, so she had to come running over. At least she'd brushed her hair this morning and even put on some mascara.

'Moll,' she admonished me, and looked up at the man. 'I'm sorry, I hope she hasn't been bothering you.'

He smiled and I noticed he had grey eyes and a crinkly smile. Excellent. 'Not at all. I think he and Bill were not getting acquainted.'

She laughed. Laughed! And looked over to where Bill was sniffing another dog's bum, taking no notice of me at all. Well, that was the idea; it wasn't HIM I was interested in. My ears pricked up; could this man be a possible?

Then I heard a voice calling, 'Kevin! Cooee! Over here!'

We all looked over to see a short, stout woman in a raincoat hurrying towards us. She didn't smell very glad to see us, and dived in to kiss Kevin on the mouth, as if she owned him. So much for not smelling of other women.

'Well, we must be going,' said Suki hurriedly. 'Bye!' and we set off. She was quiet as we walked along the beach, and I wondered what she was thinking. Then I heard her voice, small and disappointed. 'He looked quite nice, Moll, didn't he? I almost thought....'

And I felt awful for having barked up the wrong trouser leg. Next time I would find a better one, I decided. One who didn't have a woman. And who wasn't called Kevin.

3

Choosing Men

A lesser dog might have felt cast down by the lack of success with Kevin, who had smelt so promising. But not me. I was determined to find a good man for Suki. Well, for us. I wouldn't be defeated so easily.

I reported back to Pip whenever we went down to Greenbank Beach at low tide. Having been there the day Pip died, I always associated it with him and I believed he could hear me. While Suki collected shells at the far end of the beach, I trotted along the shoreline and had a quick catch up.

'It's not going very well, I'm afraid, Pip. I'm doing my best but there's always something the matter with them. Why can't we just find somebody like you?' The waves rippled in and out, in and out, in a soothing fashion, but there was no reply from Pip. Then I thought oh, perhaps he's offended. 'Not that we could ever replace you. Really, we just want you back,' I yipped. 'Couldn't you just come home? I know you didn't want to go, so couldn't you say you've had enough and come back to us? I'm sure they wouldn't mind. Perhaps they could take someone else instead?'

I was getting a bit off topic, here, which was unlike me. 'OK, well, perhaps not. Anyway, just to let you know that we really miss you. And I'll try harder.'

I strained hard to hear a reply, and while the waves hissed gently on the sand, I thought I could hear a faint rumble of Pip's voice. That was enough. For the moment.

As I ran through the checklist on my paws, every morning I scouted the fields and the beach to see if there was anyone promising. I'd had a few near misses: a few days ago there'd been a guy who smelt great – home made bread, all yeasty and full of promise, but on closer inspection I could smell cat. No thank you!

Then at the weekend there was another one but he had a small child with him. Now, I've nothing against children, but this one screamed the whole time, dragging her boots in the mud. We didn't need that kind of behaviour .

The following week we were walking through the churchyard which might sound gloomy, but I loved it. There were so many squirrels to chase, and some fascinating ghosts to spook. The smells were amazing too: you'd be surprised at the number of dropped treats, especially underneath the bench by the gate, where people sat and ate their sandwiches, overlooking the sea.

We were nearing the end of our walk but had met no one suitable, sadly, but lots of squirrels, and Suki had only cried once which was a bonus. We rounded the corner and a retriever with an elegant head and a very aristocratic wavy tail came up to us. He was posh, you could tell because he paused to the left of me and looked down, saying 'May I?' before he sniffed my bum. All very courteous and old fashioned which I rather liked. We sniffed away and I could tell he was younger than me, came from a loving background, had recently eaten bacon. That was promising. I looked round to see who his owner was, and a short fellow came round the corner, calling, 'Bertie!'

The man was a bit older than Suki, at a guess, with glasses and a beard. I ventured forth and sniffed. No Other Woman smell. No cats. Recently eaten bacon sarnie. Excellent.

Bertie sniffed Suki and we both approved of the other's owner. Even better. We turned towards them and I wondered how to start the conversation. Then I noticed Bertie's owner had a ball in his hand. I bowed, fluttering my eyelashes and the man laughed.

'Your dog's gorgeous. What's she called?'

'Moll, or Mollie,' said Suki, smelling shy all of a sudden. 'Bertie's very handsome. How old is he?'

'He's two next month,' said the man cheerfully. 'He's my first dog, but I don't know what I'd do without him now.'

Suki nodded. 'I know what you mean. Moll's my first dog too, and she completely changed our lives.' She drooped a bit after that and I wished she hadn't said 'our'. Quickly I barked, while the man smiled and threw the ball. Bertie and I rushed after it, but I felt I had to grab it quickly and get back to make sure Suki didn't make a mess of things.

When we returned, I dropped the ball at the man's feet and he laughed; a nice deep laugh. 'She's quick, your Moll,' he said. This time he threw it nearer Bertie and I let him get it – it was his ball, after all, and I wanted to keep tabs on things. 'We usually go for a coffee down at Gylly after our walk. Would you like to join us?' he asked.

Suki looked at me, smelling doubtful. I knew she was thinking about getting home because it would be dark soon, and it was tea time. But that could wait. I nudged her with my nose, gave a yip of encouragement. She smiled. 'That would be lovely, thanks.'

So we ended up having a coffee with Geoff, as he was called. I was so pleased, my whiskers stood to attention, and my fur bristled with pride. I was so good at this! I'd found her a man!

Lying underneath the table, I listened to their conversation, which seemed to be going well. He lived in a town called Redditch which was in a place called Midlands, he was staying down here on holiday and he was divorced. 'I love it down here. The air's amazing; you can really breathe here, can't you?'

Suki nodded. 'I'm biased as I'm Cornish, but whenever I've lived away it was always lovely to come home,' she said.

He was an engineer, he said, which didn't mean much to me, but Suki brightened, told him about the problem with our telly in the kitchen. Geoff frowned, then said something about tubes and aerials and stuff. I could tell Suki didn't understand: she got this glazed look, as if a shutter had come down. 'Right,' she said, which I knew meant she didn't have a clue.

'To be honest, it's probably not worth repairing,' he said. 'You'd be better off getting a cheap second-hand one.'

She nodded. 'Yes, I might do that. Thanks.' Though I knew she was thinking that would cost money which we didn't have.

Geoff smiled, as if he knew she didn't understand, but it didn't matter. 'I tried this new recipe for cooking sea bass last night; it was really lovely. Do you like cooking?' I nearly cheered – this man was too good to be true! Practical AND good at cooking! Say yes, Suki! He's the One!

'I like watching Jamie Oliver,' she said. 'But I'm not much of a cook. I sort of lost interest at the idea of cooking for one.'

'So you don't have a partner?' he said hesitantly. He glanced at her hands where she still wore her wedding ring. Then he looked down, at his phone. It was very similar to the one she'd got Pip.

'I did,' she said, and her voice dropped as she noticed the phone. 'But he died, two months ago.' And oh dog, she was off again. Big fat tears plopped onto the table. Damn and blast, as Pip would say. And it had been going so well.

'I'm so sorry,' said Geoff. 'Here,' and he passed over some paper serviettes which she took and blew her nose with.

'Sorry,' she said. 'I keep embarrassing Moll by crying all over everyone. It's very difficult. I seem to have an inexhaustible supply of tears.'

He smiled. 'Don't worry. I was like that when my cat had to be put down. Couldn't speak or work for ages. Utterly hopeless.'

There was a silence while she mopped herself up and I wondered if she'd ruined it. Please, don't mention the phone, I thought. Please. She didn't. But it was worse, for she said nothing. The conversation just dried up.

Eventually she said, 'Well, thanks for the coffee. It was lovely meeting you. Sorry to blub all over you.'

He frowned. 'It's not a problem. I'm just – I'm really sorry. If ever you feel like meeting up for another coffee, here's my card.' He handed it over. 'I'm here for another five days, but I'll be back again soon. It's been really nice talking to you.'

Suki looked up, with snail trails of mascara running down her cheeks. 'Thank you,' she said croakily. 'That's very kind.' She looked down and fumbled for my lead. 'Come on, Moll. Time for your tea. Thanks again, Geoff.'

And she marched us out of the cafe, quick as that, with me thinking that he seemed a really kind and decent fellow. What was the matter?

She usually told me what the matter was, but that evening all she did was cry into her glass of wine. Eventually she looked up and patted the sofa next to her. I jumped up, snuggled close and waited.

'I'm sorry, Moll,' she said with a watery sigh. 'It was the sight of Geoff's phone that did it. I kept thinking that Pip never got the chance to use his.' Big tears slid down her cheeks and landed on my nose, salty and warm. 'And he seemed a really nice guy, but for two things: he doesn't live in Cornwall, and most importantly, he ISN'T PIP.'

I wasn't going to admit defeat, of course. The tide was in at Greenbank, so I couldn't seek Pip's advice for the moment. But I felt short changed. Geoff was so right for Suki. It was so frustrating. He was coming back to Cornwall, so why couldn't she just meet him for coffee again and see what might happen? But she didn't seem interested.

Well, I thought. Maybe Geoff wasn't quite right, but there must be others who were. Surely? So I continued to try. Next we met a very tall fellow who spoke funny, and looked down at me as if I was a rat; he had a Great Dane, which summed it up really. I wasn't going to waste time with snobs like that.

Then there was John, who we used to see every morning while Pip was alive. He'd got a terrier called Mousie who looked a bit like me, and we were friends. John's partner had just left him, so I thought, perhaps he and Suki could help each other. But they were both too miserable. She needed someone to cheer her up.

Then there was Colin who had a spaniel called Buster with ADHD, like most spaniels. Colin was nice but there was no way I could put up with Buster. He gave me a headache after five seconds. And he had bad breath. Eat some bones, I told him. Clean your teeth! But would he listen?

One weekend there were two gay guys (I learned about gay men from listening to Anne and Suki one evening). I hadn't yet come across a gay dog, but I supposed there probably were some. Anyway, I thought perhaps two men might be better than one, but then another dog told me that they don't like having sex with women. So that was that out.

We even met a lovely woman who was really kind and clever and funny, who had a Border Terrier called Twig and I liked them. I wondered if perhaps Suki might like to have a woman partner rather than a man, but it turned out this woman had just ended a long relationship and was happy on her own. Did two women have sex? I asked around and no one was quite sure. Anyway, I thought I'd keep her in reserve, just in case.

But Suki's words kept ringing in my whiskers, no matter how hard I tried to ignore them: that none of these men were Pip. And that got me wondering if I was doing the right thing here? Why hadn't I asked Pip exactly what he meant by making sure Suki was happy? How? It was all so confusing and had laid the first seeds of doubt in my nose, making me question what I was doing, and more importantly, what I *should* be doing.

I did what I usually did, and observed Suki closely. I never let her out of my sight if I could help it, and tried to notice what made her happy. At least she didn't cry so much nowadays.

Over the next few weeks, what I noticed was this: she liked being with people. She interviewed them for her job, and she was very good at getting them to talk to her. She was even better at writing it, apparently, but I drew the line at reading. There was only so much a dog could do.

People at work liked her and really cared about her. So did her friends who were always ringing up to ask her to go to the pub, or a film, a walk or a meal. So. She liked wine, she loved her friends, she loved reading and always had a good time at her book group, she enjoyed seeing films, and when she came back from singing she always seemed lit up from inside. So that was quite a list of things that made her happy.

At home she was content with just me and her. She hadn't invited many friends back, since Pip died. As she said to me, "It feels wrong somehow, without him." Which didn't make sense – and then it did.

She still talked to Pip a lot, and I wondered if he could hear her. Could he see what we were doing? He would hate to see her unhappy. But what else could she be, without him? How could such a steady, massive source of love just not be there?

I looked at other people with their dogs. Some couples looked really smug in their togetherness. Some of them argued and, on Suki's behalf, I wanted to bark at them and say, 'don't waste what you've got!'

I missed watching my people's everyday happiness. Kisses in passing. Holding hands while watching TV. Rapid arguments that ended in her flouncing off, but she always came back. They would both grin. Burst into laughter. Cuddle.

People didn't realise that happiness was catching. It smelt warm and inviting. It tasted good and earthy, like fox poo. It felt smooth and sensuous, like the best back-scratch ever.

When you were with people who loved each other, it rubbed off on you. But it didn't just get in your fur. It got right inside you.

A few weeks later, we were at work when the editor called everyone into a meeting. All seven of them crammed into a room while I listened at the door. Even I couldn't squeeze in, they were packed so tight. But my hearing's better than theirs, so I didn't miss anything.

'I'm really sorry but I'm afraid we've had more budget cuts,' she said. She had a calm, considered voice and I'd never heard her lose her temper. 'This means that we will have to cut everyone down to one or at most, two days a week.' You could hear the stunned silence as her words sank in. 'That applies to me, too.' She sighed. 'I appreciate many of you will need to look for work elsewhere; we all have mortgages and bills to pay. If it was up to me, I'd keep you all on because we have a great team here, and I know how talented you all are, and how hard you work. However, it's not up to me.' She got up. 'I'm really sorry, everyone.' He voice cracked as she squeezed her way out of the room, narrowly missing my left paw.

There was a buzz of chatter as everyone tried to come to terms with the shock.

'What shall we do?'

'Dunno. What about you?'

'Not sure, but I've had enough anyway.'

'We wanted to move back to Devon; I guess now's a good time.'

'I'm staying put. She's great to work for. But I'll have to find other work as well.'

And last of all, Suki, who slumped down at her desk, so I jumped onto her lap. 'Shit, Moll,' she said, stroking me absently. 'I'd taken work for granted. But we can't survive on one or two days a week. What the hell are we going to do?'

And once again, I had no answer.

4

Selling Things

After the news about work, Suki stopped crying. It was as if she'd been jolted her out of her grief, albeit maybe temporarily, and her mind had refocused. 'We have to find some way of getting work, and until then, we have to sell some things,' she said to Anne one evening. 'The only things we have of value are Pip's boat and his phone.'

There was a silence while I could sense Anne was trying to decide what to say. 'Are you sure?' she said. 'You won't regret selling Pip's things?'

Suki shook her head. 'No. I've thought about it and I'm never going to use the boat and I can't stand seeing it every time I go into the shed. It's only rotting there, and he'd hate that.'

'And the phone? I know how special that was to him.'

Suki bit her lip. She smelt unsure, like chalky powder. 'I can't bear to look at it, either. It just reminds me of him holding it when he died. The phone's never been used and it's worth some money, so I'd rather it went to someone who'll use it. Otherwise it's just a waste.'

'Well, as long as you're sure, I think that's a very good idea,' Anne said. 'There's this local network I use where it's free to advertise – you could try there.'

'Perfect,' said Suki. And from the tone of her voice, I could tell she'd made up her mind.

Boating didn't make any sense to me. Why sit in the water and get wet when you could have a long walk with lots of sniffs and smells? But I knew that Pip had different tastes, and it had been important to him.

This boat was a big rubber thing that Pip called Inflated Ego, as it had to be inflated, and it took ages to do so. I think he liked the anticipation, the standing and chatting while he used an old foot pump to blow it up. Then he had to put it in the water, and off we went. I didn't like it much as the sides were very slippery and Suki had to hang onto me or I'd slide down into the water. And it was a bit boring, just sitting there, getting splashed.

Back home, Suki had second thoughts about selling the boat, so she rang Pip's brother. He was a lovely man called Pete, and they were very close. 'I know we hadn't used the boat for ages, and it's only sitting in the garage rotting,' she said. 'But to sell it seems such a big thing. You know, it's so much a part of him.'

'Pip had the sea in his blood I think,' Pete said. 'He always floundered when he didn't have a boat.'

She nodded. 'Pip didn't really count this one as a proper boat, 'cos it was too small, but he wasn't well enough for anything else and at least it got him on the water which was really important to him.'

The final spur was that we needed the money, so she advertised the boat. 'It'll take ages to sell, Moll,' she said. But almost at once she had a phone call from a lady who wanted it. She arrived the following weekend and smelt nice. She said she had dogs, and she smelt friendly, like warm biscuits.

They stood in the garage, talking about the boat and the pump and the cover and Suki seemed to be doing really well until she handed the booklet over. Then she started sobbing. Again.

The lady smelt really embarrassed, but Suki said, 'Don't worry, I'll be fine,' while tears rolled down her cheeks, so the lady got in her car and drove off, and Suki carried on crying and crying and crying. At least dear Pete was there. They stood outside the garage and held each other and the smell coming off them was like burnt rubber, there was so much hurt.

I wished I could make them both happy, but at the moment it was hard enough looking after Suki.

I thought she might go downhill after selling the boat, but that bout of crying seemed to clear something inside her. Then along came Easter, and that floored her. Bank Holidays (what a ridiculous name) had a strange atmosphere.

'I feel like I'm the only person in the world without a partner, Moll,' she said. She meant, without someone who loved her, when she knew I loved her. But of course I wasn't Pip.

The sound of her weeping, when I thought she'd finally got over that awful stage, made my whiskers go into overdrive, and my stomach churned. It seemed as if life was pressing in on all sides; first losing Pip, now losing work. It almost put me off my food, I felt so helpless. All I could do was take her for walks and cuddle up to her, which I knew she loved. In between crying, she said, 'Bank Holidays should have a government health warning for widows'.

But it wasn't just the long weekend. 'Someone wants to buy Pip's phone,' she wailed the next day. She sat down on the sofa and tried to wipe the tears away, but they fell thick and fast, like winter rain. I snuggled up to her, and realised why people said their hearts had broken. It sounded like hers really had.

'Remember when we thought he was going to get better, Moll? And he said what he really wanted was a new phone, so I ordered this one for him for his birthday,' she blew her nose, 'but because of the bad weather, all the deliveries were held up so it turned into a Christmas present. And then it was too late.'

She sobbed and sobbed and stroked me with the hand that wasn't holding the phone and finally said, 'Oh Moll, he had such hopes for it, for us, for life. My poor, darling Pip.' Cue more tears. 'It just seems so cruel. Why couldn't we have had longer?' She started hiccuping and I licked her hand. 'But at least we had 14, nearly 15 years together.' Sniff. Lick. 'And it would have been much worse if he'd got ill when he was living on his own. Like he was before we met.'

I licked her very hard after that, and glued myself to her side so close, you couldn't have put a biscuit between us. Then I looked up at her and winked. For some reason, humans seem to like this. She gave a watery laugh, blew her nose and sighed. A long, long sigh that smelt of so much sadness. Trouble was, now she'd talked about it, I couldn't stop seeing Pip lying on the bed, clutching the phone as he stopped breathing. It was not the kind of image I wanted, so I tugged at Suki, suggesting we went out for a walk. If in doubt, keep moving, I barked. So we did.

Anyway. Now someone wanted to buy the phone. 'She's called Tess and she wants to buy it for her partner,' Suki said. 'I've arranged to meet her in the Tesco car park in Truro.'

I was worried about how Suki would feel, but she seemed calm enough on the day and handed the phone over to this lady. Tess was tall and had a big smile and smelt warm and kind, like honey. 'Thanks so much,' she said. 'My partner will be delighted. He's been longing for one of these for ages and the one we ordered never turned up.'

I could see Suki's face wobble a bit and thought oh, no. She bit her lip and tried to smile, and hurried back to the car where she shut the door, put her head on the steering wheel and wept.

Suddenly there was a gentle knock on the passenger window and it was this Tess woman. 'I'm so sorry,' she said. 'May I come in a minute?'

Suki mopped her eyes and opened the car door and Tess put her arm around her and Suki leant on her shoulder and gave a horrible wail. Finally she said, 'It was my husband's and he never got to use it.'

'I thought it must be something like that,' Tess said. 'How incredibly hard for you. You are brave.' She handed Suki some tissues and said, 'Listen, have you got time for a coffee?'

'Moll needs a walk,' Suki said, 'but I'd love a coffee. Thanks.'

'How about we drive to that place at Devoran?' Tess said. "I've got my dog in the car too. We can have a coffee and walk the dogs as well. How about it?' And the way she smelt; strong and certain, like Cheddar cheese, and the way she took charge, made me think we could trust this woman.

Suki managed a watery smile. 'Thanks, Tess,' she said. 'That would be brilliant.'

Tess grinned a lovely smile that smelt of a summer's day. 'Excellent. Follow me.'

So we followed her to a cafe that we hadn't been to, and Tess treated Suki as if she was ill. She guided her to a table inside a little hut where she sat with me and Tess's dog, a terrier called Titch, while Tess ordered coffee and some flapjack. To be honest, I preferred cake, but she wasn't to know.

As they talked, we found out that Tess was a veterinary nurse. 'What I'd really like to do is set up on my own as a dog trainer,' she said with that open smile. 'There are so many dogs with problems, particularly rescue dogs. We see them every day at the surgery and I've been doing classes at work, but so many more people need help.'

'People?' said Suki. 'Don't you mean the dogs?'

Tess grinned. 'It's the owners as much as the dogs who need support,' she said. 'I love working with people, too. It's difficult walking away from a regular salary though.'

'If you started to put the word out, you could see how many clients you might get,' Suki said. 'I could write a press release for you. And you'd need a website, or at least a Facebook page, and a social media presence.'

Tess frowned. 'I'm hopeless at that stuff.'

'But I'm not,' Suki smiled. 'I'd happily do that for you.'

'Really?' Tess said. 'I've applied for one of those start-up business grants and if I get that, I could pay you.'

'Even better,' said Suki, and once again she smelt of hope and optimism. Like roast chicken with sage. 'Thanks, Tess, I feel so much better already. Come on, shall we take these two for a walk? And tell me, how long have you had Titch?'

I was interested to hear this, so listened carefully.

'My last dog was very old and died in her sleep. I was so distraught that I couldn't contemplate having another dog for at least a year,' Tess said. 'But my ex-partner turned up with Titch and asked if we could look after him while he and his girlfriend went on holiday. Rather grudgingly, I said yes, and a month later, Titch was still here.' She giggled. 'My partner asked when Titch was going back to my ex and I just said, 'He's not. He's staying here now. I won't let him go.'

So Titch got his paws under the table at Tess's place. He was a very bouncy, Plumber Terrier which meant he had long legs like a Parsons Jack Russell but with a short coat. He was a good-looking boy, so we made a handsome couple: me with my long soft hair, long black eyelashes, brains and innate charm (I know this sounds boastful but it's true) and him with his youthful exuberance.

At first I thought he wasn't the brightest woof in the pack, but very soon I realised he was very affectionate and I loved his optimism, his zest for life. I hoped we could have many more walks together. It looked promising, as Tess and Suki never stopped talking.

As Titch and I foraged and barked, trotting alongside together, I found myself wanting to know what he liked to eat. Where he liked to snooze and when. Which squirrels to chase (it was bad manners to go after the same one) and when his whiskers twitched, meaning he needed to be left alone. It was important, knowing these little things about those we may become close to.

5

I hadn't given up on finding Suki another man. I'd just realised what a near impossible task it was. I had naively thought that I could trot up to someone who would look at Suki, realise what an extraordinarily special person she was and fall in love with her, like Pip and I had.

But I began to suspect that wasn't going to happen, or not in the way I'd imagined. I reported back to Pip when I could, but the lack of response was a bit off putting.

I realised I would have to come up with another plan. I consulted my other dog friends but none of them had any ideas that made my whiskers jump. So I told all the dogs that we saw regularly to keep a leg cocked in case they came across a kindly man on his own who deserved an extra special partner.

Regarding the rest of Pip's promise, I was doing all I could to look after Suki, and as for making sure she was happy, well, with him having left us, she wasn't going to be barking with joy, was she? But I was doing my best. And I began to think, well, perhaps that was all I could do for the moment. I wasn't giving up. Rather, I thought, let nature take its course. Until I came up with a better plan.

Then, a few weeks after we met Tess and Titch, I met a dog called Errol who made me rethink everything. He was a terrier/collie and a real flirt, with huge dark eyes and a wicked sense of humour, who lived in Penryn.

We met on the fields above the sea, and he gambolled over to me and ran away, back and forth, urging me to follow him. Which after a bit I did. He had a musky scent that drove me wild, and we had such fun that afternoon – racing down onto the beach, over the rock pools and back. I felt like a puppy again.

He made me bark with laughter, and nudged against me, and teased me and nuzzled my muzzle until all my cares and worries over Suki disappeared. When I was with him, I felt as if I was the most important dog in the world.

We met several times that week; Suki knew Errol's owner, and she was friends with his wife (so no matchmaking there). Errol made me feel like a different dog. I noticed that I was walking strangely, swaying my hips a bit. My tail looked longer and I waved it upright, higher in the air. Even my coat looked glossy. Other male dogs started sniffing around me, but I wasn't interested in them. I only had a nose for Errol.

Soon, Errol suggested going off in the bushes for a frolic. I wasn't sure what he meant at first, but I had this overwhelming urge to, well, frolic, I guess, though I didn't know what that involved. But I'd never had such a strong desire to do something like that with another dog. It was all I could think about for days, and I got so excited, lying at home, imagining what it would be like. Him sniffing my butt, then my ears, then.... I wasn't sure what we'd do, but I knew we'd have to do it or I'd go barking mad.

So one day we sneaked off into the bushes – 'we'll have to be quick,' Errol barked.

We were, and it was – well, not quite what I expected. It hurt a bit, but it was over very quickly, and all he did afterwards was bellow, then he scampered off. I could have done with a bit of a cuddle, paw to paw, and a nose-to-nose chat, but perhaps male dogs weren't like that.

After my initial disappointment, I felt invigorated and emboldened. Desired. The experience went right to my nose. He was all I could smell for days. I got quite dreamy for a while, remembering his scent, imagining doing it again – but better this time. But he'd disappeared. I was barking to some other dogs who lived nearby, and then I heard he'd used the same chat-up to several other dogs, and my tail and my whiskers drooped. I felt a real fool.

I almost went off my food, and my tail remained down for several days. But it was never down for long. I couldn't afford to be, as I had to look after Suki. I mentioned Errol's name to some other dogs, who laughed about him. He was a bit of a joke, they said. After a certain amount of nose bumping, we all agreed he was hopeless. Charming, un-neutered and out of control, but harmless. And he was very cute to look at. We just wouldn't fall for it again.

While my pride was injured for a few days, gradually I saw the funny side, and it got me thinking. If this was what it was like for us dogs, surely people were the same?

I'd been barking up the wrong tree, looking for a man who could cook or mend things. What Suki needed was someone to have sex with! Not someone who would rush off afterwards, but would stick around and chat and cuddle. But how would I find someone suitable? And how would I know if they were the right sort of person?

I would have to ask around, sniff my research thoroughly.

The next morning, I found Suki frowning at her computer screen. 'If we don't go out, and don't get any big bills, we can survive this month,' she told me. 'But I need to get some more work soon, Moll. Still,' she turned round and tickled my tummy. 'I've started work on Tess's website and social media, and once I've got those up and running that might generate some more work. Actually, I need to update my own website and spread the word online.' She sighed. 'It's just a question of seeing if anyone wants my services. There are a lot of us writers about.'

At least Tess's website kept her busy and focused. As we were only in the office one or two days a week, Suki needed something to do, as well as bringing some money in.

And then, three months after Pip died, after several months of very little money, Suki had some good news. At last. We had done lots and lots of walks for a Cornish magazine, and she'd been trying to find a publisher who would make a book out of some of them. She sent off email after email, but they all came back saying, "no, sorry".

One afternoon, she and Pete and I were sorting out Pip's clothes in the bedroom when her computer bleeped with a message coming in. She glanced over, said, 'Oh it's from a publisher. It'll just be another no.' So she ignored it. But I had a funny feeling. This smelt different; like a smoky puff of promise.

After Pete had gone, I nudged her to look at her computer and, 'Moll!' she cried. 'Alpha Press want to publish a book of my walks!' She laughed and we ran up and down the hallway and she gave me a big hug, and she said, 'Wouldn't Pip be pleased, Moll? he'd be saying, "Go for It, Flowerpot!" and' –

she stopped and smiled at me, a really huge smile. 'Just think, I'll be a proper author!'

She was right; Pip would have been so proud. A real author! I mean, being a journalist was important, but books lasted longer, didn't they? You could hold them in your hand. You could take them with you. Give them as presents. Not much good to dogs, of course, but people seemed to like them. They were one step up from papers and magazines, it seemed.

She scanned the email again, reading it more slowly. 'They're sending a contract in the post for me to sign, and they'd like to discuss the book with a view to publication later this year! Oh, Moll, I'm so excited!'

I barked with her to celebrate, and we twirled around a bit and then she said. 'Hang on. I don't know what they're paying.' She read the email again and her shoulders drooped. 'Oh. It's not very much.' She sighed. 'No wonder Victorian artists and writers always starved and lived in garrets. It hasn't improved since then. But a little is better than nothing, eh, Moll? And who knows where this may lead?'

The following day, we were in the office celebrating Suki's good news. She'd bought a fruit cake and carved it into slices for everyone. I wasn't supposed to have any, as she'd heard that dried fruit was dangerous for dogs. Ridiculous! Luckily this fruit cake was very crumbly so I managed a few fruity snacks without her noticing.

Suki had just gone back to her desk when a man who worked in the upstairs office came in. He smelt of salt, fresh air and warm bread. Yum. He came over and stood before Suki's desk and smiled, smelling a bit unsure. She looked up and smiled. 'Hi Ted,' she said.

'Are you celebrating?'

She grinned. 'Yes. I've got a publishing contract!'

'That's fantastic news,' he said, with an equally large grin. I edged closer. He smelt kind, like soft butter. And there was another smell, that I wouldn't have recognised, but thanks to Errol, I did now.

Looking up, I could see he had green eyes that twinkled. Fair hair that curled over his shirt collar. He looked a few years older than Suki and reminded me of someone.

'Thanks,' she said, but instead of looking down at the floor, as she usually did, I noticed she was looking straight up, into those green eyes. 'Do have a piece of cake, and there's coffee over there.'

'I've got to go and see a client,' he said. 'But another time, maybe?'

I barked, loudly – just once – to get the message across. She looked at me, then at him.

'OK,' she said, and I could hear her smile, though I could sense that she was a bit puzzled.

But my whiskers bristled excitedly. Could this Ted be a Sex Candidate?

The next day, we had to call into the office and we bumped into him again. He had very long legs, in jeans that smelt of salt and sea air. 'Got time for a coffee?' he said. 'I'm just going over the road.' He had a gentle voice. I could smell kindness and – that something else. That musky, happy scent that meant Sex.

'OK,' she said. She smelt a bit unsure but that was to be expected.

We went to the bakery opposite which was also a cafe and I had a fabulous sniff around. I loved it in there; such wonderful smells of yeasty bread and chocolatey cakes and masses of rich, fatty croissant crumbs.

They chatted and then he stopped and I could smell hesitation. Go on, I thought. 'I was so sorry to hear about your husband, Suki. Do you mind me asking, what happened?' he said. 'I remember meeting you both at that party last year. He was such an interesting, vibrant man.'

Party? I hadn't been invited to that. She nodded, told him what happened. In a very matter of fact way.

There was silence, then, 'It must have been so difficult for you,' he said.

She shrugged. 'Yes it was terrible,' she said. 'It still is, sometimes.' Interestingly, I could tell she felt safe saying that. Him being a stranger. I could also smell that she really needed a cuddle. Would this Ted person do that? Whoa, too soon.

'You could do with a break,' he said. 'I'm so pleased about your publishing contract.'

'Thanks,' she said. 'Just think, I'll be a proper author!' I could sense her face lighting up. Pride burst through her words, and I was very glad she was sharing it with someone else.

'That's fantastic, Suki!' he said, and the excitement bubbled out from his words. At this point the coffee arrived and two croissants. Good, I loved those greasy, flaky bits.

'Though I do need to find some more work,' she said. 'So if you hear of anyone who needs help doing press releases, or research, or anything, please let me know.'

He stirred his coffee thoughtfully. 'I might know someone,' he said. 'I'll make some enquiries and get back to you.'

'Great.' She passed over her business card and he took it, put it carefully in his wallet. 'I don't know if you can help, but I need someone to help with the photographs for my books.' She spooned the froth off the top of her coffee. 'I got Pip this camera for his birthday but it's very high tech and I don't know how to use it. Do you know anyone?'

'I could help,' he said. And I got a strong flare up of that happy scent.

'Really? I thought you were a graphic designer.'

'I am, but I also work as a freelance photographer.' He paused. 'You can check me out online.'

'Really?' she said again. 'What's your website?'

He told her and she quickly tapped on her phone. 'You're really good!' she said.

He laughed. 'No need to sound so surprised!'

I could sense her going red. 'I didn't mean it like that.'

'I'm only joking,' he said. 'I'd be delighted to take some photographs for you.' The happy scent was so strong I was amazed they couldn't smell it.

She looked at me. I could smell hesitation. 'Thing is, how much do you charge? I don't really have a budget,' she said apologetically.

'I'd do it as a friend,' he said firmly. 'Absolutely no payment.'

'But you're freelance. You need the money,' she insisted.

'Not for this job,' he said firmly. 'My day job pays the bills, so I like to help friends where I can. I insist.' He picked up his croissant, broke it in half. A few lovely crumbs just floated down onto my outstretched tongue.

'Well, thank you. I really appreciate it. But let me buy you coffee, or lunch or something.'

He shrugged. 'When you can afford it. Not yet.'

Again she paused and I could almost hear her thinking. 'So you work part time?'

'Yes, I do the photography from home.' When he said the word 'home' there was a funny smell. Stale and fearful.

I don't think she smelt it, for she said, 'I work part time from home too,' as if that was the most extraordinary coincidence. 'So you really think you might be able to help?'

He swallowed a mouthful of pastry. 'Sure,' he said. 'What do you need?'

'Well, the trouble is, it involves coming on the walks for my next book,' she said, hesitation in every syllable. She picked up her croissant, bit into it. I hovered closer, snaffled up her lot of crumbs. Delicious. Rich and fatty and superb.

'No problem,' he said firmly. 'As long as I have some notice. Weekends are probably best, but I can sometimes do the odd afternoon.'

'That would be perfect,' she said, and I could hear a smile bursting through her words. 'How about this weekend? I need to do a walk near Looe.'

A cloud crossed his face. 'Oh, sorry, this is the one weekend....'

'Never mind,' she said quickly.

'But I could do next Tuesday after 11 if that's any good?'

'Yes,' she said slowly. 'I'm free after 12.'

'Why don't I pick you up? Silly taking two cars. All my equipment is in mine so it's easier if I drive.'

'Oh, OK. Thanks,' she said, her voice brightening. 'That would be great.'

They exchanged phone numbers, and as I sat at her feet and listened to them talk, I realised who this man reminded me of. He was very like Pip would have been, twenty years ago.

Pip? What do you think? If I strained my ears, I was sure I could hear a reassuring rumble of his laughter. But what did that *mean*?

A spark of hope rose up inside me. Could this man do sex and make Suki happy? Or was it too soon?

6

A walk with Ted

The following Monday night, she didn't sleep much. She tossed and turned. By 11 the next morning she was pacing up and down, checking and double checking she'd got everything. Map, tape recorder, spare batteries, notes about the walk, bottle of water and snacks.

She stood in front of the open fridge, then looked down at me. I was giving her my best I-haven't-been-fed-for-ages look but it didn't work. 'I was wondering whether to make sarnies,' she said, shutting the door. 'But I don't know what he likes. I'll ask him if we can stop somewhere and I'll buy some.'

Then the doorbell rang and I ran to meet him, barking my head off to distract her. I could smell her nervousness as we sat in his car which smelt of dust and dried mud. I jumped in the back, seeing a few crisp packets there, but they were empty. Just his camera and lenses, and some big folders which he said contained work. The seats were warm and slippery to my paws. Nothing interesting to eat.

I decided to get in the front and sit on Suki's lap so I could look out of the window. I liked seeing where we were going and it meant I could listen to what they were saying.

They chatted about some television programme they'd both been watching, then Suki asked where he lived. I could see him stiffen. I smelt fear and hesitation. 'Behind Kiln Beach,' he said. Rather abruptly.

'Flushing? Lovely spot, lucky you.'

I saw his hands tighten on the steering wheel and he said, 'My wife and I bought it five years ago. Before she became ill. I loved it at first, but it has a lot of difficult memories now.'

There was a dense silence, while we tried to digest this information. Wife? Ill? 'Your wife...' said Suki hesitantly.

He glanced at her sideways. 'I thought you knew. Your editor's a friend of hers.'

'No, she hasn't said anything.' Suki hesitated. 'What's the matter with your wife?'

He looked straight ahead, out of the window. 'She's got dementia.'

'I'm so sorry.' I could smell Suki's confusion and dismay. We'd both thought he was unattached. But a sick wife.....

A muscle clenched in his jaw (I don't miss much). 'I had to put her in a care home six months ago, because I couldn't handle her needs.' He swallowed hard. 'It was one of the worst things I've ever had to do.' His voice had dropped, and he was staring hard at the road ahead, but I could see his knuckles white on the steering wheel. Could smell the fear and guilt seeping out of him. Poor fellow.

'I'm so sorry,' said Suki, and her eyes filled with tears. 'Where is she?'

'Unfortunately there's a huge shortage of beds for specialist dementia care in Cornwall,' he said. 'She was getting quite difficult to manage at home and her GP advised that she should move into care as soon as possible. The only specialist care place we could find was near Derby.'

'But that's hundreds of miles away.'

'Yes,' he said shortly. There was a pause and then he said. 'At least it's a very good place. She's well looked after and she's much happier than she was at home.'

Silence. 'It must take hours to get there.'

'Between five and six hours, yes.'

Suki was quiet for a moment, swallowing this information. 'And do you have somewhere to stay up there?'

'It's not far from her parents, but it's difficult staying with them because they're naturally desperately upset about it all. I usually stay in a B&B but I take them out for a meal, and we visit Jane together. They see her most days but a lot of the time she doesn't recognise us anymore.'

We sat in stunned silence, trying to absorb what he'd said. Six hours? I'd never been in a car for that long, and I didn't expect Suki had either. She hated long drives, got a sore back from sitting still for long. I could almost hear what she was thinking about that really long drive, and having to stay, for how long? Then seeing a wife who wasn't like your wife any more. Be pleasant to distraught parents. Then that hellish drive back again.

'I'm so sorry,' she said softly. 'That must be very draining.' She paused. 'How long has she been ill?' Her fingers stroked my head absently.

He glanced at her. 'She was diagnosed four years ago. Early onset dementia. At first it didn't seem too bad, but over the last year she went downhill fast.' He cleared his throat. 'It's awful to see someone you love just disintegrate like that.'

'Yes, I know,' she said softly. 'I'm so sorry, Ted. Is there anything I can do to help?'

He looked at her again and this time gave a proper smile. 'This sort of thing; getting out and walking, seeing nature, exploring. That makes a huge difference.'

'Good,' she said, but her voice wobbled.

'And people to share things with. Friends are so important, don't you think?'

This time she looked at his profile as if committing it to memory. 'Yes,' she said. 'They're vital.' And she gave me a quick squeeze which, in the circumstances, I tolerated.

I could feel her heart rate plummet. I could smell how much she wanted to help him. And on top of this, I could sense she was thinking that this wife could live for a very long time. Run, Suki, I wanted to say, but I had a strong sense that she wouldn't.

I thought that might have made things awkward between them; after all there was a lot to take in. A wife. With Dementia. Not that I knew what dementia was, but it obviously wasn't good. The smell coming off him when he said it was like rotten chicken (I tried some once, by mistake. I wouldn't repeat that).

There was a brief silence, and he put on the radio and a song called *Bridge Over Troubled Water* came on and he started singing at the same time as Suki did. They glanced at each other, grinned, and carried on singing, loudly. Somewhat out of tune, to my sensitive ears.

When it ended he said, 'I love that song. I remember hearing it at a terrible party when I was an art student. One of those student houses with warm beer and nowhere to sit. You know.'

'What did you study?'

'I've got a degree in illustration,' he said, sounding almost embarrassed. 'What about you?'

Suki shook her head. 'I hated school so much I couldn't bear the thought of prolonging my education. Anyway, I didn't get good enough A Levels.'

'Really?' he sounded astonished. 'But you're so bright.'

She shrugged and I could smell her embarrassment. 'Well, I'm no good at exams.'

'I don't hold much store by university anyway. Most of the people I know had a great time partying, but didn't seem to learn much.' There was silence for a moment, then he said, 'I thought we'd stop and get some food at the farm shop along here. I was going to get sandwiches but I didn't know what you like, so I thought this way we can both choose.'

'Thank you. That's very thoughtful.' She laughed. 'I was going to make some food but I didn't know what you'd like either so this is a much better idea.'

A bit further on they stopped outside a long low building and left me in the passenger seat. They came back with a huge carrier bag that smelt delicious. Hot meat, potato, pasties, by the delicious smell coming my way. Olives (not so keen on them but they'd do) plus some cheese and drinks, a couple of peaches. What a feast!

By the time we reached Looe I knew Suki would be getting hungry. She needed to eat every few hours so her stomach was rumbling and they both laughed.

'I was going to say do you want to eat now or later but I don't need to ask,' he said and his eyes twinkled.

He drove down to a car park by the river which was near some trees, and we got out and sat on a rug he produced from the back of the car, and looked out over the mud banks. I had some nice bits of cheese while they ate, and the sun shone on my fur and I felt warm and toasty. I snoozed in the sunshine, listening with half an ear to what they said, but we didn't stop long, because Suki said, 'That was delicious. But we need to do this walk, so we'd better go.'

'Certainly. We can take the rest for snacks along the way,' said Ted, and parcelled up bits of cheese, apples and drinks.

'You are organised,' said Suki. I was impressed, too, and glad we weren't going to starve along the way.

They consulted the map and Suki pointed at it and said, 'So we're here, and we go up through Kilminorth Woods and do a loop and then come back along the lower path. It should take about two hours if that's OK with you?'

Ted nodded. 'Sounds great. I'm ready.'

So we set off, the three of us in single file with me leading the way. I love woods as there are so many great smells of fox and badger and rabbits and all kinds of birds and toadstools and different woods and leaves and oh, so much to enjoy. I ran ahead, making the most of the terrific sniffs, but I could hear them behind me, chatting and laughing, and I relished the sound of my Suki being so happy.

It really was stunning with the sunlight slanting in through the trees which stretched far, far above us into the blueness of the sky. The ground was soft to my paws: fallen leaves, moss and decayed twigs made an easy-going carpet. I circled back to hear her telling Ted about the book she was writing. 'It's a collection of walks to do with different writers,' she said. 'This one's connected to Katherine Mansfield. Have you heard of her?'

'Yes, but I don't think I've read any of her books,' he said.

'She was born in 1888 in New Zealand and wrote a lot of short stories,' said Suki. 'She became friends with DH Lawrence and Virginia Woolf and came to Looe in 1918.'

'Was she married?'

'Yes, to John Murray, who was the editor of a magazine. From what I gather it was a pretty up and down relationship, and she was also very ill with TB. She had lots of other lovers, of both sexes.' Suki laughed, a bit nervously. 'Not sure how she had the time when she was ill.' She paused. 'She kept writing till the very end. She was only 34 when she died.'

Her words dropped like stones. I could almost hear the effect on both of them. I bet they were thinking – wife, died, very young. Ted looked like he was in his late forties, so presumably his wife was around the same age as Suki. After that there was a silence that smelt a bit stinky but luckily we came to a gap in the bank and they studied the map.

We walked along a bank and then came into a field and stopped and looked out. We were very high up.

'What amazing views,' said Ted, getting his camera out. Every time he took a picture there was a click click click. 'That must be Looe down there and then there's Whitsand Bay and Rame Head over there.'

I couldn't see that far and wasn't interested in those names when there were far more interesting things under my nose. Then I smelt sheep and felt like chasing them but Suki must have seen them too as she put me on the lead. Further on we reached some cottages and headed down into a steep wooded valley with a stream gushing at the bottom. The peace of the woods settled around us and it was like taking a drink of cold, pure water. Which I did as well.

'There are so many different types of trees here,' said Ted. 'Look – beech, oak and holly, and what amazing lichen.' He stopped in front of one that had star shaped moss on its trunk. 'Do you know how to tell where north is?'

Suki shook her head. Much though I loved her, she had no sense of direction. 'No idea,' she said.

Ted just grinned. 'North is where the moss grows.'

'So if I get lost, how's that going to help?' she said, but I could hear laughter in her voice. 'I'll know which way is north, but not how to get out of the wood.'

They both laughed though I couldn't see what was so funny. She was lucky she had me to rely on when it came to direction. The number of times she'd headed off in completely the wrong way and I'd had to show her the right path.

We stopped and had a rest and a snack and I enjoyed hearing the blend of their voices – his low and humming, whereas hers was higher and more melodic. They sounded good together and that made me happy. There was no doubt it made them happy too.

The last part of our walk took us back through the lower part of the trees and eventually we returned to where we'd entered the woods with the river below us. The tide was coming in as we walked beside the water, and Ted pointed to a yellow boat tied to a big yellow blob in the river. 'That's just like mine,' he said.

'You've got a boat?' she said, and I could smell her interest. 'Do you use it much?' I could tell she was hoping we might have a go in it.

'Not as much as I'd like,' he said. 'If you'd like to come out some time, you'd be very welcome.'

'I'd love to,' she said and I could hear the joy in her voice. 'What's she called?'

'Echo,' he said, and I could hear the echoes of his past. Happy times with his wife on the boat? But then he said, 'My wife never liked boating much, that's why I stopped going.' And he sounded really sad and wistful.

'Well, we'd love to come, wouldn't we Moll?' she said.

I chose not to reply. As I said, I wasn't sure about boats: a lot of wet and cold and damp fur. But just then Ted said, 'Why don't we have a drink before we head home?' And I thought, now you're talking. Crisps?

We walked through Looe and came to a hotel where this writer lady had stayed in 1918, according to Suki. We sat out on the terrace and ate crisps and peanuts (he didn't know I wasn't supposed to eat nuts) and they had their drinks, and I had some water, and finally he drove us home.

I snoozed most of the way back; it had been a long but satisfying day and I was tired. But it was lovely hearing their voices tumbling over each other. I could smell the connections they were building up with every minute. And the musky, happy scent was growing stronger, lurking underneath every sentence like a strong fart.

When Ted dropped us back home, I could smell his regret that we had to part.

'Thank you so much,' said Suki, yawning. I could tell she didn't want him to go either. 'It's been such a lovely day.'

'Thank you,' he replied. 'I'll select the best pictures and send them over in the next few days if that's OK? Do you have a deadline?'

'End of the week would be great,' she said. They stood, looking at each other, then she gave him a hug and he held her tight before pulling back. The happy scent was so strong I could hardly breathe. But instead of asking her into the bushes, he got into his car and waved out of the window saying, 'See you soon!'

We stood on the pavement and watched him drive off and then we went inside and suddenly everything seemed very quiet. Even my tea didn't taste the same.

Suki said nothing. She didn't have to.

7

Getting closer to Titch

We didn't see Ted for a few days after that, though I heard him ring her when he was sending the photographs over. 'I often go over to Stones and get a coffee and a bun at around 11, just to have a break from my drawing board,' he said, his voice coming down the phone as clear as a loud bark. 'If ever you feel like a coffee, I'm usually there.'

After that, quite often Suki decided she needed to pop into Stones, mid-morning. She usually took me, but sometimes she didn't and at first it made my whiskers quite twitchy. I wanted to know what she was up to, in order to rescue her, if necessary. Then I realised she needed to make her own decisions. After all, I would always be around to pick up the bones afterwards.

Despite the fact that Ted had a poorly wife, Suki would come back from seeing him smelling of warmth and happiness. Like sun-warmed honey. 'He makes me feel safe. Cared for,' she whispered to me. He was also practical and one day he chopped some wood for our woodburner; another day he fixed a broken door handle. The sort of thing that Pip would have done.

He smelt almost like a boy, with his sense of fun. That outdoors, fresh air and clean socks smell. I loved jumping up for food, and he seemed to think this really funny. I don't know why – I mean, it's food. I want it to eat it. Simple.

Several weeks after our Looe trip, we were walking into town when we heard a hoot and looked round. Ted was waving from his car. We walked over and he wound down the window.

'Off anywhere exciting?' asked Suki. I could tell she wanted to jump in the car with him.

'I'm off to see my wife,' he said, and he smelt rank. 'Then I'll go and see my in-laws.' He sounded as if someone had hidden his favourite toys. 'I'll be away for about a week.'

There was a second's silence. 'Well, I hope it goes OK,' she said, her voice falling.

'Perhaps we could have another walk when I get back?' he said.

Suki beamed. I could smell the primrose smell of it. 'OK,' she said. 'Give me a ring when you're home.'

He nodded and smiled. 'Certainly will.' He looked down at me. 'I'll look forward to seeing you both soon.' It was the sort of pointless thing that people often said, but I could tell he meant it; it smelt genuine, like a good bone.

He drove off then, and we watched his car disappear down the hill. As we continued to walk into town, she said, 'You know, I'll miss him, Moll. It's really nice just knowing he's there.' She sighed. 'But at least he'll be back soon.'

And I thought, good. As I said to Pip, on the beach the next morning, 'She needs someone she can be relaxed with, and laugh with.' I waited. Was Pip jealous? Was that why he didn't answer? However, I felt I must continue. 'He's thoughtful and generous and lifts her spirits. Well, when he's not talking about his wife, he does.' Still nothing. I tried again. 'It's too soon for her to meet The One, but I think this Ted will do for a stop gap. Just for some sex. Don't you?'

Still there was no reply. I was beginning to think there never would be.

A few weeks later, she announced we were going away. 'We're going on holiday next week to Penzance, Moll. Our first holiday without Pip. But I've booked a cottage we've never been to before, so there won't be any Pip memories.'

She didn't say anything more, but I could smell she was worried about going: a sharp tang, like sweat. 'We won't be on our own,' she continued. 'Tess and Titch are coming for a few days.'

I was delighted; more time with Titch! How fabulous.

And it was even better than I imagined. The cottage was hidden in a secret garden with the best smells ever – pigeons, rabbits and the odd fox regularly used the garden as a shortcut. The house was a bit dark but it was tucked away from traffic and smelt safe and she was happy having time to ourselves, as well as time with friends.

We had an especially nice time when Tess and Titch came along. We'd seen them once or twice a week since that first meeting, and it was very pleasant, barking as we scampered along, sharing bits of information – 'lovely bit of fox poo over there' or 'remains of a ham sandwich, I'll split it with you,' though Titch wasn't as keen on food as me.

We had four whole days of fantastic walks and great food (they got a whole leg of lamb from the butcher and we had lamb tea several nights running. What a treat! My whiskers shook at the very thought of it).

Every morning, when we woke up, Suki would take tea into Tess's room where Titch was sleeping, and I would sneak in for a cuddle with both of them. What a way to start the day! Tess always had a few biscuits with her tea so I had a few as well, and she would read in bed while Titch and I dozed with her. Then after breakfast we would walk along the seafront and if the tide was out we'd run along the beach which had big pebbles rather than sand but was still good for sniffing and running. We came across strange, long bits of seaweed, the remains of an upturned boat. Next to the sea was a weird park where people skated up and down huge ramps and made a terrific noise as they whooshed along. It was all very mysterious but we had fascinating smells and sounds.

'Thanks so much for doing the website,' Tess said one morning. It was cool but quiet, the waves whispering far out to sea as we walked down to the beach. 'I've had several enquiries already about dog walking, and I've decided to put a few puppy training classes on my Facebook page to see what response I get. I might do some classes for nervous dogs as well.'

'Brilliant idea,' Suki said. 'I know several people with rescue dogs who could do with some help.'

'That would be great. I was going to give my notice in at the end of the month, but my Mum isn't well, so I'm going to have to go and see her first. Otherwise I'm ready to go.'

'I'm sorry about your mum, but it's brilliant news about your business, Tess. I'm really glad for you.'

'And,' said Tess, sidestepping a large puddle. 'I have a client who lives in Flushing who happened to mention he's looking for a freelance researcher. Might you be interested?'

'Yes!' Suki said. 'Did he say what's involved?'

Tess shook her head. 'No, but he asked if you could give him a ring and discuss it.'

'That's amazing,' said Suki. 'Oh, just think how great it would be to get some more work! Thanks so much, Tess.'

'Well you haven't got it yet, but see what he says.'

'Certainly will.' Suki skipped along the beach, curls flying, looking like a little girl. It was catching, this joy; Titch and I scampered along after her, barking and feeling our ears blowing in the breeze.

Later she rang this fellow, put down the phone and said, 'Oh! He sounds really nice. It's not overly exciting stuff, but it would be regular and I can work from home. He wants help for at least the next three months. Oh, Tess, I can't thank you enough!'

Tess gave her a hug. 'You helped me – I help you. That's how friends work, isn't it?'

'It certainly is,' Suki said. And she smelt so happy, like warmed honey, it was a joy to smell. At last, she was content!

Later that night, Tess was upstairs talking to her partner, and Suki and I were sitting on the sofa watching telly. I was pressed close up to Suki; I liked to feel her body warmth, and know she could feel mine.

'You know, in a way it's good knowing that we've only got ourselves to look after, Moll,' she said. 'I don't have to worry about whether Pip's OK, if he's warm enough, or got a drink, or coughing too much, or anything. No matter how much I loved him, it's a relief not having to worry about all that.' She gave a sigh and hugged me close. 'And now, at last, I've got some regular work again. I can't tell you the difference that makes.'

Over the next few days, we met lots of people she knew through her writing, we went to some great cafes and had bits of cake, sausage rolls crumbs, bits of pasties. Such a treat. We also walked along the coast and explored different beaches, and it was the best time ever. Well, apart from times with Pip, of course. I liked having friends to stay, and

Tess always slipped me the odd treat when she thought Suki wasn't looking.

So it was a healing time for both of us. It was good to get away from home, have some new smells and adventures. Eat different food. Hear different sounds and meet different dogs. But all too soon the week was up and we had to come back to real life.

In that short time, we had become close, me and Titch, and I could feel my ears drooping when it was time to go. Titch's tail fell between his legs as we snickered goodbye and kissed whiskers. At least we knew we'd see each other again soon, but parting was a decidedly sombre affair.

8

Over the next few weeks, Suki had a run of bad luck. First of all someone tried to steal all the money from her bank account. I didn't understand how that worked, but the air was thick with stress and she smelt terrible. Finally, after several days, she got the money back.

Then the front door lock broke but luckily Pip's brother Pete got a locksmith to come. Then she heard that an old friend was very poorly, but Suki couldn't go and see her as she didn't want visitors.

While all those horrible things were going on, the air in the house smelt so rank it was difficult to breathe. But one morning I woke up and knew that something had shifted. I could smell it as soon as we went out. The sun was shining (at last), so we walked through the fields down to the sea, smelled the bluebells in the cemetery, and I chased a few squirrels. She even hummed a bit and it was as if someone had switched a light on inside her.

Later on we met Tess for a drink. Our local pub was called the Star and Garter and they had treats on the bar in a big jar. Suki liked me to jump up to get the biscuits so I always obliged, and everyone thought I was really clever. Well, I was.

The things I did to get some food, sometimes, but if it kept her happy, that was fine with me.

She and Tess always had lots to talk about but once we'd had our treats, Titch and I tended to lie by their feet and snooze, unless some more food came our way. There were usually crisp crumbs on the carpet if you searched hard enough.

Anyway, they had a good chat and I could tell that cheered her up, and it was always good to see Titch. We were walking back from the pub after their drink, when who should drive along but Ted! He leant out of the car window and I could see the way his eyes lit up.

'How are you?' she said.

'It's been a very long week, and a long drive, but I'm glad to be home and very glad to see both of you,' he said, exhaustion oozing from his words. 'How about a walk sometime?'

'That would be lovely,' she said.

'Shall I ring you in the morning?'

'I'll look forward to it,' she said, and waved as he drove off. Very slowly.

We continued walking home and it was as if someone had turned up that light inside her so it shone much brighter. Extraordinary the effect some people had. But then I could understand that. I felt all warm and fuzzy when I thought of Titch.

We were lying in bed, later, when Suki said, 'Moll, I feel as if there are bubbles of happiness fizzing inside me'.

A light turned on was one thing. But bubbles? Fizzing? What on earth was she talking about?

Something had definitely changed inside her, with Ted being back. She smelt like a flower opening in spring sunshine. Perhaps she was beginning to heal?

When Pip became ill, most of Suki's energies were focused on him. The rest was on me, of course, and trying to keep herself together, on her work and her friends. Then when he died, we missed him in a way that ate us up. Still did. He was too big a presence to just not be there any more. Who could live up to him? No one.

But there was a growing spark between Suki and Ted, even though they were both wary. My gut instincts told me (and her, if I smelt correctly), that he was essentially just what she needed. He was kind, generous, thoughtful, had a great sense of fun. And of course there was this very strong happy scent. As she said to me, when we were lying in bed one night, 'He's like a younger Pip.' Which of course I'd already realised. I'd found that humans often took longer to understand things than we did.

But underneath it all was this business with his wife. I could smell hesitation, fear and confusion. Like food going off. Though I didn't see why they couldn't have sex, like Errol and I did.

While there were lots of pluses, there were also a few question marks. But it was early days. So much had happened so quickly. One minute she was bawling her eyes out over Pip, the next a kind man with green eyes came along. Why shouldn't she be cheered by his kindness? I could almost see her loneliness sometimes, like sharp bones poking through her jumper. Grief seemed to do that. It was like we shed layers of skin or fur so that everything felt much more painful.

I still held onto a faint whisper of hope that Pip might come back. I suspect Suki felt it too. I could imagine it so well. Hearing his footsteps soon the pavement, and I would bark and bark, then the door would open and he would call, 'Suki?'

and I would bark and run to greet him, and he would give me a lovely cuddle, and she would cry, 'Pip?' as if she didn't believe he was there. And she would run along the corridor, laughing and crying all at once, and hold him so very very tight and never let him go again. And we would pick up and go on as we had done, just the three of us.

We both knew that wouldn't happen, but it was Wishful Thinking that got us through the early, bad days like a tantalising treat. She was writing in her diary the other day and I leaned over (I learnt to read human language quite quickly), and this is what she said.

'His absence is a slow, steady ache that burns its way up my guts, like a hot river running upstream. There can be no going back – no holding on to any bits of him – for life continues relentlessly. Which is a good thing in a way. The only thing we can do is try to swim with it.'

Quite poetic that. In fact, I might try my hand at poems myself, one of these days.

Ted rang and said would we like to go for a walk on Sunday? Trouble was, it was pouring with rain and it seemed he wasn't keen on getting wet, so Suki and I had our wet walk first thing and then met him for brunch.

They talked about where they'd travelled. What their childhoods were like. Who their best friends were, then and now. What they liked eating. Funny things that had happened to them. What they loved doing – he loved surfing, walking and climbing; she loved singing, reading and exploring. What they were good at. What they didn't like. They talked about their work; a difficult design he was working on. An interview she did that nearly went wrong, but was saved at the last moment. It was almost like they were trying to cram years worth of knowing each other into hours.

He didn't mention his wife, I notice, whereas she did mention Pip a few times. His wife was like this massive Great Dane in the corner that they both knew was there but pretended they couldn't see or smell.

We spent a long time in the cafe and they laughed a lot and although they didn't touch at all, other than to hug goodbye, it was clear to me that they really wanted to, and the musky smell was overpowering. Why didn't they just get on with it?

I wondered if Suki and Pip had smelt like this when they first met. In a way, it must have felt like going backwards in time for Suki because Ted was so like a younger Pip. The Pip who died must have been very different from the man Suki fell in love with.

As we walked back from the cafe it was almost like she floated up the hill. She smelt like freshly baked bread (Pip used to make it a lot). All soft and rising and warm and full of promise. It was like having a warm belly full of food, but this had bubbles in it as well.

But when we finally went to bed, Suki tossed and turned all night, so I wasn't able to sleep either. I could feel shivers of excitement running through her. It was like part of her had woken up after a long sleep. And all because of Ted.

They met at least once a week after that, more if they could. I could sense how comfortable they were together: she could say anything to him. He came round one night to mend a catch on a window and they had a few glasses of wine and played music, and he stayed till midnight. They didn't touch but just talked and talked and talked. You'd think they would have run out of things to say, but words and laughter and more words poured out of them. It was good to hear.

Even when Suki met Tess, all they talked about was Ted, and how she felt, how he felt. Why didn't they just get on with it?

This arousal thing interested me, having felt it with Errol. I could understand why it was such a very powerful drug, though from my limited experience I thought that dogs approached it differently from humans. Sex was exciting but essentially a functional thing for us, designed to make pups, whereas humans did it to make children, but they made sex much more complicated by involving their feelings. But then, humans made everything more complicated by involving their feelings.

I could sense this really strong sex urge inside Suki and Ted, but they were both holding back. Yet the feeling was so powerful that I felt one of them would burst if they didn't do something. If only they'd hurry up!

A week later it was Suki and Pip's wedding anniversary and I thought this would really upset her, but you know what she said? 'I'll be OK, Moll, 'cos Ted's around. In a funny way, Pip is much nearer. He'd faded right away and now he's back and happy.'

Very odd that, but if she was happy, I was happy.

There was no denying that she was behaving very out of character, but I'm sure this was because of wanting sex. She said to Tess last night, 'I feel like a teenager again. I'm all tingly and excited and nervous and I can't sleep. I don't know whether I'm terrified or delighted.' She giggled. 'I keep having these outrageous fantasies about him.' She sighed. 'My sexuality, which has lain dormant for so long, has decided to resurrect itself with a vengeance.'

Tess rolled her eyes and said, just as I felt, 'Well, get on with it, woman. You're driving us all mad.'

'Sorry,' she said, with a huge smile. 'I don't know what on earth's the matter. I can't sleep, can't eat, and seem to spend the whole time in a state of perpetual excitement. All because of Ted.' She looked at Tess, then added, 'I'm frightened of getting involved. He's wary, too, but that's a good thing, don't you think? I mean, I'm still very vulnerable.'

Tess leant over, and said, 'If you don't shag him soon, I think I'll explode.' But she gave her a hug, so I don't think she really meant it.

We had a much-needed breather because Ted had a friend to stay for two weeks. I was glad for it was all getting a bit frustrating. But Suki was was busy with research work for this guy in Flushing and she'd started singing again. She was happier than she'd been since Pip died, and she was surrounded by people who loved her. And me, of course.

At night I dreamt beside her, wondering what it would be like having a man in our lives again. To sleep in our bed again. Someone who'd be there for meals, come for walks – all the important things in life. I twitched while I thought and she laughed. 'Your paws drum when you dream as if you're running, Moll,' she said.

It occurred to me that I was possibly more pragmatic (I haven't used that word for a while) than Suki, and certainly less emotional than her, though that didn't mean I missed Pip any the less.

But we were both getting used to our new life. We had to. Pip had settled into the space that he needed to occupy. Even though he wasn't in our physical lives any more, he was still very much in our heads and our hearts. We carried his love everywhere we went, which was a lovely warm feeling that smelt like a casserole cooking; all that tasty meat, and onions, and garlic, carrots and stock and salt and pepper and a bit of cumin or curry powder. Love was all enriching, like all those different ingredients mingling around us.

Pip was a complicated person, but whereas he had his hidden sadness, he never faltered in his love for us. It was like a long, solid tunnel of love. Admittedly he was ill a lot of the time I knew him, but I never doubted his love, and it made me feel safe and secure. At least, I did until he became very poorly and smelt so bad. When I realised I was going to lose half of my family at one go I did panic a bit; my whiskers turned grey overnight.

But I sensed that he did all he could to stay with us. As Suki's brother said at the time, 'If anyone can get through it, you know he will. He just adores you.'

OK, so Pip lost that particular battle. But I knew I was safe with her. She wouldn't let me down. She wouldn't ever leave me.

9

Ted started to come out with us more often, and walks were always more interesting with him. After the Looe walk, he took us out one Sunday to a car boot sale, though all we did was walk up and down rows of stuff piled on blankets on the ground. The best bit was being near the food lorries which had bacon baps, so I had a bit of bread, and bacon. Yum. Suki never let me have things like that normally.

After the car boot sale, we drove a long way. It was a sunny day and I lay in my special bed in the back of the van, which Pip had put a metal grille in front of, so I wouldn't fall into the front if we stopped suddenly. He was clever like that. Also, when the windows were open, I got a nice breeze in my face as we drove along.

Eventually we got to a place called Lizard, which Titch had said were like little snakes, but I couldn't see any. We parked in a layby and walked a long way along the coastal footpath which smelt of warm grass and hot flowers and the wind blew ozone off the sea. It was salty and you wouldn't want to eat it, but it still smelt good.

The ground was nice and springy under my paws and was lovely to walk on after pavements; I liked to feel grass between my claws.

We walked until we saw a little beach and there was hardly anyone else there. We had to scramble down the cliff to get to it, and there was a rope hanging off the last bit so they could swing down onto the sand. I ran straight down onto the rocks, which were jagged but warm and the sand was smooth and very fine.

We played down there for a while and they had sandwiches and I had the crusts and a bit of his ham. The bread was all soft, and tasted plasticky, not like the stuff that Suki usually bought, but it was easier to eat.

And then we swam in the sea which was cold but very refreshing. I didn't like swimming when there were too many waves, but it was calm and I loved the feeling of cool water on my hot fur. They splashed each other and shrieked and laughed and I swam in a little circle as I was a bit unsure of getting out of my depth. I had to keep an eye on my people, after all. Someone had to be responsible.

Later that day we came home and I had my tea and he said he'd take her for something to eat so they left me at home but I was very tired. It had been a long day, and I had lovely dreams of beaches and sandwiches and the only thing I wished was that Titch had been able to join us. Suki came back later smelling tired but happy and I snuggled up to her and felt pleased that we were both safe and content. Pip couldn't complain about that.

That was the first of many days out. I loved our regular walks but it was always exciting going somewhere new: seeing what strangers had left messages, and if there was any fox or badger poo. Rabbits or unusual birds. You never knew what you'd find.

With Ted we often went to different places. If he was driving it meant I got to sit on her lap and look out of the window, but if it was hot we took the van which was cooler for us all.

We climbed up jagged rocks and scrambled down steep cliffs. We ended up in a sandy, soggy pile on the beach. They laughed for no reason. They often took picnics and I always had some; sandwich crusts, bits of pastry or corners of cheese. Ted smelt great and was really good at running around the beach with me. I could outrun him of course, but I let him win occasionally.

Those days were long and bursting with lovely smells and tastes and sensations like no other trips out. It was like seeing things in three dimension after looking at everything flat. Or tasting lots of different, exciting foods instead of my usual kibble.

We often went to the pub afterwards and the best bit was cheese and onion crisps. I loved Pip's crisps, but they tasted even better when I'd been running around the beach for ages.

Sometimes they'd go out for a drink in the evening after work, and I usually went too. My ears twitched as I eavesdropped, and I could inhale the lovely smells of people's dinners. Roast meat, veg and gravy which made me drool just to think of it. Fish and chips. I LOVE chips and that nice fatty stuff the fish was wrapped in.

I loved hearing the rumble of their voices. The smells of how they were feeling. Some couples sat in silence, smelling of boredom and despair, like stale biscuits. Other young couples would giggle and kiss, couldn't stop touching each other.

These two smelt of the live yeast that Pip used to make bread. Sweet and bubbly, about to rise. Full of promise. Except that it had gone past the rising stage and was fizzing like mad and I knew something would have to happen soon. Why didn't they just do sex?

But for all the tasty, exciting times we shared, there was a downside. It seemed so unfair, that she'd found someone who was right for her in so many ways, but there was this wife stuff holding them back.

At least once a month he drove away and he always started smelling sour about a week before he went. He would become distant, and distracted, like his body was here but his head wasn't. He looked all droopy, as if his whiskers had sagged. And finally, looking downcast and miserable, he would leave.

Sometimes, when he was away, we'd walk on the beach at Flushing and go past his house. It looked dark and shut up, cold and lonely, though I could still sniff him on the gate. That was comforting for me, but of course Suki couldn't sniff like I could, so she just wilted.

At least, I knew she wilted, but to most people I'm sure she appeared her usual bouncy self. She was much more back to normal now; she had more research work, she went singing, to the pub, to music gigs, to the cinema. She talked to her closest friends, and I knew they were concerned about her. Or rather, Ted.

'So when's he coming back?' was the usual question.

And she would shrug and say, 'At the end of the week,' as if she didn't care. But I knew that he'd crept into her head. He'd lodged in her soul. He flowed through her blood. And from what I'd seen, she'd done the same to him. She didn't tell anyone but I knew.

He rang up when he was away, but the phone calls were usually short. Sometimes she smelt happy afterwards, but other times she smelt really quiet and miserable, like stagnant water, and I hated him for that.

When he was here, life smelt different. Like a really good bone, it was fun and exciting, full of possibilities, whereas when he was away, life was much flatter.

On the surface, she had a busy life and everything seemed to run along fine without him. But underneath it all, there was now a pulse ticking while she waited for him to come back. Sometimes she was angry, sometimes she was upset and I hated that. It tasted of Marmite which I had the misfortune to eat once. It was much too salty and sharp and made even me feel a bit ill.

As the summer wore on, whenever Ted was away, she would say things like, 'He's done a lot for my confidence, Moll. He helped me get over Pip. He's made me feel attractive and desirable.' He was always telling her she had beautiful eyes, or amazing eyebrows. Lovely legs, looked great in shorts, that sort of thing.

'But he evidently has no place in my future. And that's OK.'

And I'd listen and think, who are you trying to fool? Why don't you just get on with it? As another friend said, 'Come on Suki, you need to get laid!'

When Ted came back from his trips up-country he smelt horrible. If you thought rotten chicken was bad, this was much, much worse. Almost as bad as that rank smell Pip had when he was very ill. Though this was different. I could tell that Ted's head was clogged up with wife stuff, and all his energy had seeped out.

I kept wondering why Ted and Suki couldn't get together, if the wife was ill and not here? It was driving me barking mad, but neither of them seemed to want to talk about it.

But one day when he came back from a visit to his wife, he knocked on the door and came in.

'I'm so sorry,' he said, and he smelt exhausted.

She glared at him, but it was as if something drew those two together, no matter how hard they tried to stay apart. It was so obvious how right they were for each other – and at the same time, how wrong. Why couldn't they just work it out?

He asked her what she'd been doing, and how she was. There was an awkward silence, then she said, 'So how was it?'

He still smelt sour, but gave a smile that wasn't a smile, and talked about how difficult it had been up there, and how unhappy he was.

Suki listened, and handed him a glass of wine. 'The thing is,' she said, as they sat on the sofa, me in between. 'Thing is, if Jane is so poorly, and there's no chance of her getting better, is there any reason why you can't have another relationship? I mean, you'd obviously still support her and visit her as you do now. But you wouldn't be so stuck. I mean, you're in limbo, aren't you?'

Ted looked as if she'd kicked him. 'I wish that was possible,' he said, his voice sinking. 'But her family don't think like that. Her parents are – obviously – desperately upset by their daughter's illness. As far as they're concerned, we married in sickness and in health. They'd be horrified if I said I'd met someone else,' he started to glow, 'and wanted to get together with them.'

Suki stared at the carpet as if there was a really tasty treat there. 'But surely, they must realise that your wife might be like this for a long time? Are you supposed to just carry on like this? And if so, wouldn't it be better to move to Derby, to be near her?'

Ted shook his head. 'I couldn't move up there.' He sounded horrified. 'My work's here, my friends, the house. Cornwall is my home.' He gulped. 'It's where my heart is.'

Suki looked up. 'So her family expect you to put your life on hold. Forever?'

'They wouldn't understand. They're devastated.'

'Of course they are,' she said.

'No one talks about it, but I don't feel able to just say – oh I've moved on, when Jane's only been in the home for a short while.' He paused. 'Maybe at some point in the future....' His voice trailed off but it was pretty obvious that there wouldn't be a point in the future.

Suki was silent, again staring at the carpet. Had I missed a crumb or something? 'I can understand how difficult it is, but I think it's very unfair on you,' she said, her voice wobbling slightly.

He looked up. 'It is,' he said. 'But it's unfair on her too. It's bloody unfair on everyone involved.' And I could sense that what he really wanted to do was take Suki in his arms and do sex with her. But there was so much Stuff between them, barricaded in by these walls of words – it was ridiculous. And made it all so much more complicated than it need be.

I sighed and lay with my nose on my paws while I thought. Surely there must be some way round this?

10

Another goodbye to Pip

In September Suki decided to scatter some of Pip's ashes.
How come he was now ashes? It didn't make sense to me, but
it seemed that when he died they put him in a cardboard box
which she'd kept beside the bed (on his side) since January.
But now she decided it was time to let him go into the river
not far from us which was, confusingly, called the Carrick
Roads, where Pip used to sail and fish for oysters.

'He loved boats and the water so much it's the perfect
place for him,' explained Suki.

We were both a bit apprehensive (another tasty new word)
about this outing, but first of all we ate a delicious lunch
provided by two friends called Michael and Andrea. I had a
tasty bit of fish, then Suki and I went with them on their boat,
up the river. The sky was a deep blue, and there were so many
other boats also enjoying the weather. And us! My first time
in a proper sailing boat!

At first I couldn't understand why people got so excited
about sailing. What a palaver. First of all we had to get in a
small boat called Tender, then Michael rowed us out to the
big boat. He clambered up onto it and then Andrea climbed
up, then Suki passed me up, then she came up too. The floor

(called a deck) was smooth and slippery when wet, so I had to be very careful. Usually on the ground there was something for my claws to grip onto, but on a boat there was nothing.

There was apparently an engine though we didn't use it but there were these big white flappy things called sails that caught the wind and took us along. So clever! I couldn't wait to tell Titch, because he liked this kind of adventure. He didn't need any encouragement when it came to Dangerous Things.

It was strange being so far from land and yet so high up in the water. The smells were different too with so many types of salt, and big birds like seagulls and cormorants that smelt really strong, and big fish and little fish which smelt oily and, well, fishy. I could feel the wind in my ears and it ruffled my fur as we went along so fast!

We stopped at a place where Suki pointed to a big granite post which was the boundary between Truro Harbour and Falmouth Harbour and Michael read a poem called "Sea Fever" by someone called Masefield, as well as Brian Patten's "How long does a man live?" Suki was going to read something, but said she knew she would be crying too much to speak at this point.

Then when they'd done all the talking, Suki said, "Goodbye darling," and emptied a tin full of Pip into the river. It didn't smell of him at all. Just dust and cardboard and lots of ash. Andrea had bought two bunches of flowers which she threw onto the water on top of him, and with each one Suki shouted one of Pip's favourite sayings – including "shoot the bastards" and his made-up German swear words. And I barked. A lot.

My ears and whiskers went all over the place. You could feel all the sadness and happiness in that boat, and all the love for him and for her and it made me so proud that he'd brought me up, and even more proud that her friends loved us so much to do this.

And then suddenly the wind caught the sails and the boat rushed forwards and I nearly went overboard. Suki grabbed me but she was laughing and said, "It's Pip saying, Come on, enough of that, let's go for a sail!" So we did and it was ever so exciting and almost took our minds off the sad bits.

When we finally got home it was a mix of an exciting, happy and very sad day. Suki said, "Wherever we go, it seems Pip will be there, somewhere. Just keeping an eye on us." And I let her give me a big cuddle. We both needed it.

Ted was away when this happened, which meant we could both focus on Pip, which we needed to do. We went to bed that night and I'm sure she dreamt of him, as she gave contented little snuffles in her sleep. She didn't do that when she dreamt of Ted.

Whenever he came back from seeing his wife, what he really needed to do was put his head on his paws and have a good long snooze. Gradually the bad smell lessened, but for the first few days it lurked underneath everything, like a really bad pong. However, the longer he was with us, the less he smelt, though every now and then there would be a nasty whiff.

As the weeks went by, I could tell Ted was getting more and more confused and frustrated; it was a bittersweet smell. He was driving back from a walk one day when he said, 'You know how I feel about you, Suki, but you are very vulnerable, and I couldn't.... it wouldn't be fair on you or...' He evidently still couldn't bring himself to mention his wife's name.

Suki sat very still, looking out of the window, instead of at him. 'I know,' she said stiffly, and they were silent for the rest of the journey.

One day we were walking along the beach at Flushing when we saw an elderly man collecting shells. 'Petroc!' cried Ted, sounding really pleased to see him.

The man turned round and smiled. I went up and sniffed; I liked the smoky scent to him. 'Ted!' he said. 'Good to see you. I was going to invite you to a game of Scrabble tonight, but I see you have company.'

Ted indicated me and Suki. 'Petroc, please meet my friends Suki and Moll.'

He bowed slightly from the waist, like I do when I want to play. 'How very pleasant to meet you,' he said, as he straightened and held out his hand. 'I haven't seen Ted look so well for a long while. You must be doing him good.'

Suki shook his hand. 'I hope so,' she said. 'I think we help each other, and anyone who enjoys walking is welcome with me and Moll.'

'I'm making some tea, Petroc,' Ted said. 'Will you join us?'

Petroc looked from us to Ted and as he smiled, a peaceful feeling ran over me. Like warm treacle. 'I'd very much like that, as long as I'm not intruding,' he said.

'Of course not.' Ted smiled at Suki. 'Follow me.'

I was intrigued to have a good sniff round Ted's house. As we walked up the path, in through the front door, I paused. No smell of wife, at least. We went into the kitchen, where Petroc seemed to be at home as straight away he sat down at one of the chairs around a big wooden table.

Suki followed him, while I scavenged on the floor, listening to them talk. Breakfast crumbs of toast, bit of marmalade. Smells of coffee, overlaid with the tea Ted was brewing right now. No bad smells here, though there was something else underneath. A hint of sadness, like an easterly wind. Smelling biscuits, I emerged from under the table and jumped onto a chair next to Suki.

'Have you lived in Flushing a long time, Petroc?' Suki asked, clasping her hands around a mug of tea that Ted had passed to her.

'My wife and I moved here forty years ago,' he said. 'Flushing became our home, even though I'm originally from Cury, on the Lizard. She died three years ago.'

'I'm sorry,' she said.

Ted joined them at the table. 'She was a very talented artist.' He pointed to a painting on the wall. 'That was one of hers.'

Suki got up and examined it. 'I love the colours. How clever.'

'She certainly was.' Petroc sipped his tea, and took a biscuit from the plate on the table. I shifted closer, nose quivering. They were dark chocolate digestives – oaty, sweet and crunchy; an extra special treat.

'How did you and Ted meet?'

Petroc smiled. 'It was one bonfire night. They always used to have a huge fire on the beach, not far from here. One year there was a sudden downpour, not long after the bonfire was lit. Everyone stood around for a bit but we were all soaked, and Ted invited my wife and I for a drink. We dried out and Ted opened a bottle of wine and we spent the rest of the evening here which was the start of many a good soiree.'

'Petroc and his wife were a real whizz at Scrabble,' Ted said, pulling a face. 'We still play, but I can't hope to compete with him.'

'Do you play, Suki?' asked Petroc.

'Well, I haven't for a very long time.'

'Perhaps we could have a game one night?'

Suki smiled and I could smell how pleased she was. 'I'd love that,' she said.

Ted explained about Suki's book and Petroc smiled. 'If ever you wanted someone to proofread, I'd be delighted,' he said.

Suki went pink. 'That would be fantastic,' she said. 'No matter how careful I am, I always miss something, so that would be really useful.'

'Petroc used to run a language school, and he's also walked a lot around Cornwall, and knows a huge amount about Cornwall's history,' Ted said. 'He'd be the perfect person to proofread your book.'

'That's great,' Suki said. 'Thank you so much, Petroc.'

'My pleasure,' he said, smiling. 'I look forward to reading it. Let me give me you my email address so you can send it over.'

Ted handed the plate of biscuits round. I gave Petroc my best Wistful Stare. He broke the biscuit into pieces and slipped a few small bits onto the floor for me. I liked this man.

They were busy with email addresses and such like, then Suki drained her tea and looked at her watch. 'My goodness is that the time?' She got up. 'Thanks very much, but I must be off now.'

'You're going?' Ted sounded upset. 'I was going to make supper.'

'No, we have to get back,' Suki said. She smelt uneasy, so she obviously had some reason. 'Lovely to meet you, Petroc, and I look forward to that game of Scrabble sometime. Bye Ted, see you soon.' And she bent down, clipped my lead on and swept us out of the door.

'Sorry, Moll,' she said as we hurried back to the car. 'I just didn't feel comfortable. I mean, he's friends of Ted and his wife, and it just made me feel a bit, you know. Awkward. Used.'

I trotted along beside her, thinking. Awkward, yes, but I was pretty sure he wasn't using her, and Petroc seemed a dependable sort of person. But I had to be on my guard. I couldn't have her getting hurt again.

So next time we went down to Greenbank beach, I told Pip what was going on. 'And I don't think Ted will be The One,' I said. I waited for some response.

I didn't hear Pip, but it suddenly occurred to me that maybe Ted wasn't The One. But did that matter? He was male and they were enjoying each other's company. And what about Petroc? I had a tingly feeling as I felt he would be a good person to have in our life. A reliable, uncomplicated one. A true friend. It looked like he'd be generous with the biscuits, too.

We continued to see Ted about once a week, but every time they met, underneath their ease with each other, the tension grew. It crept up my whiskers and into my mouth and it tasted bitter, like almonds. It was so loud it drummed in my ears sometimes. I wanted to shove them together, do anything to burst that tension. But they had to work that out themselves.

On midsummer's evening, Ted came to listen to Suki singing with her choir on a big beach on the north coast of Cornwall. I went too and we had a huge picnic on the beach with all the other singers (I had several sausages and all sorts of strange vegetarian things on the quiet) and we had a fabulous run along the sand. It had been a hot sunny day but when the sun went down, the sand was beautifully cool and smooth under my paws and I wished we could stay there for ages. But I got a bit tired and eventually we got a lift back and while we'd all had a fabulously different day, I could smell Ted's frustration, lurking like a sick smell.

Several times after that he asked her out for a drink, but she kept saying no. Why not, I barked? She seemed to understand me at last because she looked down and smiled. 'Because he's not free and I don't want to get hurt,' she said firmly. Well, I know that 'hurt' meant something different to humans than to us dogs. So I yipped, quietly. I understood.

Ted continued to ask her out, and eventually, she said she would have dinner with him. Not at the pub, where I could have gone with them, but to what she called a Posh Restaurant. She spent ages getting ready. She tried on one dress after another, then different shoes and make up and sprayed this smelly stuff all over her and finally, she was done.

Would this be the night that Something Happened? I was longing to know, so I had a snooze and eventually she came back. She didn't say anything but she smelt strong. Like steel. In charge. We went to bed and I cuddled up next to her and thought, what will he do now?

He had to go and see his wife the following week, so we didn't see him for a while but one evening we were watching telly and there was a knock on the door. She jumped up and I could smell hope on her skin, anticipation in her footsteps. She opened the door and there he was, with a bunch of flowers.

'For you,' he said, sounding hopeful.

She looked down at them. 'They're lovely,' she said and looked up at him. I could see her wavering. 'I would ask you in, but you must be exhausted,' she said.

His smile slid off his face. 'I, yes, I am rather,' he said and he smelt so tired I was amazed he could stand up. He turned to go. 'Perhaps we could have dinner again soon?'

'Maybe,' she said carefully.

'Or, something else?'

'Maybe,' she repeated, and we watched him retreat down the path, back to his car.

She didn't say anything to me but her hands were shaking when she poured herself a glass of wine that she drank a wee bit too fast. She looked at the telly, then got up and looked out of the window and then she said, 'Come on Moll, walkies,' and we had a long walk around the streets which we didn't usually do at that time of night. Usually it was just round the block.

Come on, I was thinking. Say yes, for dog's sake.

11

A boating picnic

'How about a picnic on the boat?' he said.

We'd gone into town to go to the bank, and met him outside the bakery. 'Picnic?' she said, as if he'd suggested killing someone. 'On the boat?' But I could smell interest.

He shrugged and smelt embarrassed, as if he'd farted. 'The forecast is good at the weekend. I thought it might be fun to take the boat out. We could go fishing, have a picnic, or a barbecue if we catch some fish.'

She stood there with her head to one side, like a bird, and Ted and I held our breath for what seemed like ages. 'OK,' she said eventually. But I could sense she liked the idea.

The relief! It smelt as if they were discussing much more than a picnic, but they arranged to meet at Greenbank Quay, not far from where we lived, at 11 on Sunday morning. Suki and I would bring a quiche and some drinks and Ted would supply the rest.

She hummed as we had our walk that morning on a day which was warm for late September. 'We might find a beach and go swimming, Moll,' she said, as she packed her swimsuit and towel along with the food, water and biscuits for me.

As we walked down to Greenbank Quay, I could sense the excitement, bubbling under her skin. I could almost see it creeping into her toes, along her feet and up through her body; she smelt like I do before Titch and I are about to go on a long walk. I wished he was with us, because I had a feeling this might be special.

Ted was already waiting for us, and he was able to bring the boat right alongside the quay so we could step on board easily, not like Michael's boat where we had to get in Tender and then clamber up.

Ted's was a motor boat with a cabin, 'so there's shelter if it gets wet or windy,' he said as we settled ourselves on proper seats with cushions. There were no sails on this one (I was getting knowledgeable about boats, you notice), and Suki and I looked out over the water as Ted pulled a string to get the engine going and we chugged along.

It was very different compared to sailing. It was noisier and smelt oily from the fuel (I wouldn't want to taste that), but we chugged up the river and there were interesting smells coming from the different scents of the salt and seaweed and the cormorants with outstretched wings, sitting on big cones in the water, and the gulls screeching overhead, and everything looked so different from the sea. The deck (see, I remembered the parts of boats), was very smooth under my paws, and made of hard plastic stuff but it wasn't wet, so I didn't slip.

It was enjoyable, taking in all the smells, sounds, tastes and stuff, but then I thought, was this all we were going to do? Sit on this boat? What about a walk? Some food?

However, just then Ted said, 'I thought we'd have our picnic over there,' and he pointed to a beach near a lighthouse, not too far away. That looked exciting, and I stood on my hind legs so I could check where we were going. The spray bounced into my face with cold wet spits but it was fine, because Suki held onto me tightly.

'Moll could do with a lifejacket,' said Ted as he steered the boat round a big pink thing that I later learned was a Boy.

'She'll be OK,' said Suki, but I could detect a sudden tinge of panic and she held me tighter.

'Of course she will,' said Ted easily. 'I just meant, if you'd like to come out again, you know, regularly, it might be an idea.'

She didn't look up but I could sense we were both thinking the same thing; we might do this again? I'd reserve judgement till I knew what it was going to be like today. But I could smell her excitement, like wild garlic.

She and Ted talked, but not as much as they usually did. They were quieter, more thoughtful. As usual, the tension was there, simmering away like one of Pip's casseroles, though it didn't smell as good or as straightforward.

As we got nearer the beach, there was silence and I thought, he's going to say something to burst this bubble, but then she said, 'What do you call this beach?'

And he sort of deflated but said, 'I've always called it Lighthouse Beach.'

She nodded. 'That's what Pip called it but it's got another name, I think. Can't remember what it is though.' I had the feeling she was talking rubbish just to stop him from saying something. 'There's no one else there!' she added, sounding pleased.

He chuckled, a rich sound like meat in gravy. 'That's why I thought we'd come here. Not many people venture out for picnics at this time of year, and not often in boats.'

She smiled at him then, a flash that he might have missed but he was quick and caught it, like when they throw a ball to me. And from then on the tension sort of leaked out over the water, and the smell in the boat changed completely.

We neared the beach and Ted slowed the engine and jumped ashore, getting his feet wet. Suki passed me over, very carefully, as it was a bit high to jump down, and Ted took hold of me with strong firm hands and lowered me gently on the beach, where the sand was warm and crunchy underneath my paws, and I was so excited I ran. It was fantastic! I was a sailor! I tore round in little circles and then looked back, and Ted was holding out his arms to her. She shook her head but she was laughing and he said, 'Come on,' but she ignored him, handed him the bag with the picnic things and then she jumped into the sea, shrieking as the water hit her feet, then her jeans.

They both laughed and I ran up and down and barked with them, and Ted walked up the beach and found a space at the back with rocks around it and we spread the picnic out in the sun. I had water, as I was thirsty, and some chicken and bits of cheese and some of my biscuits and it was the best picnic I'd ever had.

They had quiche and boring stuff like coleslaw and just as I was thinking I could nick a few bits of leftover quiche without them noticing, Suki tidied all the food away into the bag and they drank fruit juice and then we all lay on the sand while they stared at the sun.

'Walk or swim first?' said Ted, his voice sounding deep and lazy.

'Oh, swim I think,' she said. 'But we'd better let our food go down first.'

I started digging then, but I always got bored after a few minutes, so I lay down between them so I could keep a careful ear on what was happening. Or not. See if I could move things on a bit. The tension was back but it tasted different. Sweeter.

After a while, Ted sat up and held out his hand. 'Walk now, swim on the way back?'

Suki looked up at him. 'OK.' She took his hand and he pulled her up to sitting and then they looked at each other but still he held her hand. I felt like something was going to snap. Then she let go of his hand and dusted down her jeans and said, 'Better get going then.'

Ted stashed the picnic back on the boat, which had a big metal thing called an anchor stuck into the sand to stop the boat drifting away, and we set off up the cliffs. There were a few puffy clouds but it was still warm and we reached the top and walked along the path till we came to a car park and some long, low houses which Ted said were let out for holidays.

'People can also stay in the lighthouse,' he added, and led the way down a steep tarmac path until we came to some big gates. They were shut, but behind them we could see a massive white thing that stuck up into the sky. It was so tall and rounded and the oddest and biggest building I'd ever seen.

'You don't want to be here when the foghorn goes off,' said Ted.

Suki laughed. 'I was walking near Lizard Lighthouse once when their foghorn went off – it was so loud I thought my eardrums were going to burst!'

We retraced our steps and set off along the coastal footpath, which was much more fun. The ground was dusty and smelt of feet and paws and sweat and happiness. We passed a bird hide which confusingly was for people to hide in, not birds, and then we came to a sign down to a beach. We looked down, over the cliffs, to the path, which wound down to a small sandy cove. 'There's no one there,' said Ted. 'How about a swim?'

'Why not?' said Suki, and we ran down the steep path, and after about ten minutes we scrambled down to another beach.

It was smaller than the beach we'd picnicked on and looked like no one had been there, ever. No paw prints, no bird or human prints, no dropped food, nothing. The sand was so fine and white it was like dust on my paws, and so clean and soft. I ran in circles to christen it, and I heard them both laughing, and then she said, 'Last one in's a sissy!' and she stripped off, pulled her swimsuit on in record time, left her clothes on a pile on the beach and ran right down to the water's edge, so I thought I'd better go with her.

I looked back and Ted was standing there, smiling. And then he stripped off too and put his trunks on and came running after us and we all jumped into the water which was really cold and she shrieked and laughed and then he got very near and flicked water at her. She flicked some back but I swam back to the beach because they were being silly. And then he dived under the water and came up beside her and he came even closer and leaned forward and kissed her. And she did nothing for a minute and then started kissing him back.

These weren't like the kisses she'd had with Pip. Those were full of slow love. These were fast and urgent, almost as if they were trying to eat each other. And I could sense that these kisses were made of a different kind of love that was changing shape all the time.

I got out of the water and shook myself and they were still kissing and I was sort of glad but I had a feeling that nothing would be the same and I wasn't sure I wanted it to change. So I barked. Several times.

They broke apart and laughed and Ted said, 'Moll's right. We'd better get a move on.' And he held out his hand and this time she took it and they ran out of the water, up the beach and stripped off their swimsuits and dried themselves, and they were giggling and it made me feel good too so I barked again and ran around the beach to get dry.

They tugged their clothes on and we struggled up the path back to the cliff top, and I could smell their happiness and it was as sweet as fox poo in spring.

By the time we got back to the boat there were a lot more clouds overhead and Ted frowned. 'Come on, we'd better head back,' he said, helping us both onto the boat. 'The weather's coming up from the west. They said it wouldn't rain till around 6 but it's coming in early.'

So we settled inside the cabin and watched Ted steer our way back. It was a bit bouncy from the waves but it was fun because we were sheltered from the wind, and he pointed out things as we went along. 'That's St Mawes Castle behind us and the one opposite is Pendennis Castle. They were built by Henry VIII and reportedly had a chain across the harbour to stop invaders coming into Falmouth.'

I looked out to see these big round stone buildings that looked all old and worn so they must have been built ages ago. As we headed back to Falmouth he pointed out Pendennis Head. We walked there sometimes, but all we could see now was light glinting which Suki said was the sun on people's cars in the car park. Then as we got nearer, we saw Falmouth Docks which was massive and full of big boats and strange bits of tall machinery and smelt of gas and oil and then we could see Flushing and the beach and suddenly the sky clouded over and it got really dark and the rain came down really hard.

We were all right as we were in the cabin, but it was quite frightening as it got windy very suddenly and the boat rocked from side to side and Ted was standing there getting soaking wet.

'Have you got any waterproofs?' shouted Suki.

'There's a jacket underneath the cushions opposite where you're sitting,' he called back, so she dug around and found a cupboard under one of the seats and there was a big jacket which she handed up to him and he put it on.

It was still raining very hard but at least he wasn't getting quite so wet. 'Do you want to come back with me and I can drive you home?' said Ted. 'You'll get soaked walking back up the hill.'

Suki looked out; he was right, we would. 'OK, thanks,' she said. And I wondered, if we're going to his house, what else will happen?

12

Ted had to tie the boat to a mooring so we sheltered by a boathouse while he did that. Even so, by the time we got to his house Suki looked drowned, and my coat was cold and matted.

My fur was fine and long and took ages to dry out, but as soon as we got in the door Ted gave Suki a towel to dry me off, and lit the fire. 'There, she can dry out in front of that,' he said. 'Would you like a shower to warm up?'

She hesitated. 'No, I'm fine thanks. I don't have any dry clothes, so there's not much point.'

'There are some spare clothes of Jane's,' he said, and went pink.

Suki smelt very awkward; a peppery smell. 'No, I'm fine,' she said. 'I'm not that wet. I can dry out in front of the fire, with Moll.' She was rubbing me hard, which I didn't like.

'Or you could borrow one of my sweatshirts,' he said. 'Though it might be a bit big.'

She laughed. 'It'd be huge! No, don't worry. You go and shower and warm up.'

'If you're sure,' he said, but she shooed him out of the room, gave me some biscuits, and we settled down in front of the fire. The warmth of the flames seeped through my damp fur and I felt really mellow as it dried. My nose started to crack from the heat but that was all right. She sat next to me and her jeans started to steam, but she didn't seem to mind. We listened to the crackle and fizz and pop of the logs and she added a few more, and we got warmer and drier, and after a bit she got up to have a look around.

Looking out of the big long windows we could see a thin garden which led to the river, and looked over to Falmouth. We could probably have seen our house if we'd known where to look.

The room we were in had a big sofa with fat cushions and a huge telly, much bigger than ours. There was another comfy looking chair and a table and chairs nearest the garden. On the walls were lots of pictures which Suki examined closely, and a big mirror facing the windows which made the room look larger.

Next she looked at the book cases, and taking down some books, flicked through them. I stayed in front of the fire. I was tired and a bit hungry, and barked at Suki who looked down, as if in a daze.

'Sorry, darling,' she said. 'You'd better have some tea, hadn't you?' And she rummaged around in our picnic bag. 'Here, you can have some leftovers. It's all bit damp, I'm afraid, but these will have to do until we get home.' And she gave me bits of biscuits and leftover cheese which she put in the collapsible bowl she carried with her.

Everything was a bit soggy but I didn't mind. I munched while I listened to Ted's footsteps upstairs. The water noise had stopped, so I presumed he was getting dressed. Sure enough, as I finished my scant meal, we heard footsteps on the stairs and Ted reappeared.

'I couldn't bear to think of you in damp clothes,' he said. 'So I found these.' He handed over a sweatshirt and some leggings. 'My sister left these here earlier in the summer when they came to stay. I was going to post them back but she said she'd pick them up next time she comes.'

Suki took the clothes and held them up against herself. They weren't too big. 'Thanks,' she said. 'These would be great.'

'If you'd like a shower, there's a clean towel just inside the door,' Ted said.

By the way they were both looking very pink, you'd think there was something really rude about having a shower. When they'd just been swimming together. And kissing!

She went even pinker, and said, 'OK, thanks,' for the umpteenth time. Then she grabbed the clothes and hurried upstairs where I heard the shower again.

Ted filled a bowl of water and put it down beside me, then opened the fridge. 'What have we got here?' he muttered, and pulled out some ham. And some cheese! I sat and looked up expectantly, my nose quivering. Other people's food is always so interesting. He wasn't to know I'd had a few snacks but that wasn't a proper tea.

He smiled, picked up my bowl and put a few lumps of ham in, then he added some cubes of cheese and put it down on the floor beside me. 'There you go, girl,' he said and I could feel him watching me as I ate. It didn't take long, it never does. My motto has always been, Life's Too Short To Chew. With six hungry siblings there was no time for table manners, it was all mouths to the bowl.

When I finished, I realised I needed a wee. I usually do after my tea, so I went and stood by the doors that were like big windows and Ted let me out into the garden. It was still raining, so I didn't stay long: I wanted to get back to the fire, so I hopped indoors again and settled back by the warmth.

Ted made himself a mug of tea and came and sat down on the big chair beside me, toasting his bare feet in front of the flames. He didn't speak at first, but when he did, his voice was low, not much more than a rumble.

'I expect you're wondering what I'm doing with your mum,' he said. His toe rubbed my stomach gently. It was rather soothing. 'Perhaps you think I should stay away from you two, but it feels as if I've known Suki forever. It's just so *easy*.' He sighed. 'She's everything I've ever wanted in a relationship. She's incredibly sexy. She's funny, she's kind, she's generous, loving and caring. She's clever.' He sipped his tea. 'And, of course, she has you.'

The toe continued rubbing. Up and down. Up and down. Left a bit, down a bit – yes!

'The trouble with me, as you know, is my wife. Jane.' The toe stopped a moment before continuing. 'I can't leave her. Well, I *have* left her to all intents and purposes, but I can't just abandon her. Every now and then, she recognises me and that's, well, I don't know which is worse really. When I go and she doesn't know who I am, or when she suddenly calls me by my name and asks why she's there, and not at home.' He groaned. 'Either is awful, to be honest, but I don't know what else I can do.'

His voice choked up and I could tell he was having trouble speaking. There was silence for another moment, then he said, 'I suppose you want to know what I can offer you both?'

I rolled over and looked at him. That was the multi-million-bone question. Also, his toe had stopped rubbing. I gave him what the vet calls my Paddington Bear Stare.

'I can offer you my companionship. I mean, we enjoy walks and days out together, don't we?'

I sneezed. Yes.

'Good. Well, I can also offer support and friendship. And I can cook,' he added. 'I'm not bad in the kitchen. I haven't got much in at the moment because I was about to do a shop, but I thought I'd make omelettes when she comes down. With salad. And French bread. Do you think she'd like that?'

My whiskers shimmered. She liked that sort of stuff. So did I.

'But, what I mean is, I want more.' He sounded awkward again. That peppery smell. 'I'd love a physical relationship with her. But that makes things more complicated.'

I have never understood why, but that was Humans for you. They always complicated things.

'And I'm pretty sure she would, too. The thing is, is it fair on her?'

Suki was old enough to make her own mind up, but I appreciated being asked. I stretched out in front of the fire and thought about me and Titch. We were very happy. We had a great time together, once or twice a week, and I thought about him a lot when we were apart. It would be fantastic if, say, they lived next door, or we moved in together, but that wasn't going to happen. I was a pragmatist (I had to get that word in again).

Well, I was pretty content, so why couldn't Ted and Suki be happy as they were? I mean, I could see that what they had was really special. She might never meet someone else she cared for so much.

On the other hand, she hated it when he went away. So did he, of course. But she hated it for two reasons. One, because he was going to see another woman, and two because it made him miserable. She hated seeing him sad, particularly when she couldn't do anything to stop his sadness.

So what did she want? I knew she wanted a relationship like she had with Pip; happy and settled, without too many complications. Would she ever find that again? It was so difficult to know. What if this was as good as it got?

I stared at the flames which were flickering and leaping and changing colour all the time. It was mesmerising and calming, but didn't help me come up with any advice for Ted.

It was terrible trying to decide for other people.

I was saved by a light tread on the stairs. I looked up, so did Ted, and there was Suki, dressed in the sweatshirt and some weird leggings.

'You look great,' said Ted, and I could hear the smile in his voice.

'Are you sure?' she said. She never usually worried what she looked like.

'Very sure,' he said firmly. 'Now how about some food?' He crossed over to the fridge and started pulling out things. 'An omelette with mushrooms, ham and cheese?'

Her stomach gave a loud rumble and they both laughed.

'And some salad,' he said, pulling lettuce and tomatoes out. 'And there's some French bread that needs heating up.'

'A feast!' she said, and moved to stand beside him. 'Now, what shall I chop?'

He handed her a big knife and gave her a board and an onion and soon the two of them were standing next to each other, chopping and laughing like they'd been doing it for years.

I sat and waited for a few scraps but they were both so intent on each other, I think they forgot about me. For once I wasn't offended. Joy ballooned out of them in a big warm cloud and wrapped round me like candy floss.

Mind you, even more joy streamed out of me when he put the omelette on the table in a big frying pan. The smells were exquisite: chopped onion, garlic, bits of bacon, mushrooms, topped with Cheddar and Emmental, lots of tarragon, and, of course, eggs. And black pepper and salt. People underestimate us dogs. I could tell you exactly what ingredients went into a dish by smelling it, as I just demonstrated.

But I digress. Suki was nearly drooling by the time the food was on the table and he served up. I sat right by her side, nose twitching in wonderment. And expectation.

They ate for a moment in silence, and then she said, 'This is wonderful. Best omelette I've ever had.'

Ted beamed. 'Glad it meets approval, but you cooked it as well.'

'No, I only did the chopping,' she said but I could hear her grin.

Silence while they ate. I could see I wasn't going to get anything from Meanie Mum so I went to sit beside Ted, put on my best beseeching face. It usually worked, particularly with men.

'You were talking to Moll when I came down,' she said.

Ted flushed and gave me a bit of bacon. That was better. I moved nearer, sat between his legs and gave him my Stare again. 'Yes,' he muttered.

'It's all right, I couldn't hear what you were saying.'

He sneaked a piece of egg into my mouth absently. 'I was asking her advice,' he said and got up suddenly. 'Fancy a beer? Glass of wine?'

'Wine, please,' she said, sounding a bit puzzled.

He fetched the drinks and came back, handed her a glass of wine, and they finished their meal in a comfortable silence.

'I always find it useful to talk aloud if I've got problems, and Moll's a very good listener,' he said, with a slight undercurrent of laughter in his voice. I nudged him with my nose. Got a bit of cheese.

'She is,' agreed Suki. 'I talk to her all the time. She is also the soul of discretion.'

'I'm glad to hear it.'

'Anything I can help you with?'

He put down his fork. 'It's about you.'

'Me?'

By the tone of their voices I realised this was probably the end of treats time so I took myself back to the fire, where I could listen and dry out.

He took a swig of beer and cleared his throat. He smelt really nervous and acidic. 'You know how I feel about you, Suki,' he said.

She looked up. 'Do I?'

'I know we've only known each other a few months, but it's made me realise that you're everything I want in a partner. You're strong yet vulnerable. You're intelligent, sensitive, caring, funny, gorgeous looking....'

She gave a gurgle. I think she was flattered and didn't know what to say.

'And incredibly sexy,' he added.

'Well, thank you.' She went very red and sipped her wine. 'But?'

He sighed. 'You know the but,' he said. 'And I'm wondering what we should do. What do *you* want to do? What do you want from *me?*'

She sat back and looked at him. 'The short answer is for us to be happy. Together.' She looked down. 'A lot of the time I know we are. I've never met someone I feel so in tune with. We are compatible on so many levels.' She paused. 'You make me think about things differently. I learn from you. We challenge each other, but in a good way. We have great adventures, but it's more than that. We seem to be connected on a deeper level.'

He looked down at his beer glass. 'But..'

She nodded. 'If we pretend that your wife isn't in existence, we're very happy. But the trouble is, she is very much alive, and I hate what that does to you.' She spoke so passionately I could see the heat coming off her.

'So what do you think we should do?' Hesitation and fear shook his voice.

She got up and walked over to me. 'The sensible part of me says Go now and Don't Come Back. Don't get any more involved with this man. He will only hurt you.'

'I would never hurt you on purpose.'

'No, I know, but every time you go up to Derby, you age about ten years. I hate seeing that, and I hate the fact that you have to go through it. And, of course, to quote Princess Diana, there are Three in this Marriage.'

There was a silence, then he looked up. 'So what would you do if you were in my position?'

She sighed. 'Same as you, I guess. I do appreciate how difficult it is, Ted. Of course you can't just leave her, but she could live for a long time. Couldn't she?'

He nodded.

'Which means you could – we could be stuck in this situation for ages. Neither able to go forwards or back. Surely you deserve a chance to be happy?'

He shook his head and I could smell his sadness. He got up, started clearing the dishes away. 'I know. It's too depressing to think about.' His voice cracked. 'But thank you for being such a good friend. I've so enjoyed the time we've had together. I really do value your company very much.' He looked over at me, stretched in front of the fire, ears extended to their limit. 'Both of you.' He ran water over the dishes. 'Perhaps we can do it again sometime.'

She looked at him and a smile flickered across her face. 'Which bit?'

He busied himself washing a dirty plate. 'The walks, the boat trip. Picnic. Whatever you feel like.'

She was silent for a moment and gave me a stroke. 'You know, I think Moll would say live in the moment. Don't worry about looking ahead.'

Well, of course I did. She was a bit slow in getting there. And? Neither of them moved. Then she got up, walked over to him and put her arms around his waist.

He turned, slowly, and looked at her searchingly. 'Are you sure? Really sure?'

She nodded. 'I'm sure.'

'Because there's no way I'm going this far and turning back.'

Turning back? What did he mean? But they were both smiling, then laughing at each other.

'Quite sure,' she said. 'In fact, if you don't hurry up, I think I might burst.'

He smiled and joy exploded out of him. He bent his head and kissed her and it was almost as if they were swallowing each other up. But in a good way.

Finally they pulled apart, gasping, and she said, 'Come on then. Let's go upstairs.'

He let out a bellow of laughter and suddenly he picked her up. She shrieked but it was a happy cry and he looked over his shoulder. 'Look after the fire, Moll. We'll see you a bit later.' And then he carried her upstairs.

I wasn't going to listen outside the door, but after a bit I heard a noise that sounded as if Suki had hurt herself, so

I shot up the stairs; Ted had better watch out! But as I got there, I realised she was laughing. So she wasn't hurting. She sounded extremely happy in a very deep way.

It sounded like he got very sad at one point, but then they carried on and I could tell he was really happy too. And then it all went quiet, so I took myself back to the fire and had a snooze and dreamed of my Titch and pretended he was lying there beside me.

13

He asked if we'd like to stay the night but she knew I liked my evening routine, so he drove us home much later, and I was glad to get back to our bed. We didn't sleep very much but she smelt really joyous: like the first day of spring.

The next afternoon, we'd just come back from our walk along by the sea, exploring rock pools, and over the beach. I loved the jagged feel of rocks under my paws, the gritty sand between my claws, and the hush of the waves. We were tired but pleasantly so. She had had less sleep than me, I think, and Ted had rung first thing, but since then, silence.

She gave me my tea and settled back to work. She'd interviewed this writer called Ian Rankin and was writing it up for a magazine, when the doorbell rang. I barked and ran straight to the door, because I could smell who it was.

Ted stood on the doorstep smiling broadly. She smiled back. Get on with it, I thought, so I barked again. Just a nudge. 'Would you like a coffee?' she said. She doesn't usually like being interrupted when she's working but this was obviously an exception.

He nodded and came in. Had he lost the ability to speak? She made coffee and then, without a word, they went to our bedroom where they played this game again. I was getting used to it by now, but I waited next door just in case she needed me. I could smell how happy she was, even if they both grunted a lot.

I popped my nose round the door later, and they were lying in bed, cuddled up together, and there was so much love pouring out of them I was quite overwhelmed. It smelt like a hot summer's day and fox poo and cheese all rolled into one.

Then they got up and she made something to eat and he had another coffee and said, 'Are you happy?' and she nodded.

'Yes,' she said. 'Are you?'

He had a great silly grin, and held her hands and they couldn't stop touching each other, all the time. They looked at each other and laughed, and it was as if they were talking with love instead of words. Just like us dogs do.

It was rather sweet at first, then it got a bit irritating, but luckily she had to finish her work, so he had to go and they arranged to meet for a walk before work the next morning.

She didn't sleep much that night, tossing and turning, but it was like she didn't need sleep. She was all lit up, inside and out and so happy I couldn't believe it.

It was a relief, as the tension had been building up for months. And now it had burst, like a huge bubble. I could sense that it had changed the dynamics between them; it was happier yet more intense.

The next morning was bright and sunny and we met Ted, as arranged, at Gylly beach. She was almost skipping along, she was so happy, but as soon as we saw him walk across the beach towards us, I could smell something was wrong. That old acrid smell was leaking out of him, poisoning all the lovely stuff.

'What is it?' she said, as he wrapped his arms around her.

'It's Jane,' he said. 'She had a bad fall last night, and hit her head. She's in hospital being assessed.' He looked down at her. 'I'm going to have to go and see her, Suki.'

I could have chewed his guts out when he said that, had he not looked so miserable. I could smell all the happiness leaking out of her. The misery caught in her throat, smelling like off milk. She couldn't speak but nodded, then shook her head, looking down at the beach. I could feel her cold despair and in that moment I hated him. Why had I encouraged them to live for the moment, when this moment was so profoundly unhappy?

She sometimes withdrew into herself when she was upset, and I wondered if this would drive a wedge between them – be the last biscuit. Well, if it did, at least we knew where we stood. I waited and sniffed, watching their body language.

He wrapped his arms around her so tight I was surprised she could breathe. 'I'm so very sorry. I hate to do this to you,' he said, speaking into her hair.

She didn't reply, but knowing her, I suspected that was because she couldn't. They clung on to each other as if they were drowning, then I decided enough was enough. We were here for a walk, after all. I barked.

They turned and she bent down, stroked my ears. 'Sorry, Moll,' she said. 'Come on then, let's go.' We walked along the beach, me running ahead, and when I looked back to see if they were following, I noticed they were holding hands so tight their knuckles were white.

We walked down to the rock pools at the far end of the beach and eventually she said, 'When are you going?'

'After this,' he said. 'I had to come and see you first. I'm so, so sorry, darling.' He pulled her to him again, and held her even tighter if that was possible.

She blinked a bit when he called her darling. 'I'm sorry too,' she said, in a voice that crackled as if she hadn't used it for ages. 'How long do you think you'll be away?'

'I'll be back as soon as possible,' he said. 'I'll ring you whenever I can, OK?'

She nodded, dumbly, and I could almost see all that lovely energy streaming out of her, into the sand.

Someone had to do something, and those two weren't capable, so I ran ahead and barked. Nothing happened. I barked again and trotted down to the sea, and then Suki laughed, faintly, but it was still a laugh.

'Come on,' she said to Ted, and she joined me at the water's edge. The waves were lapping gently over the sand, and it couldn't make everything better, but it was cleansing and gentle and just what we all needed.

Ted ran down with us and chased me along the waterline, waving a big bit of seaweed, and for a short while we all pretended that nothing was the matter. Every minute counted, as we put off the inevitable. We really were living in the moment, but with a sense of desperation.

During that run along the beach I vowed that if I couldn't make her happy, I would fight even harder to protect her, and keep her safe. It would be harder for them both, this time he went away. For they'd crossed a line, hadn't they? The knot that tied them together had tightened even further.

Suki was working at her desk at home one morning when suddenly she let out this huge squeal as she read something on her computer. She got up, danced around, sat down and read it again.

'Oh, Moll!' she breathed, and the most wonderful smell of hot baked meat rose off her. 'My publishers like the idea I sent them for another book. It's going to be called *Walks in the Footsteps of Cornish Writers*. So I can start writing that one!'

She danced around the room and kissed me (I suffered that for I wasn't quite sure what was going on, but if she was happy that was fine with me). Then she rang Tess and I heard a lot of garbled giggles down the phone.

Finally, she sat down on the bed beside me with a thump, so I bounced upwards. Her eyes were sparkling, and the most amazing fizzy smells were coming off her.

'That means a book launch for the first one this year, then they're going to publish the Cornish Writers book early next year, and they'd like ideas for another one,' she breathed. 'Oh, Moll, I wish I could tell Pip.' She sighed, and I could almost see her spirits sinking. 'I wish I could tell Ted, for that matter. I mean, I'll tell him when he rings, but it's not quite the same as being able to ring him when I want...'

She looked at the computer again and smiled. 'Just think, Moll, soon I'll have the first book in my hands, and we'll have a proper book launch. I'm going to be a real published author and I can invite all our friends to the party!'

The following week time sped by slowly. By which I mean that she was busy with work, but I knew she was counting the time till Ted got back. Wondering what he was doing, how he was feeling, how his wife was. It was exhausting, smelling that rollercoaster of emotions. She'd been up and flying with Ted, and life smelt like a really good bone you could get your teeth into. And then suddenly it was taken away from her. Taken away from them both. And now here she was, up again.

She and Ted were completely swept away by each other; I could smell it all oozing out of them. Besotted is the word; I heard it the other day. Sounded like a really tasty biscuit. As we walked along, she said, 'Well, whatever happens, I don't regret sleeping with him, Moll. It was just amazing and I'd do it all over again.' She kicked a pine cone that skittered along the path so I chased it.

And I thought, well perhaps she and Ted won't last. Perhaps it was a One-Night-Wonder. I'd heard this on the television and wondered what it meant. Now I thought I knew. Like me with a bone; after the initial excitement and chewing and chewing till my jaw was sore, I lost interest.

But then I thought about the two of them together. How we'd walked along the cliff path the other day and he'd said, 'Isn't it lovely, just the three of us?' and I thought, no, there's more to this. Their feelings were too strong to be blown apart by this hiccup.

But now, despite being busy, there was a sadness to her. Disappointment, that's what it was, and it smelt of old, wet dog blankets. It was heavy and dragged her down. The only person she told was Tess, when we met for a walk. Which, of course, meant I got to see my lovely Titch. We ran ahead while I filled him in, then we ran back to eavesdrop on their conversation.

'Oh Suki, I'm so sorry,' Tess said as they walked along, avoiding the muddy puddles. 'He sounds such a lovely fellow. Poor man. But awful for you with him coming and going like that.' She glanced at Suki. 'What do you think you'll do?'

'I really don't know,' she replied. 'I mean, I knew this was part of being involved with him, but I didn't think he'd have to go away again quite so soon.' I could smell the hesitancy in her voice. All that bottled-up love and desire and confusion that overflowed into his bed the other night.

'At least you got to talk to him about it,' Tess said.

'Yes, but it didn't get us anywhere,' Suki said, sounding so desolate my whiskers drooped.

'Think of the pros and cons, that's what I always do,' Tess said.

We came to a big open bit of field where Titch and I could run ahead a little and chase rabbits. I could still hear them by staying reasonably close.

'OK, the Cons are, obviously, The Wife,' said Suki. 'But I have to say, that's the only con so far.'

'But quite a big one. What about the Pros?'

'Oh, lots,' she said, her voice lifting. 'He makes me laugh, he's brilliant at playing with Moll and teasing her. He loves walking, days out, picnics. He's got a boat so that's more exploring. He's got his own business and he got an award for his design work last year. He's good looking. And,' I could hear the smile in her voice. 'He's bloody good in the sack!'

Silence while they walked along. 'That's a lot of Pros,' said Tess thoughtfully.

'So what do YOU think?'

Another silence. 'Well, normally I would say go for it. But I can see how upset you are, and I would guess he's feeling terrible about letting you down. It's an incredibly difficult situation for him. But *you* don't have to put up with *his* problems. And I think you deserve someone who can give what you had with Pip. Undivided love and attention. Not be some guilty secret.'

Her last words floated out over the grass and I could feel Suki flinch. 'Guilty secret,' she muttered. 'That's a bit harsh.'

'I'm trying to see things from both sides,' said Tess, giving her a hug. 'I want the best for you. So I'm trying to be objective.'

'It's been such a rollercoaster recently,' Suki said. 'When I look back on this year, I've been grieving for Pip, which has been necessary but exhausting, and then I met Ted which knocked me for six.' She sighed. 'The trouble is, there's so much about him that's right. As if we were made for each other.' She jumped over another puddle. 'Except for his wife.'

'That's the stumbling block, isn't it? And it isn't going to go away.'

She shook her head. 'Nope.'

'Is there, I mean, do you know how long she might be like this?'

'You mean, is there any chance she might die soon? No, apparently not. She could go on and on for years. Poor woman.'

We came to a kissing gate where they put us on our leads to cross the road, and walk along to some gardens. There was a cafe where we usually stopped for a coffee. Well, they had coffee and there were always really good cake crumbs on the floor. Perfect halfway stop for a walk.

'So,' said Tess a few moments later when they'd bought their coffee and cake and sat down. We sat looking hopeful by our owners. 'If you want to be involved with him, you have to accept his circumstances, and the fact that he's a good man. Think of it this way; what man would walk away from a woman in that situation?'

She nodded. 'Yep. But I hate what it does to him. When he comes back, every time he looks utterly wrecked. I can't bear to see it.'

'But that's his choice. You need to remember that and get on with your own life regardless,' said Tess stirring her coffee. I wished she'd hurry up and eat her cake. The smell of her lemon sponge was driving me crazy.

'Yes, I suppose. Though that's easier said than done,' said Suki. 'Anyway, I'll see how the next week goes.' She looked up and smiled, ate a piece of her fruit cake.

Obligingly a few crumbs fell just by my left paw. Sultanas, raisins, honey and a bit of cinnamon. One of the better ones.

'But that's enough about me. How's your mum?' Tess's mother was very old and lived on her own in a place called Exeter, and had been ill recently.

'Not too good,' Tess replied. 'We've got to go back to see her.'

'Your poor mum,' said Suki as we all got up and walked out. I was glad: the concrete floor was so cold my paws and my bum were aching. 'How long do you think you'll be up there for?'

'I don't know,' Tess said as we all walked down a narrow path through the woods which smelt of pine and lichen and lovely thick, rich earth with pockets of all kinds of poo. 'I'm hoping we'll be back in a week or so, but we'll have to see how she is. She's got a hospital appointment next Friday so I said I'd take her to that.'

Suki was quiet and I knew what she was thinking. First of all Ted had gone, now Tess was going. 'What about work?'

Tess shrugged. 'I can't afford to leave and start a new business while Mum's like this. I'm going to take a week's holiday to look after her.'

Titch came running over and nudged me so that his whiskers shimmied against mine. 'What did she say?' he barked.

I relayed the information. 'So we won't see each other for a while,' I said, my tail drooping.

'I'll miss you,' Titch sniffed. He sat and scratched his neck; something he often does when he's thinking. 'Why don't you come too?'

I barked. 'I'd love to, but Suki's got her work so we can't just get up and go.'

He nodded and shook his head. 'Well, we won't be away for long. We can compare notes on walks when we get back. It'll be colder then,' he shivered dramatically. He had a shorter coat than me and didn't really feel the cold but he liked to pretend he did so that Tess made a fuss of him.

We didn't talk about their impending departure for the rest of the walk, but it lingered over us like a black rain cloud. We ran and chased as we normally would and tried to forget it. But our parting was, as some famous bloke once said, Such Sweet Sorrow. Except that it didn't taste sweet, it was like dismal, damp fog, and tasted like wet cardboard.

I sat in my bed in the back of the van and watched Tess and Titch drive off and hoped it wouldn't be too long before we saw them again. I needed my man for support, too.

14

Petroc and a review

Ted rang every day and sometimes he sounded reasonably cheerful; dogs' hearing is so much better than humans', I could hear what he said on the phone even if I was in the next room. But often he sounded worn out and desperate, his damp fog seeping down the phone. I was sorry for him, but she was my priority and this wasn't doing her any good.

'I was hoping to get back tomorrow, but they're doing some more tests on Friday, so I really need to stay till next week,' he said.

'Next WEEK?' I could smell her desperation, her rancid fear. It caught on my whiskers and I couldn't swallow properly.

'I'm so sorry, darling. I'd be back today if I could.' His voice dropped. 'I miss you so much.' He sounded so desolate that I knew he was telling the truth.

She whispered, 'I miss you too,' and put down the phone, staring into space. I jumped onto the bed so I could lean over and give her a lick. A tear fell on my back. 'I don't know that I can do this, Moll,' she said. 'This is just too hard. It feels like everything's against us.'

The longer Ted was away, the more it hurt her. And she'd suffered enough for my liking.

That afternoon we walked over on Kiln Beach. The tide was out and the beach was deserted but on the rocks in the distance was a stooped figure that looked vaguely familiar. I trotted over to have a sniff and, yes it was Petroc, who greeted me then bent down, rummaged in his pockets and produced a biscuit. I knew he'd be good for food.

He looked round to see Suki climbing over the rocks towards us. 'Hello, my dear,' he said. 'How nice to see you. I was wondering when we might meet again.' He looked at her closely. 'How are you?'

'I'm fine,' she said quickly, though her red eyes told a different story.

Petroc looked at her, then nodded ahead. 'I'm walking up to Trefusis Head. Would you join me?'

I barked loudly, just so that Suki wouldn't refuse. She smiled, 'Yes, we'd love to.'

He held out his hand, revealing a cluster of tiny yellow shells. 'I love these little fellows. I remember showing them to Ted, just after we first met. He was fascinated.' We scrambled over the last few rocks, then up a few steep steps up onto the grassy area of Trefusis. 'How is he?'

Suki hesitated. 'He's up with – Jane.' She paused. 'She had a bad fall, and it's proving more complicated than he'd thought.'

Petroc sighed. 'I am sorry.' We walked close to the edge of the cliff, looking down onto the waves hitting the rocks with a booming noise. 'I can see how much he cares for you.'

'Really?' she said. As if she needed proof, when it was blindingly obvious to all of us.

'Really,' Petroc said. 'You are clearly very right for each other. He can't take his eyes off you.' He frowned. 'I'm just sorry life is so complicated for you. It must be very hard.'

She nodded and I could sense tears filling her eyes. 'It is,' she said. 'I feel so helpless. But it's difficult to know what to do when you feel so strongly about someone.'

They walked on in silence for a while, then Petroc said, 'Before I met my wife, I found myself in a similar situation, so I can understand how you feel.'

'Really?' Suki bit her lip. 'Do you mind me asking what happened?'

'Of course not,' he smiled. 'I met Rita at work. She was going through a difficult time with her husband, who'd been diagnosed with cancer. We got talking, went for a coffee, had a walk, and we fell in love.'

He said it as if it was the most normal thing in the world. Which I suppose, for humans, it was.

'We saw each other several times a week. She'd come to my flat, and we had many joyous afternoons together.'

'But...?' Suki's voice wobbled dangerously. It was obvious where this story was going.

'I loved Rita very much,' Petroc said simply. 'I would have done anything for her, but she felt a certain duty towards her husband, as she should have, and made it clear that she wasn't going to leave him.'

'Ouch.' Suki sounded pained.

'It was a bit of a blow to my ego, but I recovered,' Petroc said, and I could hear his wry smile. 'After a while I wondered what I was doing. It was like loving in a one way street. So I took myself off and not long after, I met my wife.'

'You make it sound very simple,' Suki said. 'I suspect it wasn't that easy.'

'No,' he said. 'Life never is. But what I'm trying to say, in my clumsy way, is that we all have choices. If one relationship doesn't work out, it's not that it failed, but that it came to the end of its time.'

Suki gave a big sigh. 'I've never thought of it like that before. The thing is, with Ted, it's so all consuming. I've never met anyone I feel so in tune with. It seems so hard that ...' her voice tailed away. 'You know.'

'I do,' Petroc said firmly. 'I have little to give you in the way of comfort, except to say that life *isn't* fair, as we both know, but I am a firm believer in taking chances when they come along. No regrets, and all that.' He paused. 'And that there are always other opportunities.'

Suki stopped and looked up at him. 'Thank you, Petroc. That's made me feel a lot better.'

'Good,' he said. 'Now, I must turn back, but perhaps you would come and have supper and a game of Scrabble one evening?'

'I would love that,' Suki said, and I could hear the warmth and the smile in her voice. 'I'm very glad we've met, Petroc.'

'Not as glad as I am,' he said, and with a chuckle he kissed her on the forehead, bent to give me another treat, and strode off in the opposite direction, coat flapping behind him. I watched him go, pleased that we'd made this new friend who made Suki happy in an uncomplicated way.

As often in life, while bad things happened unexpectedly, so did good ones. The next day she got an email which she read out to me. 'It's from a dog magazine, Moll. They're asking if we'd like to review some dog-friendly accommodation for them.' There was a lightness to her voice that was welcome. 'Listen, we go to the place that they want reviewed, stay for two nights, and in return all I have to do is write a short review and take pictures.' She read on, 'and we can take a friend!'

She was quiet for a moment, and I knew she was thinking what fun it would be to go with Ted. Or Tess and Titch. 'It's starting from next month, so Tess and Titch will be back by then.'

So that was something to look forward to. In the meantime, she was busy with her research work, and singing and walking, but each time Ted rang, at least once a day, he said nothing about when he'd be back. As a result, the tension mounted, smelling like rancid fish.

The weekend loomed ahead. Time which we'd hoped to spend with Ted. But he rang and said he wouldn't be able to get back till later the following week, and she went very quiet. That was never a good sign.

'I'm so sorry,' he said. Which was what he said every phone call. 'I wish I could be back with you now. This very minute. So we could spend the weekend together.'

'So do I,' she said, but her throat sounded thick with un-cried tears, and she said goodbye and put the phone down.

'We'd better plan something else for the weekend, Moll,' she said. She was about to ring her friend Anne when there was a ping on her computer, announcing the arrival of a new message.

It was from the dog magazine asking if we'd be able to do a review this weekend, at short notice. One of the other reviewers had dropped out, apparently.

Instantly she perked up. 'I think we should go,' she said to me. 'Let's ring Anne and see if she'd like to come.'

Anne didn't have a dog but she loved long walks and going to the pub so that was fine. 'Oooh I'd love to come,' she said. 'What time shall we leave?'

So the following morning, Anne came round and we set off for this hotel on a place called Roseland. It was a cold day with grey skies and I could smell rain: a distinct powdery smell that turned soggy.

'What do you know about this place?' asked Anne as we drove through Truro. I liked to smell where we were going but the windows were shut as it was too cold.

'It was an old mill, apparently, that was turned into a hotel,' Suki said. 'It looks nice, and it's not far from the pub.'

'Sounds brilliant, can't wait.' We waited to board the King Harry car Ferry and Anne said, ever so casually, 'So how are things with the new man?'

'Ted?' said Suki, also casually. Then her face fell and I could hear her voice drop too. 'Oh, Anne. I don't know what to do.' She told Anne what had happened, and slowed down as we drove onto the big ferry going over the water. 'What would you do?'

Anne looked out of the window. 'Well, with four ex-husbands, I'm probably not the right person to ask.'

'You've got David,' Suki said.

'Oh yes,' Anne said. 'I don't have any trouble attracting men. It's keeping them that's the problem. And David's a lovely man but he never wants to DO anything. Out of bed.'

I could smell Suki's amusement. It was gentle, like soft rain. 'So is he on the way out then?'

Anne nodded. 'I think so. But we're not talking about me. Regarding Ted, why not just enjoy it for what it is?'

Suki eased the van down the ramps and off the ferry. 'And what is it?'

'An exercise in seeing other men,' Anne said promptly. 'You don't have to look to the future, Suki. Just enjoy good sex and his company. At least if he has to go and see the wife every now and then, you won't get bored with him.'

127

'No,' she said, but she sounded doubtful. I think we both knew that Ted was more than a casual fling. Their relationship was already bound with steel ropes.

The hotel was tucked into a valley which led to the sea; you could smell it from the room we were given, though they couldn't see it. It was a huge room on the ground floor that led out onto an enclosed lawn via some big doors that looked like windows.

'Good, that means Moll can have a wee out there in the morning,' said Suki, ever practical.

Inside the room were two big beds, a big card saying WELCOME to the Mill End Hotel, and a goodies pack for me containing a blanket, some treats, poo bags and a map of dog walks in the area.

The blanket smelt new but Suki put it on her bed so I could sleep on it and it was very soft and warm, and by the time I'd rummaged it round a bit, it smelt much more normal. The treats were a bit sickly but OK and I thought I might get used to this sort of thing.

First of all we walked through the hotel gardens, which had huge trees and bushes and lawns and a terrace where people sat eating. I snaffled some lovely scone crumbs before Suki dragged me away, but it was worth it because the path wound down to a tiny beach.

It was long and narrow but we were the only ones on it and the sand was really fine and almost white. We saw a few small paw prints, and I charged up and down, making it mine. Suki and Anne followed, and they ran after me down to the sea, where they stopped, panting. I knew what she was thinking. This was the kind of trip that Ted would have loved. He should have been with us! Damn Ted and damn his wife.

Suki and Anne paddled in the water which was very clear. 'Looks just like Greece, doesn't it?' said Anne wistfully. 'It's almost warm enough to go in.'

'Come on,' said Suki, and looked at Anne. 'Shall we?' And before I knew it, she'd stripped her clothes off, leaving them scattered on the sand, and run into the water. Anne didn't need much encouragement, and soon they were splashing around and Anne swam out a long way. Suki didn't like going out of her depth, so I went in to supervise. After a bit she got out and we ran up and down the beach to warm up, and then as the sun was out, we lay down and waited for Anne to come back.

They talked a lot about this and that, and it was easy and relaxing, as we walked back along the coastal path and they discussed having a glass of wine, what they would eat that night. And lovely as the afternoon was, it would have been so much better if Ted had been with us. Or Titch. Preferably both.

Later, Anne and Suki and I entered the dining room and decided to sit by a big window looking out over the garden. My whiskers twitched in anticipation. So many smells drifting by; steak, fish, gravy, barely cooked vegetables, freshly baked bread, herb butter; my nose went into overdrive. I sat between them as this was the best way of getting some crumbs, or maybe trip up the waiter as he came along; if any food dropped, I'd be there. I'd also found that if I tilted my head to one side and fluttered my eyelashes, my chances of getting food were much higher. Humans loved this kind of thing.

'Oh, isn't she gorgeous?' Anne said, as I fixed her with my Tilted Head, Wistful Look. 'Is she allowed a tiny bit of bread?'

'Not really,' said Suki. 'But—'

I'd already snaffled a bit of bread that Anne dropped on the floor. She would have picked it up, but I was too quick. Very spongy it was, with a crispy crust and a bit of herb butter. Parsley, I thought: I was becoming quite the gourmet. They'd ordered a bottle of wine and were sipping that while they decided what to eat, when Suki's phone rang and I knew who it was.

I could sense her face going pink, and she turned away from Anne slightly, to look out of the window. 'Hi,' she said, her voice soft and gentle. 'Listen, we're in the dining room. Can I ring you later?' She laughed, slightly self-consciously, and said, 'Yes. It's great. You'd love it here.' Another pause. 'Yes, OK Ted, I'll ring you in a bit.' Pause. 'Miss you too.'

Suki turned the phone off and looked back at Anne. 'Decided what to eat?' she said in a bright voice. I could smell how much she missed Ted. It was like peanut butter and jam: I managed to snaffle a bit of toast that fell on the floor. It was out of this world.

'Yes,' said Anne. 'I'll have the sea bass.'

'Me too.' Suki looked up as someone came to take their order.

When we were alone again, Anne said thoughtfully, 'It's quite serious, then.' It wasn't a question.

Suki swallowed. 'Mmm.'

'Not just a quick fuck?'

She smiled – I could feel the tension lessening in the air around her. 'No, not just a quick fuck.'

Anne sipped her wine. 'You two sounded very comfortable. Not as if you'd only just got together.'

Suki sighed. 'Yes, I feel like I've known him forever. It's weird. I feel like part of me is missing when he's not here.'

'Oh lordy. You have got it bad,' Anne said.

Suki smiled awkwardly, and looked at her wine glass.

'What do you think Pip would think of all this?'

Suki frowned. 'Good question. I like to think that he'd know what to do.'

'So why not ask him? Take a walk and ask Pip his advice.'

'That's a very good idea,' Suki said slowly.

There was silence while I edged forward: a tasty bit of potato was on the floor, just beyond the reach of my lead.

'So when's Ted coming back?' Anne said.

'In a few days. Fingers crossed.'

'Good,' she said shortly. Then she looked up. 'He'd better not hurt you, that's all. Or he'll have me to answer to.'

It was so different staying in a hotel, but Suki liked not having to cook, or think about what to eat. The breakfasts were amazing; help-yourself bowls of cereals, ham, cheese, croissants, bread, jam; every cold food you could imagine, and then the cooked breakfasts. Oh my! Crispy bacon and eggs and sausages and mushrooms and eggs and hash browns and beans and tomatoes. I was in seventh heaven.

The walks were great, too. We found a long twisty path that took us down a wooded valley with wonderful smells and fantastic fox poo. We found another beach but there were people surfing and although the sun came out, it wasn't warm enough for Suki and Anne to swim again. And we walked for miles along the coastal footpath which had different smells of different paws, different feet, different food.

So we all enjoyed our break, though I was glad to get home and sleep on our bed, and catch up with the local messages. It did Suki good to get away: I could smell that she was more relaxed, and she slept better, and stroked my ears while we were in bed, which I always loved.

However, the day after we came back, her editor rang to say she was going to be off on maternity leave soon, and because of more budget cuts, a lot of the work that she'd commissioned might not happen.

'Bugger, Moll,' said Suki. 'We need that money. And I need the work to keep sane. Still, at least I've got the work from Andrew. I'll see if he needs me anymore, or knows someone who might.'

We went off to Truro for a meeting which resulted in me getting some chocolate brownie, but no confirmed work for Suki, and I could sense the worry starting to eat away at her again. She sounded all discordant and smelt like vinegar.

That afternoon we set off for a long walk, as we often did when she was upset, and I knew she wanted to talk to Pip.

We drove over to Mylor Quay and walked along by the river. It was quiet there, with a few ducks swimming in the river, and a lot of old boats moored up. Across the water, we could hear hammering coming from the boatyard, and a blackbird sang very loudly in a tree next to us. For a while we walked in silence, greeting the odd dog walker.

Knowing Suki as I did, the conversation with Pip was in her head, but this was the gist of it. 'So, darling, looks like most of my work's cancelled.'

'You'll have to look around, won't you? Don't put all your eggs in one basket and all that.'

'Yes.' Sigh. 'You're quite right. At least I've got Andrew's work.'

'That's good, and it pays well, doesn't it?' Pause. 'And Ted?'

She kicked a pinecone along the ground. 'I don't know what's the right thing to do.'

'There very often isn't a right thing to do, Suki. It's whether he makes you happy or not.'

'He does. Very much – when he's here. Not in the way *you* did – no one could ever do that. But differently.'

'And when he's not? That's the difficult bit, isn't it?'

'Yes. And I keep coming up against this brick wall of The Wife which isn't going to move.'

'No, it won't. So you have two choices, don't you? Stay as you are and put up with his comings and goings. Or stop it now.'

'I don't know that I *can* stop it now.'

'In that case, you've only got one option.'

She sighed. 'I do miss you, darling. So much. I really wish you were here.'

A chuckle. 'If I were, you wouldn't be in this situation.'

'I certainly wouldn't.'

'Well, you've got plenty of time to make up your mind. But either way won't be easy, remember that.'

Another sigh. 'I wish you weren't so bloody wise all of a sudden.'

A roar of laughter. 'Me? Wise? That'd be the day.' Pause. 'Just remember, I'll always love you, Suki.'

A happier sigh. 'And I love you more than anyone else ever could. Bye darling. Don't go, will you?'

'I'm always here for you, Suki. I'm not going anywhere.'

And then she burst into tears. She cried for a good half an hour, all the way up the stony track towards Flushing. Then she carried on crying along the road towards the river. And it wasn't till we got to the big field where I love to run around that she finally stopped.

She sat on a log and I could almost see a wave of exhaustion sweep over her. Crying seemed to do that to humans. I jumped onto the log and sat down next to her and she stroked my spine, the way I like it, sending ripples down to my nerve endings. She didn't speak but I could almost hear thoughts turning over in her head, like biscuits clunking in a tin.

Finally she stood up and we walked down the path, back towards Greatwood. It took about an hour and I knew she was still thinking, cogs whirring. But when we got to the little bridge where there's a sunken boat and you can look over to the other side of the river, she said, 'I don't know how I ever thought anyone could live up to Pip. I was crazy.'

No you weren't, I thought. You've been swept off your feet by Ted. He's nuts about you, too.

'So I've decided I'm not going to see Ted again.'

I stopped in my paws. Not see him? Was she bonkers?

'It's too much, all this disappointment and having to play second fiddle to that poor woman. It makes me feel I'm not good enough. And I don't like that.'

Quite right. But.

'The last few conversations we've had, he's sounded so down and I'm sure a lot of it is guilt. And I don't want a relationship that's full of guilt and ups and downs, and being made to feel second best. So, I've decided. I'll tell him on the phone, then he won't have to come back and be disappointed. He can spend as much time up there as he wants.'

She threw a pinecone for me into a ploughed field. I ran after it, bouncing over the muddy earth, thinking, really?

'So that's my decision, Moll. And I feel so much better having made it. We can go home now and I'll see if Anne wants to meet for a drink. We can celebrate having made up my mind.'

Hmm, I thought. Did she really mean what she said? Surely not.

15

Wobbles on both sides

Ted rang before she had a chance to ring him, and Suki just plunged in there, no preamble.

'I think, Ted, that it's better if we don't see each other.'

'What?' Stunned silence. 'Are you sure? I mean, I love you, Suki, and...'

'I know, and I love you too, but we have no future. And I don't want to live like I'm always in the background. Not being acknowledged.' Her voice dipped. 'It's not good for you, either.'

'What do you mean?'

'Well, you must feel so guilty when you see Jane and her parents.'

'Oh I do. But it's worth every second of it.'

Suki got up and started walking around. 'I want more than this, Ted. I want a proper relationship. One where we can go away together. Be open about how we feel. Do whatever we want, when we want, instead of being restricted all the time. I feel as if you're ashamed of me.'

'I could never be ashamed of you, Suki. Never.'

'No, but you can't be open about us, can you?'

He cleared his throat. 'No. You're absolutely right. It isn't fair on you.' Pause. 'And I do feel guilty, you're right. But ...' his voice dropped, as if he was sensing defeat. 'I don't know what else I can do.'

'There isn't anything you can do, really,' she said, sounding so sad that I wanted to lick her face, very hard. 'I mean, you're not free, are you?'

I waited, holding my breath.

'No,' he said, but it came out more like a sigh.

She was clutching the phone so hard her knuckles went white, and I could smell her anguish. I jumped onto the bed and scrabbled at the duvet. It helped me think, sometimes.

'I just wish...' he said, but his voice tailed away.

The duvet wasn't helping. A stinky silence hung heavy in the air.

At last he said, 'Well, thank you for everything, Suki,' and the smell of defeat smothered everything else, even down the phone. 'You're amazing and I will really miss you. So much.'

She swallowed hard. I could smell tears were on the way. 'I'll miss you too, Ted.'

'Perhaps we could have a walk – every now and then?' He sounded desperate, poor fellow.

'Maybe.' She wiped her eyes. 'I'd better go now. Bye, Ted.'

'Goodbye, Suki. Thank you, and Moll, for everything. You're right. You do deserve better. And the man you choose will be the luckiest man in the world.'

She finished the call then and threw herself on the bed. 'What have I DONE?' she cried. I lay down beside her, knowing she needed to get it out of her system. She cried and cried, and I snuggled up to her and decided that we'd go out later, take her mind off it a bit. Plan the rest of our week. Our life. Without him.

Petroc proved to be a steady friend, particularly as Tess was away, and I know Suki missed her close friendship, just as I missed Titch. We went to Petroc's for supper (fish pie, and I had a little bowl of my own. Mashed potato was the best ever). Scrabble seemed long and boring to me, but they seemed to enjoy it. A clever man, they talked about all sorts of philosophical stuff which did her good. And he kept her mind off Ted.

'How did you and your wife meet, Petroc?' she asked as we sat over supper.

'We were both at a march protesting about closing the libraries,' he said. 'I feel very strongly that everyone should learn how to read, and have access to free books because not everyone can afford to buy them.'

Suki nodded. 'I agree. Libraries were a big part of my childhood. I don't know what I would have done without one. So what happened?'

Petroc smiled and sipped his red wine. 'A group of us gathered outside County Hall in Truro one December afternoon – the weather was terrible, typically: it rained, then we had hail, and high winds. But a TV crew came along, and radio, and eventually the local MP turned up and he said he'd do what he could.' He chuckled. 'We were all freezing after that, and it was early evening, so some of us headed off to the nearest pub. We started talking and realised we had a lot in common.'

'What was she called?'

'Heather. We found that we both loved languages, and she'd started her own language school, and was looking for someone to help teach Russian. So I said I'd help.'

'You speak Russian?' Suki said, her eyes growing large. 'My goodness. What other languages do you speak?'

'French, German, Spanish and Italian,' Petroc said, rattling off these names as if they meant nothing, which they didn't to me. 'It was good for both of us, and we ran the school until she died.'

'I'm so sorry.' Suki reached over the table and squeezed his hand.

Petroc shrugged. 'It was Heather who led me to meet my current partner, actually. They were friends, you see, and Megan used to help with teaching German and they belonged to the same book group.' He smiled. 'She's eighteen years younger than me which causes a few raised eyebrows, but it's no one else's business but our own.'

'Absolutely,' Suki said. 'I had the same thing with my husband; he was seventeen years older than me, and a lot of people said it wouldn't work.'

Petroc got up and started to clear the table, so Suki helped him. 'Most people love a good gossip,' he said. 'Megan is very into local politics so I have become more involved as well. I do think we need to try and stand up to the government. But that's a conversation for another time.'

'Let me wash up,' said Suki. 'Does Megan enjoy walking too?'

'She does,' Petroc said. 'If you don't mind washing up, I will dry as I know where things go.' He turned and put the rest of the dishes on the draining board, slipping me a nice bit of mashed potato; good for him. 'Megan is also very interested in the arts, and there is a thriving artistic community in this area, so we are very active locally.'

'She sounds great,' said Suki. 'Perhaps I could meet her sometime?'

'I'm sure you would both enjoy that,' Petroc said. 'We don't live together. She has her own life and we spend time together when it suits us both. I find that can be a good way of maintaining a relationship.'

Suki nodded thoughtfully. 'Absolutely,' she said, and I presumed she was thinking about Ted.

'And any time you wish to talk about Ted, or anything else, you know where I am,' he continued in his soft, gentle voice.

Suki looked up and there were tears in her eyes. 'Thank you,' she said. 'That's very kind.'

'You looked as if you were about to ask something,' Petroc said.

Suki smiled. 'Yes. Would you be able to come to my book launch?'

'Of course,' he said. 'I'll bring Megan if I may.'

'That would be great.' She hesitated. 'And, I know this is a lot to ask, but would you be able to come for a quick drink or bite to eat afterwards? We get thrown out of the room at 8pm and I suspect I'll feel a bit flat going home on my own.'

'I would be delighted,' said Petroc, and I could tell that he really meant it. 'I know exactly what you mean about after a launch party. I felt the same when I had private views.'

'You're a painter as well?'

'Well, not much now,' he said with a twinkle. 'My hands are too arthritic. But I did in the past.'

'My god, Petroc, you're incredible,' said Suki. 'Can I see some of your paintings sometime?'

'You may,' he said. 'Now, shall we have a game of Scrabble?'

I was glad she had her book launch to focus on. Sadly, I couldn't go, as the building didn't allow dogs. Ridiculous. But from the amount of phone calls, and running around in the van, and the smell of her panicking, it was a Big Deal. Mel and Joe who lived upstairs said they'd help, as did other friends, so the days sped by and Book Launch day loomed ever larger.

The day before, she was in a terrible state. 'The books haven't arrived,' she wailed to Petroc. 'The book launch is tomorrow and I haven't got any bloody books!'

'You've rung the publishers?'

'Yes!'

'What about the courier people? Can you track the delivery? Ring the depot?'

'Oh, good idea.' So followed more phone calls, and finally, three boxes of books arrived the morning of the book launch, by which time Suki was in a terrible state.

She was so nervous, as she got ready, her anxiety spilled out of her like gone-off milk. 'I just wish Pip was here,' she muttered, changing her dress for the fourth time. 'Or Ted.' She looked at me, and I could see she was trying really hard not to ring him up and invite him. 'But Petroc's coming, and so is Anne, and quite a few of my other friends.' She turned and looked at herself in the mirror. 'Well, that'll have to do. Bye darling. See you later! Wish me luck.'

And she kissed me, patted my head, put on some high heeled shoes, and headed out of the door.

Well, what could I do but wait? Luckily us dogs are good at that, so I snoozed and lay underneath the bed, which was always nice and cool and a very good place for thinking, and before I knew it, the door opened and she came back in.

I bounced up to meet her, as I always did, wagged my tail, sniffed her, gave a few appreciative barks, that kind of thing. She smelt happy, though with an undertone of sadness, but I guessed it had gone well. I followed her down the hall, into the kitchen where she poured herself a glass of water, kicked off her shoes.

She gave me a few biscuits which I devoured swiftly, and waited. She sighed, sat down. 'It was good, Moll,' she said. 'I sold 35 books, which was amazing. Lots of people turned up, and everyone seemed to have a good time, and Sally took lots of pictures, and Petroc was brilliant...' she sighed, and I waited for the But. 'But I so wished that Pip had been there. Or Ted.' She sipped her water, and I went and sat beside her, so she'd rub my head and keep talking. 'It was really good, better than I'd expected, but oh, I really, really wanted someone to share this with. I mean, I shared it with all my friends, of course, and I'm so glad Petroc and Megan were there but, you know, it would have been lovely to have shared it with someone of my own.'

She got up and filled the kettle. 'I know I shouldn't complain, but I felt really lonely. I just wanted Pip, or Ted, to go for a drink with afterwards, and mull it over. Or just talk about it in bed, with a cuddle.' As she spoke, a tear splashed onto the floor, followed by another. She wiped them away busily. 'Silly, isn't it?' she said fiercely. 'That a happy event should make me feel so miserable. GOD I miss him so much.' She paused. 'I miss them both so much.'

Every night she lay in bed, staring at the ceiling. She tossed and turned, put the light on, read for a bit and turned it off again. Repeat. It was almost as bad as after Pip died.

She didn't say anything else about Ted; she didn't have to. I could sense all this yearning seeping out of her. I could feel it in her fingertips when she scratched my back. I could feel it when I snuggled up to her back, or her hip. Waves of longing that crept down my spine, down my fur. It was most disconcerting.

It was different to missing Pip. This was more immediate, and sharper, because of course, Ted was not only alive, but we could see his house out of our window. She knew he'd be down the road at 11 o clock every morning. So we avoided going into town then.

One day she had to interview a couple who ran a local cafe, so I went with her. We went late afternoon, which was the cafe's quietest time, and trotted through town which I always liked. So many interesting messages on the litterbins and drainpipes. A whole new collection of dogs, all saying different things. And the scraps; choice pasty crumbs, discarded sandwiches, chips, cake, melted ice cream; the selection was like a running buffet. She never let me eat enough, that was the trouble.

Still, we got to the cafe and the interview seemed to go well: they were chatty and gave her coffee and a bit of cake and just as we were about to leave, the bell jangled on the door to announce the arrival of the next customer.

I heard him before he came inside; he often wore boots that made a distinctive clip clop noise. When the door opened, she froze, like I do when I've seen or heard something threatening. Then she flushed. I could almost see the blood roaring round her body.

The tension pouring off both of them was so strong, I felt quite ill. Ted stuttered, 'Er, no worries,' and shot out of the door as if a police dog was chasing him.

We walked down to the beach which helped her calm down a little, but I could sense how shaken she was. She needed extra cuddles that night and I lay beside her and despaired. How could I ever fulfil my promise to Pip?

Another time she had to go to the bank, and on the way back, decided we'd go to the cafe on the pier, which is my favourite. She ordered her coffee (and cake, hooray) on the way in, then we sat outside and looked out over the water, at the seagulls strutting their stuff, watching the boats bob around, and the tourists setting off for Flushing, St Mawes and Truro. There was often a man singing and playing the guitar, and of course, usually a plentiful supply of good quality crumbs; bread, cake, bits of bacon, egg. It was great for dog and people watching; always a plentiful assortment of smells and sounds.

This time, we were sitting outside when I smelt him. Coffee, mixed with the smell of the sea; I knew that distinctive mix anywhere. She didn't clock him until the coffee and cake arrived. I sat with my head to one side, my nose twitching like nobody's business, and my whiskers strained in his direction, but she didn't notice at first. And then she did.

I could feel her whole body tense, like me when I'm about to chase another dog, or a squirrel. But this was different – she was more in the running away mode. But what could she do? 'Shit,' she muttered. 'I can't just leave the coffee.'

So she blew on her drink because it was too hot and she was so rattled she gave me a huge lump of cake without thinking about it. She's usually pretty strict. Then, as she took a gulp of coffee, he got up, turned round and saw us. I could smell the pleasure racing through his body, shortly followed by a peppery smell of hesitation.

'Hello,' he said, as he came and stood by our table. 'You – er – don't usually come here, do you?'

'No,' she said, carefully not looking at him.

'Thought I'd go somewhere different,' he said.

She nodded, and gradually looked up. 'Me too.'

They stared at each other, and I gave his leg a nudge with my nose. 'Sorry, Moll,' he said. 'How rude of me,' and he bent and stroked my ears just how I liked it. Gently. I miss you, too, I barked, just so that he knew.

He straightened up and said, 'Well, better go. Lovely to see you both.' And then he walked off, without looking back. And while I could smell that part of her was relieved, the other part wanted to run after him and say, Come back!

She didn't though. She stayed and finished her coffee, though her hands shook and she gave me the rest of the cake (unheard of!) and then we walked home. But her footsteps were slow and pensive. He'd jumped inside her head again, I could tell, and his shadow stayed with us for the rest of the day.

Ted was the subject of intense discussion with her friends. Opinion was divided between those who felt she should just have a good time and not worry about the future, and those who felt she Deserved Better.

'The trouble is,' she would say, 'I might *deserve* better, but it doesn't mean I'm going to *get* it.'

Still, she kept saying, 'I'm better off without him.' But I knew she was thinking of our outings, the way that we'd had such special times together. Was she really better off without him? 'The trouble is, when we're with him, it's as if everything's in colour instead of black and white,' she said to me one night. And she wasn't just talking about our walks. I'm sure she was thinking about the times they went to bed together.

About three weeks after the coffee shop incident, he sent a text, which she read out. *Would you both be free for a walk or a boat trip this weekend? No strings attached, but it would be good to see you both. Ted X*

She hesitated, read it again. Then she sat down on the bed with a thump. 'Oh, Moll,' she said, and the smell of craving wrapped round those two words. 'Shall we?'

I barked sharply, which meant 'Of course.'

'I won't reply just yet,' she said. 'He can wait.' But it was as if the text was burning a hole in her phone. She kept looking at it, putting her phone away, checking it again. Oh, get on with it, I felt like saying, but she had to make up her own mind.

She left it till the Friday, then sent a quick text saying sorry she was busy. Busy! Busy going bonkers. There was no reply.

I sighed, rested my head on my paws and was very grateful I wasn't a Person.

The following week, we were collecting bread from the Farmers' Market one morning when who should we bump into but Ted at the fish counter.

'I hope you didn't mind me asking if you'd like a walk,' he said. He reeked of awkwardness and his voice had gone very low.

'No, that's OK,' she said. I could tell she wanted to run. Or jump into his arms.

'If ever you feel like meeting..' he said.

She nodded, looking at the ground. 'OK.'

There was a long pause.

'Forecast's good this weekend, if you're free,' he said.

Still she stared at her feet, and gave me a treat. 'I'm not sure what I'm doing,' she said.

Liar. We weren't doing anything.

'Well, just let me know,' he said.

When we got back home, she paced up and down the hallway. 'It'll only end in tears,' she said. 'I'm not getting into all that misery again. I'm not.' She walked into the living room and looked out of the window. 'I'm not,' she repeated, but she sounded less sure. She turned and looked at me, gave a big sigh. 'But we do get on so well, and I'm miserable without him.' That was certainly true.

I looked at her with my head on one side. I was very good; I didn't bark. I just looked.

She gave a glimmer of a smile and went back to her computer, where she thumped the keyboard hard.

She stuck it out till Friday evening, when she looked at me and kissed the top of my head, which I permitted, given the circumstances. 'Let's go, then,' she said, and I heard bubbles of excitement in her voice. She sent the following text: '*Saturday good for walk.*'

There was silence. She paced up and down the hall again. Tried to watch the telly, couldn't concentrate. Finally, hours later, there was a ting on her phone and she rushed to have a look.

She showed me. He'd sent a message with two thumbs up. Thank the Lord Dog for that.

Saturday dawned wet and windy and I do not enjoy getting wet in the rain. Swimming is a different matter; that's a choice, but rain is a No No. We had a quick round the block for a wee first thing, then sat and listened to the patter of rain on the window. Then, a text.

Horrible out there, shall we try again tomorrow? Ted Xx

Despite playing it cool, I could smell the disappointment dragging down her spine, along the chair and down to her feet. Her excitement, which had been dancing like butterflies overnight, came to an abrupt halt. Wings stopped beating. Silence.

Yes, good idea. X. She got up and peered out of the window, as if she could will the rain away.

How about brunch? He wrote. *At Stones? Moll too?*

She laughed. A joyous sound that made my fur shiver in delight. 'What do you think, Moll? I should say no really.' I gave her my best Paddington Stare. 'Oh, OK.'

What time?

11.30?

Done. X

We headed down to the cafe to find him already there. He was sitting at a small round table at the back, away from everyone else, where he could watch people coming in. I could smell his coffee-and-salt smell from the door and it was nice and familiar, like sleeping on Pip's tummy.

Ted stood up as soon as we came in, and I could sense his excitement, his fear and his love. It was like opening a cupboard and finding a year's supply of biscuits. She could sense it too, though I suspect in a different way.

He kissed her cheek, awkwardly, and they sat down, discussed what to eat. Bacon and eggs for him with sourdough toast. Mushrooms and poached eggs for her with a croissant. Cappuccinos all round. I sat and waited. I like sourdough, though the crusts are a bit chewy for my receding teeth. Croissants are nice and soft and flaky. I love the hot milky froth and the chocolate sprinkles on a cappuccino. The day was looking up.

Having ordered, Ted came back and sat down. 'So. How are you both? You look well.'

'Fine,' she said, a shade too brightly.

Silence. The coffees arrived and Ted added sugar, though his hand was shaking so much he scattered granules over the table. I caught a few; all crunchy and sweet.

'I just wanted to say...' he said, just as Suki said,

'I'm glad...'

They both stopped, laughed clumsily. Then Ted said, 'I'm so glad to see you.'

I could sense the confusion jumping around in her head, like flies buzzing. 'It's good to see you, too, but I meant what I said, Ted.'

'I know.' He looked down and stirred his coffee again. 'I'm sorry. I have no right, I mean, I really appreciate you coming here. And I do enjoy your company. Just as friends, of course.'

Silence.

'Because, no, it's not fair on you.'

'It's not fair on you either.'

He shrugged. 'All I have to offer...'

She looked up, alert, like when I smell something interesting. 'Is what?'

'Is me. My support. My backing. If ever you need a friend – I'll be there.'

Suki smiled and sang, *You've got a friend* by Carole King. 'It was one of my favourite albums when I was a teenager,' she said.

Ted nodded. 'I love it, too. And yes, I will always be there for you.'

She looked at him. 'When you can be. But not as a partner,' she said.

He sipped his coffee and I could smell him trying to get the right words out. 'I would be honoured to be your partner. But I can't, at the moment, be your partner in the conventional sense,' he said slowly. 'I'm sorry, but I really can't abandon

Jane. Not in her state. I really couldn't live with myself if I did that.'

She sat very still. I could sense that it was like someone poking a sharp stick in her side.

'But I always think of you first, and I have, and always will put you first, as much as I can.'

She sipped her coffee and sat back. She wasn't going to make it easy for him, and I was proud of her for that.

'I found it really hard the last time you were away,' she said. 'It made me feel worthless. Or at least, second best. And that's horrible. Demeaning. Made me hate myself as well as you.'

'I felt like that too. I felt guilty because I couldn't be with you, and even more guilty because I didn't want to be with Jane.' He sighed. 'I'm so sorry, Suki. I shouldn't have dragged you into this.'

Her hand reached for me, and began stroking my ears. I'm a sucker for ear stroking. I could feel despair and longing creeping down her fingers and into my ears.

'All I have to offer you is my heart,' he said. 'And I will do my best never to let you down again.'

'Though I bet you would,' she said. 'Maybe not through choice, but you would.'

'Oh, Suki. I would do anything not to hurt you.' He closed his eyes for a moment, then opened them again. Love spilled out of him like that time I spilled Pip's tea. Who knew there was so much liquid in a mug? It flooded everything. 'I wish things were different, but you will never, ever have cause to doubt my love for you.'

She looked up, as if she was catching all that spilt love, and scooped it up. Still she said nothing.

'If you don't want to be anything more than friends, that's fine. But, oh, Suki.' His voice cracked. 'I have missed you. So, so much.' He put down his coffee cup and one hand reached across the table towards hers. Go on, I thought. Take it. I know it's a really difficult situation, but the guy LOVES you, and you love HIM.

Her hand crept across to join his. They held on tight. White knuckles to white knuckles. They didn't speak, just smiled at each other, and both faces went pink. Tears blobbed in their eyes. I yipped. This was getting embarrassing.

And then the food arrived. Phew. They disentangled their hands and got stuck into their brunch and talked and talked about, well, nothing really. I don't think they knew what they were saying and it didn't matter, because they'd found their way back to each other. I mean, it was inevitable. And no, it wasn't ideal, and there would be troubles ahead, but if you were sitting where I was, and could feel how they felt about each other, you would have cheered them on, too. As Pip said, there were no definitive rights and wrongs. It was just what was right for them at the time.

Anyway, I got some very tasty bacon, a bit of sourdough crust and a knob of croissant. Very acceptable, as they said in the Olden Days.

And then, as it was still drizzling, we went and had a look around the art gallery, where they welcome dogs, I'm glad to say. Then we went and had another coffee.

Then he came back to our house and they spent an hour or so in bed. I joined them later, when he got up and made tea and we had biscuits. Digestives. My favourite.

Later on, it stopped raining and we had a walk in the woods at Budock. It was damp and drizzly, but not cold and the smells rose up even stronger. Lush. Then we all went home and they cooked a chicken stir fry and opened a bottle of wine and there was laughter and bits of chicken for me and I was as happy as they were.

He stayed the night, this time, and he fitted in so well, it was difficult to imagine that he'd ever been away.

16

Together and first Christmas

After that, they were inseparable. How they got any work done is beyond me, but the smell and the sound of their happiness was infectious. I had been feeling a bit achy in my joints, but I bounced off the bed in the morning like a pup, all pains forgotten.

Her Ted Happiness had a different smell to her Pip Happiness. That was like a long walkway, peaceful and strong, lined with solid, sun-baked bricks of their love. In the treetops, birds sang loudly of their steady joy.

Ted love was like an avenue of trees, bending in the gusty wind, but springing upright again. It was full of excitement, of newness and of discovering each other. It was like they were chasing squirrels together through woods, down to the sea and up to the top of the moors. It was fast and slow and new but as if they'd always known each other, and a bit like I felt when I was with my Titch. And oh, I did miss him.

To celebrate their new-found love, once a week they would go out and have dinner with a friend of Ted's who'd opened a small restaurant near the seafront. 'It's only open two nights a week, but one of those nights is a special price steak deal with wine thrown in as well,' he told her. I liked the idea of the steak, until I realised that I wasn't invited. But he laughed. 'Don't worry, Moll, we'll bring you back a doggie bag.'

Pip and Suki had never gone out for meals, so this was a new venture for her. She also had her hair cut short. She started putting things in her eyes which meant she didn't have to wear glasses all the time. She started wearing jeans that fitted tightly, and short skirts and dresses. I'd never seen her wearing those before. She showed her legs!

When Pip was alive she had never really thought about what she looked like. Now she looked so different and smelt like a rose that had come into bloom. Sensuous and ready to be picked. And bone, was she picked.

Ted wore a smart jacket and clean jeans when he came to pick her up. You could tell by his walk, by the way he looked at her, how proud he was of her. His feelings streamed out towards her like sinewy tendrils of ivy. Strong and persistent, drawing her to him. She sent back equally strong ones, and they twisted together until you couldn't tell where one started and the other one ended.

Humans seemed to tie themselves into proverbial knots over Christmas. I mean, it was just another day! But the fuss, and the stress, and the waste of money buying stuff that no one wanted. Ridiculous. That's why I admired Pip and Suki for keeping it quiet. But of course, this year would be the first without him.

Christmas had always been a dodgy time for Suki. I don't know what happened when she was young, but I do know that it wasn't good, and even when Pip was alive, she found it difficult. A few times she even stayed in bed till lunchtime, which wasn't at all like her. A wet blanket of fear surrounded her.

I would like to say something about ghosts, or spirits as I'd rather call them. As far as I was concerned, they weren't like the ones I'd seen on TV. But they definitely existed. Take Pip, for example. Technically he was a ghost now. He didn't wear grey or clank chains or make woo-woo noises, but he was very much here, with us.

Sometimes he appeared when we were least expecting him. Other times, when we wanted him, he was nowhere to be seen. Rather like Ted, come to think of it.

But Pip was a friendly, familiar and loving spirit, whereas the ghosts of Suki's Christmas past were nosey and noisy and smelt of rotten fish and were so dark they almost faded into the cracks between day and night. Then suddenly they'd jump out and terrify her.

Every year I saw this happen. She'd think she was doing all right and then suddenly one of them would trip her up, and the others would all shriek, 'She thought she'd got away with it, this year. Can you believe it!' amid gales of cackling laughter. They were a rotten bunch and I really wished I could bite their ankles and bark loudly enough to frighten them off for good.

There was one ghost that crept down her throat, into her stomach. I still hadn't worked out how it got there, but it sneaked in silently and the next thing she knew, there was a smell of sileage and she had a terrible knot in her stomach. Couldn't eat.

It was difficult for me to ask her, so I was very glad when Suki was on the phone to Tess and the C word came up. 'I'm not a great fan,' Suki said quietly. 'I'd rather just ignore it to be honest.'

'Of course, Pip died on Boxing Day, didn't he?'

'It's not just that. It's always been a difficult time.'

Tess waited. Suki didn't speak, so Tess said. 'Why?'

Another silence, then Suki said, 'I don't really like talking about it, but...'

'But it's me, and I won't judge you,' said Tess's calm voice.

Suki took a deep breath. 'Well, first of all, my dad was very ill one Christmas when I was young, then he died in the January – so that was one thing. Then the first boyfriend I fell in love with, he dumped me just before Christmas. Also, I was anorexic for a while, and Christmas is all about food, isn't it? So it's a really difficult time for anorexics. And then of course, Pip died.' She exhaled loudly. 'There. So that's why. Too many ghosts.'

'Poor love,' said Tess thoughtfully.

Suki nodded. 'And now, even though it's been a long time since I was anorexic, it's as if at Christmas whenever I look at a big plateful of food, a crowd of these chattering ghosts start mocking me. I feel like I've got something in my throat and I can't swallow.' Tears came to her eyes and she fondled my ears, then a few tears slid down her cheek and landed on my nose. I licked hard. I couldn't bear seeing her like this.

'I wish I was there, but we're going to Mum's,' Tess said. 'I'm just wondering what might help you. You need to overlay those horrible memories with good ones, don't you? What about Pip? Did he help?'

'Sort of,' she said. 'But Pip hated everything Christmas stood for; all the commercialism and overspending and everything except the booze. So he usually drank his way through it.'

Tess was silent for a moment then she said, 'What are you doing this year? Why don't you come up to us? As long as you don't mind coming to Exeter. We'd love to see you.'

'That's very kind, thanks,' Suki said. 'Can I let you know? I'm trying not to think about it at the moment, but I know I'm going to have to make some plans.'

This Christmas, as Pip had died on Boxing Day, it seemed more important than ever that Suki should have a happy time. Obviously, we wanted to be with Ted, but he usually spent it with his father (his mother had died some years back) or with his brother.

'This year I want us to be together,' he said to Suki.

Suki looked sceptical but didn't ask him his plans.

Then, a few weeks before Christmas, he arrived at our house, beaming. 'What would you like to do for Christmas?' he said. He smelt of newly mown hay: fresh and sweet.

She looked at him, hope and doubt shimmering in her eyes. 'What do you mean?'

'My dad's going to my brother, in Devon. They're going to pick him up. So we can be together!'

I could see a tumble of emotions clash across her face. 'What about Jane's parents?' she said stiffly.

'Her sister is taking care of them.'

She hesitated. I could almost hear her thinking, if this was a proper relationship, she would have gone with Ted to see his dad.

'Have you made other plans?' he said. The sweet smell of joy had vanished, was replaced by sour smelling doubt.

'No,' she replied. 'It's just that...' and she stopped.

'I know,' he said. 'No way are you second best. But I had to make sure both lots of parents were looked after.'

Pause. 'What did you tell them?'

'I said I had spent a lot of time up there over the last few months, I was exhausted, and I wanted to be with friends at home. Which is perfectly true.'

She considered what he'd said, then nodded slowly. 'OK. If you're going to be here, we can spend the day together.'

Ted's happiness burst out of him like a firework (nasty, noisy things) and he pulled her into his arms. 'I can't wait,' he said, and kissed her long and slow. All this smooching; ugh. Titch and I never did that.

In fact we had one of the best days ever. Certainly the best Christmas Day ever. We went to the pub together on Christmas Eve, and everyone smelt happy and Ted stayed the night. The next morning he made tea and biscuits for us in bed which was a very positive start to the day.

Later on, Suki made breakfast; bacon and mushrooms and eggs and things and I had a bit of bacon rind and toast. He gave her some spotty scarves to wear round her neck and she was delighted. When she put them on, they floated out behind her. And he gave me a big chewy bone which was delicious and kept me going for days. And she gave him a book he really wanted, something to do with art.

Later, we went down to Lizard again. We still didn't see any lizards, but they were so happy, and the air was cold, but the sun was shining, and everything always smelt so much better when it was dry and bright. Messages came across clearer, and it was easier to hear things more clearly; the rustle of a bird or the thump of rabbits' feet.

The ground was springy beneath my paws, which gave me an added bounce. I had noticed that my legs were a bit stiffer these days, and Ted gave me a lovely massage round my back legs which helped, too.

We walked and walked, and the sun shone on the sea so that it was sparkly and hurt my eyes, and we scrambled down the cliff and played on the sand and it was lovely and smooth and we were the only people there.

'Isn't this magic?' said Ted. 'It's our own desert island!'

Suki nodded. 'Just for us,' she said, and she smelt so happy I almost weed myself.

By early afternoon I was tired and they wanted to go to the pub (hooray!) so Ted found one that was just about to shut at Lizard Village. It was hot in there because they'd lit the fire and people were red faced and laughing as they ate and drank. We had some crisps and everyone said how lovely I was, and gave me a biscuit and a bit of roast potato, which quite made my day. I even had a little bit of beer on the end of Ted's finger. It smelt yeasty and tasted bitter and I was sleepy after that, so I had a doze on Suki's lap on the way home and once we got there, they went to bed. Again.

After another snooze, we all got up and I had my tea. Suki had put a casserole in her magic cooker. In the morning she plugged it in, and by the time we came home, it was ready. Incredible!

Petroc came round and they all shared the casserole and I had my own little bowlful as well and afterwards they played music and sang and then played funny games and I still had my bone and it was one of the best days of my life.

The next day was exactly a year since Pip died and it rained all day. Ted went home; I think he felt awkward because it was Pip's special day. He did ask if we wanted to meet up, but Suki had arranged to meet some friends, so we had a wet walk and then lovely brother Pete came round for supper. I liked Pete, he was a very kind, restful person. Even if he did smell very sad. I didn't get any treats, but he gave me very lovely strokes and he was just the right person to have around even if he smelt bad sometimes. I realised he couldn't help it.

It was sad to think we'd had a whole year without Pip, but in a way it was also happy because we'd survived that long without him. Pete said, 'He would be really proud of you, Suki. You brought him so much happiness.'

I think she felt a bit guilty for having Ted in her life so soon after losing Pip. But she didn't say anything about him, and Pete didn't ask.

For New Year's Eve Suki went to her friends early on and then we met Ted in the pub later, but that was very quiet so we went to another pub and that was great fun. Lots of people and noise and everyone said how cute I was and gave me crisps and I went to sleep on the seat next to them.

We went to bed very late, tired and happy. Having had such a brilliant time, I thought that Christmas and New Year would always be like that from now on. Fun and laughter with our friends and Ted. Little did we know.

17

Herons and night sky

Tess and Suki talked a lot on the phone. Mostly in the evenings, after work. The original idea had been that Tess and Titch would be gone for a few days. It was weeks, now.

'So how is your mum?' said Suki one evening. She'd finished work and poured herself a glass of wine.

'Not too good. I've got to take her to the hospital again on Thursday for more blood tests. They're not sure what's wrong.'

'I'm so sorry, Tess.'

I nudged Suki. How I wished dogs could talk to each other on the phone. She laughed gently and scratched the top of my head. 'Moll is sending her love to Titch. She really misses him, you know.'

'Titch misses her too. Whenever we get ready to go for a walk he gets all excited, then we go out and there's no Moll and he looks all forlorn.' She paused. 'Talking of which, is Ted with you?'

'No. He's gone for a long weekend,' she said. 'He's been down here for ages so his monthly visit was very overdue. We're both missing our men.' She stroked me gently and I looked into her eyes, to see if I could send my love to Titch

160

through her. 'But at least Ted will be back on Sunday night, whereas we don't know when we're going to see you and Titch again.'

'I'm going to pop back for a few days next week. As long as Paul's here to look after Mum, she'll be OK.'

'What about work?'

'I'm on compassionate leave at the moment but that can't last forever. I'm thinking about bringing Mum back to Cornwall, but we'll have to see how it all goes.'

I tuned out slightly after Tess said that she and Titch were coming back next week. It would be so lovely to see dear Titch again. I could hear him whimpering down the phone, then a cheery bark sending his love. I replayed that bark over and over that night, as we lay in bed, and wished I could fast forward the clock until we met again. But anticipation was a wonderful thing, I realised. I would make the most of it.

Over the next year, life ticked along happily. Ted spent a lot of time with us and I became very fond of him. The nights that he stayed over, he would wake up in the morning, throw back the duvet and go and make tea. He would give me my breakfast and I would go out through the cat flap for a wee.

Then he would come back to bed, place a mug of tea by Suki's side of the bed and, if it was a weekend, he'd whisper, 'What shall we do today, Moll?' in such a way that I couldn't help wagging my tail with excitement. 'Let's go to the Roseland!' he said one day, or, 'Down to Penwith!' but whatever he suggested sounded, and always was, fun.

If it was a work day, he would sometimes say, 'how about a drink after work?' which, in summer, often meant a trip out on his boat, Echo.

After our trip over to Lighthouse Beach, and getting soaked on the way back, I wasn't that keen on boats. But we had several gentle trips which were really fun, because they involved food, walks or the pub.

The next time we took his boat out was one winter afternoon. There wasn't much light left, and we set off just as a few other people were coming back. That didn't deter Ted, though.

Suki and I sat up in the cabin, but after the second time we went out, he said, 'Now, you should learn how to cast off and steer.' He smiled and added, 'Nothing's going to happen to either of us, but you should know what to do, for safety reasons.'

So after that Suki untied the boat and cast off, and the next time he taught her how to drive the boat. It seemed like driving a car: it had a wheel and I could see she had to concentrate hard, and look around us all the time. Sometimes idiots in other boats appeared from nowhere, and we had to get out of the way fast.

On this trip, we headed out into the bay and the wind was cold and whistled in my ears, and I kept getting all these amazing smells across the water. Fish and birds and seaweed and cormorants and fuel from boats and a bonfire from a distant garden. I could hear a tractor in a field, the deep chug of the engine, seagulls crying above us. There was so much going on!

The cabin smelt of salt and felt a bit damp under my paws, but I snuggled against Suki and felt the soft, reassuring warmth from her jacket. She smelt happy and alert, with the buzz of a little adventure, and that trickled down my fur and onto my paws.

After a bit we came to a little beach where we dropped anchor (I had been learning all these nautical terms) and had a sandy walk along the beach, up through some woods where there were even better sounds; robins and blackbirds with their very distinctive songs. Rabbit poo, which is great to eat, like hard little bits of extra special kibble. It had rained so the ground was a bit muddy and soft and squidgy under my paws which I love. Everything smelt better when it was damp.

After a while Ted looked at the sky and said, 'Come on, we've just got time to go the pub,' so we jumped back in the boat and Suki steered us down a narrow little creek with houses on one side and suddenly we came to the Pandora pub, with its jetty alongside.

We tied up and walked along a pontoon which led to the pub where it was dark and warm and smelt of beef cooking and burnt logs and pine and yeasty beer. We sat by the fire which was very hot, but I liked that: I toasted my back, but my paws were cool from the slate floor. Ted had a pint of beer and Suki a glass of ginger beer and we had pork scratchings which were a bit tough on my teeth at first but made lovely crunchy noises and I liked them more as the packet went down.

We couldn't stay long as Ted said the light was fading, so we went back to the boat and Suki got the engine going and steered back along the creek and although it wasn't dark, we had to put the lights on and it was all moody and misty and mysterious. The water was black and oily, and we slipped past the other boats, like dark and silent ghosts, and it smelt really exciting.

Soon we headed back towards Mylor and Ted pointed towards an old tree with bare branches showing dark against the sky, like an old person's knobbly fingers. 'Look,' he said.

We looked up and saw these huge great birds, silhouetted against the sky. 'They're like flying dinosaurs,' said Suki softly, as these creatures made weird cries, circling in and out of the branches. 'Wow,' she said. 'What are THEY?'

Ted laughed. 'That's a heronry.'

'They're amazing,' she said. 'I've hardly ever seen herons flying. They're usually standing beside the water looking mournful.'

'I know,' he said. 'What amazes me is that they always look so Eeyore-ish and here they are flying around having such fun. I didn't realise they had a sense of humour!'

Suki gazed up at the sky and then looked over at Ted. 'Thank you,' she whispered. 'I will never forget this.'

We chugged back in silence after that, and as we rounded the corner going back along the river towards Flushing, they looked past Falmouth Docks, and back over Penryn river. 'Oh,' cried Suki. 'It's like the sky's on fire!' She turned to Ted. 'I read that dogs can't see colours like we can,' she said. 'So, Moll, it's like someone's painted the background rose pink.'

'And on top of that are streaks of purple, and slashes of red,' said Ted.

'And the red's tinged with flames of yellow and bursts of orange,' she added.

It all sounded a bit barking to me, but I could see how delighted they were. We dogs knew how spectacular nature was; we weren't as surprised as Humans were.

Suki kept looking at the sky. 'Look, the colours are deepening by the moment,' she said, as we motored along, and then suddenly, even I could see they had faded.

'It goes so quickly,' she said sadly. 'As soon as the sun sets the colours just vanish. Oh, I wish I had my phone to take some pictures.'

'Sometimes it's better not to have photos,' Ted replied. 'I find I remember things better if they're in my mind rather than on my phone.'

Suki nodded. 'Well, I won't forget this outing for sure.' She put her arms around him. 'That was the most amazing trip ever. I can't thank you enough.'

'I'm so glad you enjoyed it,' Ted said, kissing her. It was too dark to see his face, but I could tell from his voice that he was smiling. Then he bent down and gave me a little scratch round the ears, and a biscuit. 'I think we'd better get Moll a lifejacket if we're going to go out on a regular basis. What do you think?'

And just as Suki said, 'Absolutely!' I gave a big bark which meant YES! It wasn't just for the lifejacket, whatever that was, but because it meant more time with Ted. More adventures, more happy times, and proof that I was doing my job: making sure my Suki was happy.

18

Dorset review

Another review came in, shortly after Ted had been away for a week. A week didn't sound long but I could sense how much Suki hated his absences.

'The trouble is, every time he comes back from those visits, he's like a broken man,' I heard her telling Tess on the phone. 'I have to put him back together again.'

'He's very lucky to have you,' came the reply.

'He hates going,' she continued. 'He has to steel himself to see her, and I just can't imagine what it must be like. At least, I try *not* to imagine. But I worry about his mental health. He's only 46, but every time he comes back from seeing her, he looks about 70.'

'Oh, Suki,' Tess said. 'Poor bloke. What an awful situation.' She sighed. 'You just have to make the most of the time you have together, don't you?'

Suki stroked my spine. 'Exactly. Are you still coming down?'

'You bet. Got time for a walk on Friday?'

'Of course!' she said, and I jumped off the bed and barked and ran up and down the hall. I was going to see my Titch again!

We had a wonderful walk, at our favourite halfway spot near Truro, down to Roundwood Quay. Titch smelt different: city smells of smoke and dusty cars lay in his short, dense coat. His nose smelt of foreign food and something powdery that he said was Tess's Mum's talcum powder, whatever that was.

But in essence he was still my lovely Titch. Our noses met, our whiskers brushed, and we had plenty of room to run and chase squirrels, dive after a rabbit and listen to the coo of a distant pigeon.

Titch, it had to be said, wasn't a great talker. He was a listener, and a thinker, so sometimes I got frustrated because I thought he was ignoring me, when actually he was just mulling things over. He said he ran in a big park up there with another terrier called Dusty. She never stopped barking, which gave him ear ache, he said. My Poor Titch. I licked his ears gently and he nuzzled me and licked my face and it made up for all the time we'd been apart.

'So how long do you think you'll be away?' Suki asked Tess.

'Hopefully no more than a few days,' Tess replied. 'I've organised someone from Social Services to see Mum every day. I wanted her to come and stay with us but she said she'd rather be near her friends which is fair enough.'

So not long before Titch was back for good!

They hugged hard, and Titch and I nuzzled noses again. We'd already been separated for longer than Suki and Ted were usually apart. Having watched and smelt her, I knew that she felt very much the same before she saw Ted after they'd been separated.

Anticipation tasted of milk warmed by the sun. Of new grass. It had all the promise of the first day of spring. If you looked at it this way, being parted for a short while had a lot going for it.

I decided I would look forward to our next reunion. It had been such a joy seeing Titch again today, but I was learning more about anticipation, which had been nose tinglingly special. For days beforehand, I had lain under the bed imagining his special scent, which blended with the lotion Tess put on her skin. The way his muzzle was beginning to go grey, just like mine. The way he trotted along in front of me, his legs slightly bowed. The way his ears twitched and zoned forwards when he smelt me coming. The cold black rub of his nose on mine. The way he snickered hello so that my heart thumped. All these things I would hold onto, and tuck into the Titch shaped hole in my heart, until we next met.

As luck would have it, a big distraction came our way, right after Ted came back from his latest visit to see Jane.

'The magazine has asked if I'd like to do a review in Dorset,' Suki said. 'It's a long way to drive, and I don't get paid much petrol allowance, but the place looks lovely.'

Ted peered at the website. 'My God. It's near where I used to camp as a boy!' He laughed, and smelt delighted; a soft, sweet smell, like honeysuckle. 'It's so beautiful, you'll love it. And I'll pay the petrol, don't worry about that. It'll do all of us good to have a break.'

All three of us gave a shiver of excitement. A proper holiday!

'The walking is lovely round there,' he said. 'It's not far from the coast. I can't wait to show it all to you!'

So the next weekend we set off on a trip that took nearly all day. We stopped along the way, to stretch our legs, have coffee and a walk. Then further along at a supermarket to stock up on food and drink for the stay. And at last, driving further on, we came to a slope, into a parking space, and Ted said, 'This is it. We're here.'

We got out, stiffly, and stretched, then walked through an arch into a huge, enchanted garden. It had little paths leading in different directions, and lots of grass, bushes and plants and trees, and rabbit poo in one corner, and the smells were strong and foreign and really exciting. I ran up a steep path with steps and it led to a big lawn and there, in the middle, was a little house.

'Oh,' breathed Suki, following quickly behind me.

'Wow,' said Ted, behind her.

She turned and kissed him. 'Come on,' she said, and we all ran the last bit to get to the house.

It was about the same size as our flat but arranged differently. The kitchen and living room looked out over the lawn, and our bedroom looked out of the back of the house. Having a little snoop around the back of the terrace, I could hear blackbirds singing their heads off. Robins perched on a nearby branch, whistling a welcome. And in the pine trees behind the little house was the tap-tap of a woodpecker.

Ted had bought me a bone when we stopped in the town for coffee, and after they'd unpacked, we all sat on the little terrace looking at the lawn while I chewed away and Suki and Ted clinked their wine glasses.

'Here's to us and our home for the next few days,' he said.

'Cheers,' she said. 'I wish we could be here for at least a week. What an incredible place.'

'It certainly is,' said Ted. And he leaned over and kissed her. 'Thank you for inviting me.'

She smelt of sunshine and happiness and love. 'It's great, isn't it? Aren't we lucky?'

As I gnawed at my bone, my two favourite people in the world next to me (apart from Tess and Titch), I had to agree. It really was perfect.

Ten minutes of exploring this new garden provided me with an incredible range of experiences. There was another small house, just like ours, not far away, and they had a big compost bin outside, full of eggshells, orange and apple peel. Left over mashed potato. Bits of gristle and fatty meat. Teabags. I could go on, but you get the idea. I was itching to jump inside and have a good munch, but all those treasures were packed inside this tank with a heavy lid, which made foraging inside it impossible.

Apart from compost, I could smell the boots belonging to the people staying next door. They were on the doorstep. A man with big clumpy ones that smelt of manure. Delicious. Hers were new, smelt of clean rubber, very little mud. Needed breaking in. The boots, not her.

At the edges of the garden were pine trees, and the cones smelt of resin and citrus; clean and outdoors and fresh. The cones were good to chew, and for playing football. Ted threw them for me, over and over, until I was nearly out of breath.

Then at the bottom of the garden was a long low bungalow with people who came in late at night and went out early morning. They smelt of strange cigarettes and their boots smelt foreign. It was difficult to define, but a bit like tobacco: musty and alien and not English at all. They had several noisy cars that woke me up when they came home late at night, and smelt of strange fuel.

And then there were the sounds: blackbirds, robins and sparrows sang from the bushes. Pigeons cooed in the trees, and a young family of buzzards gave strange mewing noises.

Pine needles dropped regularly, but that was such a high, tinny noise, that I don't think Suki could hear it. But we could all hear the wind that howled and whistled through the branches of the pine trees at night and was quite spooky at first. I heard the cows lowing several fields away, and some cars in the distance.

I could hear rabbits running in the next field, but I could also hear Ted and Suki in our little house, so they never caught me with my nose near the compost bin as I was too quick. Or they were too noisy.

The couple in the next-door house didn't shout, but they had arguments that smelt bad. Then they would go quiet but I think they went to bed, and then there were different sounds; a bit like Ted and Suki in bed, and when they came out they sounded and smelt completely different. Calmer and happier and they talked in normal voices.

I could also hear the sea when the wind was coming from that direction. It wasn't far away: we could see the bay from the bottom of the garden, and every now and then the sound of the crashing waves and the salt smell would waft up through the garden and take me by surprise.

The other thing I could hear (and smell, of course) were meals being made. At home, I had my breakfast early then sometimes Suki went back to bed with her tea. She had her own breakfast later, and it was boring; usually a bowl of muesli that didn't smell of anything interesting, or toast that was a bit better as she had peanut butter and jam and I got the occasional crust.

But holiday breakfasts were made by Ted and they were a real adventure. He cooked eggs: boiled or fried. Or mushrooms with cheese and garlic. Thick slices of yummy granary bread, all washed down with tea. Well, I didn't have the tea, but the smell of those breakfasts, when I was sniffing around outside, made my nose go into overdrive. If this was what life with Ted was like, I thought, we'd better kidnap him.

We had several splendid walks along the coast, which was very different to Cornwall. The hills were higher and grander and more rounded and spacious, somehow; the landscape was on a larger scale than we were used to. The rabbits smelt similar, as did the foxes, but apart from that the smells were satisfyingly different and I had a sense of wonder at who had trodden these paths before us. What fascinating messages they had left through their paws, their boots and their feet.

We visited the nearby town, where there was an open-air market, and had coffee at a cafe there. There were several walls and corners just rammed with so many messages that I had trouble reading them all. I could have stayed there all day, but Suki and Ted wanted to go to the antique stalls, and there were plenty of smells there, too. Fusty smells of old metal boxes and wooden furniture, which weren't very interesting, but the owners of the stalls always had sandwiches or coffee or biscuits – there were crumbs everywhere if you looked hard enough.

We found a massive old castle in the middle of nowhere and walked around the outside, which was called a moat, and was like a vast bowl which smelt of rabbits, masses of different dogs, and thousands of different boots, to say nothing of all the cars and vans and lorries that pulled up there.

Underlying our exploring was the tick-tick that meant our time was limited, so it was more precious than usual. We had to cram every second full of good stuff to last us through the times when we weren't together.

The only downer was when Ted had a phone call one morning. He went outside, talked animatedly for a while and then came in. There was an awkward silence, and he smelt like rotten eggs.

'Everything OK?' she said. I knew she'd been trying to hear the conversation.

He hesitated. 'Jane had a bad night so they're thinking of adjusting her medication.' He came over and pulled her to him, and held her tight, her head pressed against his chest. They said nothing, just hugged each other so I went out into the garden to give them some time to themselves.

A little while after that she came out and called me. She sounded better, so I relaxed, and after that we had a wonderful day, walking by the sea, jumping over rock pools and digging in the cliffs for fossils.

Ted took pictures of us, and I enjoyed being a model. Me on the beach. Me jumping up for a treat in the garden. Me outside the house. Me on the terrace. Me in the water. Me on the bed. Me watching television. Me, me, me everywhere.

Not so many of Suki. She hated having her picture taken, though he said she must as she was a real author now, and needed publicity pictures. He took pictures of her by the sea, holding me, walking along. 'I don't mind them as long as I don't have to pose,' she said.

Suki went to interview the family that owned the house for the review while I stayed with Ted. She came back saying that if we wanted to come again, they'd give us a special deal.

'In that case, let's come again soon,' said Ted. 'Let's put a date in the diary so we've got something to look forward to.'

She grinned. 'Also,' she said. 'I was just thinking... how busy are you the rest of this week?' This was Wednesday.

'Nothing too urgent. Why?'

'Well,' she looked at him with a lopsided smile. 'I told them we were having such a lovely time, and they said that the house is empty until Saturday. So, we could stay a few more days if we wanted.' She waited. 'For free.'

I could see Ted's burst of happiness, like a firework, as he walked over and put his arms around her. He kissed the top of her head and looked down at her. 'I can't think of anything I'd like more,' he said with a huge grin. 'I might have to do some work tomorrow, but that's all manageable.'

'Brilliant!' Suki danced over to me. 'What do you think, Moll? Shall we stay another few days? More holiday?'

I bounced around too, and barked, and they had another cup of tea, and she went to tell the owners that we were staying until Saturday. A proper holiday!

Those days felt even more special, like an unexpected present. Everything was tinged with warmth and smelt of love, and we felt quite drunk with it all. If only Titch had been with us, it would have been perfect.

On the Friday, the day before we had to go back, it rained. Suki took me for a quick dash round the field first thing, but by the time we got back, the rain was getting heavier until it was torrential. It seemed like an omen.

Ted made breakfast again; stuffed mushrooms with garlic and blue cheese, but the sunlit joy had gone out of the morning. It was a poignant reminder that our lovely time was coming to an end.

'I'm going to have to do some work this morning,' Ted said. 'Do you want to go into town or something?'

She shook her head. 'I'll go and see our hosts, book us in for a week in January. I can write up the review now, and post the pictures, then I don't have to do it when we get back.'

So our morning was almost like a normal work morning, with both of them crouched over their laptops. It was comforting, though, knowing that Ted was with us. Every now and then one of them would get up, make coffee and pass it over with a kiss or a smile. I lay by the window feeling warm and contented. Pleased that I'd fulfilled my promise to Pip. Wishing that life could always be like this.

19

Operation

There was no doubt that our time in Dorset brought them even closer together. It was almost as if they breathed the same air, they were so attuned. The downside, of course, was that when he had to go away, she suffered all the more. He did, too, I'm sure, but she was my priority.

Still, the year sped by, and we were happy, for the most part. And before we knew it, another Christmas loomed.

Tess and Titch were finally back, as her mum was a lot better, so we were back to regular walks which was such a joy. I hadn't believed it possible to miss him so much. 'What are you and Ted doing for Christmas?' Tess said.

'I don't know. I'm happy to do the same as before. Just have an easy day,' said Suki. 'What are you doing?'

'I want to bring Mum down here, but she wants us to go up there. It's under negotiation,' Tess said, giving a faint smile.

The week before Christmas, Ted rang, saying he'd be round after work. He sounded tense, and my hackles went up. This wasn't good, I could smell.

I was right. 'My dad's in hospital,' he said, when he arrived. 'He's had a stroke.'

'Oh, Ted, I'm so sorry. Can I do anything?'

He shook his head. 'No, but it means I'll have to stay with him when he comes out of hospital. I've told my brother, but he's not able to stay with him for long, so I've got to organise a carer and stuff. Oh, darling, I'm so, so sorry...'

Suki swallowed hard. 'Can I help at all? With your dad?'

Ted looked down. 'It just makes it a bit complicated,' he said, his face going red. 'He doesn't know about us, and....'

And he was too chicken to tell his father. My hackles went up – this wasn't fair on Suki. I could see tears stinging her eyes. She so wanted to be a part of his family life. And now the Christmas that they'd been looking forward to was disappearing faster than you could say biscuit. And all this around our anniversary of Pip's death. At a time when her ghosts made her most vulnerable. I barked sharply. It was so unfair.

'OK,' she said, although it obviously wasn't.

'What about Christmas? What will you do? Oh, I so wish I could be here with you.'

'I'll go to my mum,' she said. 'We didn't go last year because my brothers were there, but she hasn't got anyone, so I can be with her.' She tried a smile. 'It won't be for long. Will it?' They were both putting up a front for the other, I could tell. But underneath was a sour sadness that dragged at my guts.

Her pulled her close, saying nothing, just breathing into her hair. They were so close you couldn't tell where one ended and the other began.

So our Christmas was a quiet time, with Suki's Mum and her carer. They both tried to be jolly, but Suki smelt terrible. All her ghosts had come back in full force and while she tried hard not to show it, I could smell she was really struggling.

Her mum didn't say anything, but I caught her looking at Suki carefully.

Her mum knew about Ted, but there was a noticeable chill in the room when he rang and Suki rushed upstairs to talk to him.

'How is Ted's father?' she asked, when Suki came back.

'He's home now but he's got a nurse coming in every day to check on him.'

'And when will Ted be back?' All these questions, each one making Suki flinch.

'As soon as possible,' she said. 'In a few days, we hope.'

But as with Tess, the few days turned into a week, which turned into another week.

'He's got an infection and I had to call an ambulance this afternoon,' said Ted when he rang. He sounded exhausted, and I knew how worn-out Suki was: she smelt like an old pair of jeans, washed so much that all the smell had come out. How she yearned to be with him.

'I'm so sorry, love,' she said. 'I wish I could help. Let me know how he is.'

His father improved, and was back at his home a few days later. 'I can't wait to see you,' Ted said. 'Won't be long now, darling.'

'Can't wait,' said Suki.

In the first week in January, Suki went off to see her doctor. A rare occurrence. My whiskers told me she wasn't worried, and I waited in the back of the van while she went in. But the Suki who came out was very different to the one who went in.

She opened the van door and slumped inside. When she spoke, her voice was croaky. 'I've got a lump just by my right hip bone, Moll,' she said. 'It didn't occur to me to worry about it, but I thought I'd better have it looked at.' I waited, my fur prickling along my spine. My whiskers twitched. This didn't smell good.

'The doctor was worried. I've got to have blood tests next week.' She looked round and stroked my head, fondled my ears. 'Oh well, it's probably nothing. I mean, I feel absolutely fine. Let's go and have a walk.'

But as we walked down to the beach, her phone rang. 'Hello?' said Suki. 'Oh, OK.' She had her polite voice on. A few minutes later, she put her phone back in her pocket. 'It was the doctor. She's referring me to the hospital next week,' she said, sounding dazed.

The next day, the hospital rang to make an appointment for her to see a consultant the following week. My whiskers twitched. What was it for? When the letter of confirmation arrived the following day, Suki burst into tears.

'It's from the Gynaecology and Oncology Department,' she wept down the phone to Ted.

What the hell did that mean? I didn't realise, until much later, that oncology meant cancer. My whiskers stilled, my spine shivered. Did that mean she was going to die?

After that, life seemed to speed up. Everything was geared towards finding out what was the matter with her. My nose felt blocked so I could hardly sniff, and my whiskers wouldn't keep still. I even went off my food for a few days, my stomach churning. Was I going to lose her as well as Pip?

'I'll come back to see the consultant with you,' Ted said.

'Don't be ridiculous,' said Suki. 'I'll be fine. Tess said she'd go with me.'

'But I can't bear to think of you going through all this without me,' Ted said.

'Ted, I'll be fine,' she said, though her voice wobbled and I knew she wasn't feeling fine at all. 'Look, I'll ring you as soon as I've seen him, OK?'

And so she went off, leaving me at home. Dogs are better at waiting than humans, I think, but even so it was an anxious time, and I was glad to hear Tess's car drive up outside, hear Suki's key in the door.

She came in, on her own, and I rushed up to her, barking as I always do. She knelt down and hugged me and I licked her tears as they fell, hot and salty, onto my coat. She smelt of that chemically, hospital smell which frightened me so much my ears went flat and I couldn't stop licking my lips. But I had to be strong for her, so I waited till she got herself together. She sat down on the floor with me in the hall and buried her face in my fur. Uh oh, not good.

'They think it might be cancer, Moll,' she said. 'Ovarian cancer.'

'WHAT?' Ted shouted down the phone, when she told him that evening. 'But it can't, I mean, you don't feel ill, do you?'

'No,' she said, clutching her glass of wine. We'd had a dismal walk in the rain and my fur was still damp, despite lying in front of the fire for ages. Suki had forgotten to change her jeans and they were still wet, though she didn't seem aware of it. 'I feel absolutely fine and they're not sure it's cancer. I've got to have more tests next week.'

'It'll be a cyst or something, that's all,' said Ted. 'It'll just be a false alarm, darling. They have to err on the side of caution.' But his voice shook so much, I had the feeling he was reassuring himself rather than her.

We went out for another walk in the rain that night. I'm not fond of the rain, but being on the move usually tired her out, helped her sleep. We pounded along the slippery streets, the familiar smells diluted by the rain, and the only sounds were the swish of wet tyres on the roads, the clump of her boots and the wet padding of my paws on the pavements.

I was cold with fear, which ran like the rain, down my spine and seeped into my already wet coat. This would mean another thorough towelling off when we got home. A night with damp fur. The things we endure for our owners.

But more importantly, what could I do to keep my Suki safe? I had tried so hard to save Pip, but that hadn't worked. At least, I thought, I had her. Yet now, she was in danger. I had to think fast. Do something. But how could I fight this?

I didn't sleep much, and that was when I realised how many different types of night there were. Sometimes the darkness was thick and impenetrable, like a solid wall. Other nights were warmer and looser, so thoughts could flow and good dreams took place. Some were dense and prickly, with strange scary smells that made my fur creep. Nights were rather like the sea, I realised; sometimes they had long, slow swells, other times they looked pewter grey and were flat calm. And others, like at the moment, were storms with shrieking winds, drenching rain and booming thunder, when we were tossed up and down, not knowing which way we'd end up.

The next week was full of more trips to the hospital, then the week after that she had another trip to see the consultant. I stayed with Nice Sheila who took me to the allotment where I chased mice and explored the smells of manure and earth and rabbits and bird droppings, the earth cool and damp beneath my paws. We had tea and biscuits sitting in her little hut, and I sat on her lap, which was bigger than Suki's and therefore more comfortable, and though she was cheerful and chatted to the people next door, I had a sick feeling in my belly.

Suki came to pick me up from Sheila's house where we were watching television, and I could smell the bad news as soon as she came in the house. It smelt like stale, rancid air.

'Well?' asked Sheila.

'I've got a tumour in my ovaries,' Suki said, her voice wavering. 'They're pretty sure it's ovarian cancer.' Her voice was small and nothing like hers.

Sheila gave her a big hug. 'You know I had breast cancer, years ago,' she said. 'I had treatment and I'm fine.'

Suki nodded, but didn't seem able to speak.

'So what are they going to do?'

'I've got to have a radical hysterectomy,' she said. 'Because the tumour is so big, they can't do keyhole surgery, so they have to make a big incision down my stomach. It's going to take twelve weeks to recover. Twelve weeks, Sheila!' And she burst into tears.

Sheila patted her back and made her sit down, and I jumped on her lap, and they both had a glass of wine, and talked about who could help, and how. And then we went home and she rang Ted.

'Oh, my darling,' he said. 'Listen, I'll come back. Now.'

'How can you?' she said. 'Your dad needs you. And anyway, I'm all right now. I'll need help after I come out of hospital.'

'And when will that be?'

'They're doing the operation in three weeks, and I should be in hospital for about five days.'

'Well, that's good,' he said, but he sounded more frightened that she did. 'Look, I'll come back this weekend. I have to see you.'

Despite her protests, Ted drove back and arrived on the Friday night, but it was very late when he got here, and although it was lovely to see him, he smelt terrible. Sadness enveloped him like a thick fog, choking the air. It seemed to sap all his energy, and he'd lost his normal brightness.

I gave him a huge welcome, of course, barking and jumping up as usual, and Suki jumped into his arms, and he held her tight, then bent down to give me a cuddle. But he was a dimmer, smaller version of himself, which made my tail droop and my ears flop.

We all went to bed because it was late and he was exhausted, and it was cosy all snuggled up together, and yet it felt wrong somehow. In the darkness, she said, 'I've postponed our Dorset holiday,' and she tried to sound cheerful.

He turned over. 'Oh, my darling, I'm so sorry. I'd forgotten all about that.'

'That's OK.' The bed creaked as she snuggled into his arms. 'They've said we can go later in the year. I explained the circumstances.'

'Good. Well, that's something to look forward to.'

'We can go when I've recovered, can't we? Late spring.' Silence. 'What's up, Ted?'

A longer silence. I began to be worried. 'The thing is....'

I could feel her pulling away from him. 'What's the matter?'

'Dad's carer's got cancer. They've got someone for this weekend but she's really busy so she can't come back next week, or the week after, and they're really short staffed at the moment. I also have to go and see Jane and her parents.'

Suki lay very still. 'So, you mean you won't be here for a while?'

'No,' he said, in a very small voice. 'I am so sorry, darling, but this is all beyond my control. I seem to be needed everywhere and I don't know what to do. I can't look after everyone and the only person I really want to look after is you.'

I could almost hear Suki battling with herself, and him. There was a heavy silence, and the darkness seemed thick and claustrophobic while we waited for her to speak. 'I think,' she said, in a voice that was small but firm. 'I think it would be better if we called this off, Ted.'

'What?' Horror and fear laced that one word.

'Ted, I know how hard this is for you, but I need someone who can be around for me, certainly over the next few months. I would love that person to be you, but you can't be there for us all. It's not fair on you and it certainly isn't fair on me.'

A stunned silence. 'You mean, we're over?'

'Yes. I think it's better this way. Then you don't have to worry about letting me down, and I can concentrate on my op, and getting better.' If you didn't know her, you'd think how strong she was. I knew otherwise. She was trying, desperately, to hold herself together.

'But...' he sat up. 'Over? We can't be. I can't live without you.' He sounded panicky.

'Ted, you've been living without me for a while now. You need to concentrate on your dad, and Jane and her parents and all that that entails. And I need to sort myself out.'

'But who will look after you?'

She turned over. 'Av rang and she said she can come and stay for a while when I'm out of hospital. And Tess and other friends have offered to help.'

'But what about Moll?'

'I've got the number for a dog sitter so I'll give her a ring. And Tess and Anne said they'd walk her too.'

'You've got it all worked out,' he said slowly. Faintly.

'I've had to, Ted, because I never know when you're going to be here,' she cried.

Silence.

'So you don't need me.'

She groaned in exasperation. 'Ted, I would love you to help me, but you can't. You have too many other people to worry about.'

Pause. 'Have you met someone else?'

'What? No. God, Ted, of course not. How could you think that?'

'It just all seems so sudden.'

'Well, everything has happened rather suddenly, hasn't it? To both of us.'

'It certainly has,' he said in a small voice.

We all lay there for a while and I waited. How on earth could we sleep after that?

The bed creaked. 'In that case, I think I'd better go,' he said. His voice was thick with tears. 'I'll go home and perhaps we can talk in the morning.'

'You don't have to go, Ted.' But it was best that he did.

'I can't stay here now.'

She didn't reply, but put the light on while he got dressed, in stupefied, painful silence.

I crawled over the bed and snuggled up against her. Firmly, to her thigh. Moral support. She said nothing but watched him put his clothes on.

'I'll talk to you in the morning,' he said. Hopefully.

'Better not,' she said gently. 'Goodbye, Ted.'

He stopped at the door and looked down at us both. 'Bye my darling. Bye Moll.' His voice cracked and he blew a kiss. 'I love you both. More than you'll ever know.'

The bedroom door closed behind him. We heard him walk down the hall, and the front door opened, then shut quietly behind him. His footsteps echoed down the path, then the muffled roar of his car engine.

That's when she heaved, and sobbed, and cried like all hope had gone. I'm not one to give up lightly, but I really came close to despair.

My poor Suki. What on earth was I going to do now?

20

Preparation

Ted rang the next morning, and firmly but gently she said, 'No, Ted,' and turned her phone off. She lay back in bed and cried such tragic tears, it sounded like they came from a gaping wound inside her. Her anguish and pain smelt like a long, dark sewer filled with festering Christmas ghosts. Her back against mine was cold and felt brittle.

Later, she turned her phone back on, rang Tess and arranged to walk with her that afternoon. Judging by the pinging of her phone, she had lots of texts, too. Then she got up and had a piece of toast. 'We've got to start planning who's going to look after you, and what happens when I come out of hospital,' she said. Despite her fear and pain, she was being thinking of me. Being pragmatic. Right now, that was her saviour.

The next week passed in a flurry of phone calls, and someone called Emma came round. She smelt of meaty treats and lots of other dogs; she was very friendly, and said she had her own Jack Russell called Joey. She was warm to snuggle up to, and had some very tasty bits of sausage and knew exactly where to tickle me, under my chin, so I decided I liked her.

I had a few walks with her, and Suki said, 'You're going to stay with Emma and Joey for a few nights while I'm in hospital, OK?'

I wasn't too sure about this, but Emma smelt calm and safe so I had a feeling it might be fun just for a few nights. Her Joey was old but reasonably friendly and her house was untidy and smelt of biscuits and old rugs and her teenage son so it was very homely.

Suki had several more trips to the hospital. Each time she came back smelling of acid stuff that was apparently antiseptic. It made my nose itch and my whiskers curled. But apparently it was all part of trying to find out what was wrong.

Every day I could smell how much she missed Ted, with every inch of her breath, her body, her mind. I did too. He'd woven into our lives, and fitted so well. He had brought joy and love and laughter and fun and even when he smelt awful, he was good to be with.

He had been the reason she jumped out of bed in the morning. Now the bed was too wide and too empty and neither of us could bear to sleep on his side. It smelt wrong.

Even though he hadn't lived with us all the time, we were so used to him being around. His presence was here, even if *he* wasn't, and now he just *wasn't*, and worse was the prospect that he wouldn't ever be again. I felt as if we'd fallen off a cliff and left him behind. Or he'd gone over the edge and we were standing looking at him smashed on the rocks far below. Both sensations left shivers down my fur and made my tail droop. I didn't feel safe any more. Everything was threatened.

Walks with Suki were always a high point of the day, but they'd lost their sparkle without Ted. I missed my Titch, too, when he was away, but now I missed Ted almost as much as Suki did,

Even when they hadn't been talking, they were communicating. The touch of a hand, a quick caress, a long kiss, an exchanged grin, or raising of eyebrows. Handing over a drink, or making a meal. It was their way of talking without talking. In that way, they were learning to be more like dogs. Though their noses were rubbish, and their hearing wasn't nearly as good as ours.

Ted had been more than her partner, he really was a part of her, and she was part of him. Without each other, they had gaping holes that smelt so rotten, and were so big you could almost see them.

Meanwhile Suki's operation hurtled towards us like a tornado, sweeping everything in its path. The only good thing was that it absorbed a huge amount of the time and energy she would have spent missing Ted, for she had an even worse problem to worry about. Her life.

One evening she finished work and, as she stretched and yawned, her phone rang. I listened with one ear cocked while she said yes and no and stuff, then she said, 'OK, I'll call in for a bit.' And something about this call made my whiskers twitch.

She looked down at me and scratched behind my ears and said, 'there's a party tonight, Moll, in town. One of the other freelancers has got a job as editor of a new magazine, so he's buying drinks for everyone.' She sat down beside me. 'I don't really feel like going but...'

I barked, sharply, and nudged her with my nose. Just so she got the message.

She grinned. 'Yes, I know, I think I should, too. I'll go and have a glass of wine and then come home and we can watch that new drama on telly.'

I licked her hand, glad she was going out. It would do her good. Loss hung around her like a wet smelly towel that had been left out in the garden for too long.

She spent some time getting ready: put on a skirt and tights and shoes with heels and a black shirt and green cardigan thing and she looked lovely. Not that I'm biased. While she was out, I lay on the bed for a snooze and dreamt we were in Dorset with Ted. I was eating a bit of toast with bacon and we were going to have a lovely long walk by the sea and chase rabbits and then, what was that? I jerked awake as the front door opened and in she came looking all sparkly.

Well, that was good news. She was a bit giggly and smelt of wine. It must have been later than I'd realised. 'I've had a lovely time and talked to several people and one of them asked if I'd have lunch in a few day's time,' she said, all in a rush. 'He's called Luke and he said he wants to pick my brains about writing. He's ever so nice and easy to talk to. A boatbuilder. Lives in Mabe.'

Well, I thought, and licked her hand thoroughly. Lunch, eh? I wondered if she'd take me, and whether they might have chips. Judging by her pink face, a bit of food with another man could only be a good thing.

Later that week they met for lunch at a cafe near the beach in Falmouth but she left me in the back of the van. I wasn't impressed. I wanted to be there, listening, and having the odd chip, a bit of bread or even better, bacon, but what could

I do? At least we'd have a walk afterwards and I could hear all about this Luke while he was still fresh in her mind.

She was gone for ages. Just as well I had a cosy bed in the back of the van or I would have been well pissed off. But just when I'd dozed off for the umpteenth time, I heard her footsteps, as well as those of a man. Big heavy treads, from someone wearing boots.

'This is my van,' I heard her say, as she opened the door. 'And this is Moll.'

I looked up, smelt hesitation and fear coming from this strange man. What was that about? He glanced into the van but made no effort to come near me. All I could see was a tall man with dark hair. Wearing a thick jumper that smelt of salt and wood and something else. Something alien.

I jumped out, so I could investigate more thoroughly, but he shrank from me, and stood awkwardly behind Suki. I could smell he liked her, so that was good.

'Thanks for lunch,' she said, and I could smell a gentle contentment wafting off her. Like primroses. Not that I ate them, but they had a lovely lemony smell.

'Not at all, my treat,' he said. 'I've learned a lot about journalism, so many thanks.'

'Well, if you'd like to borrow my notes from the course, you're very welcome,' she said, smiling up at him. He was taller than I'd realised. Taller than Ted.

He smiled back, and all his hesitation and fear vanished. He must be frightened of me. But why? I stood back, didn't want to crowd him. 'That would be very useful,' he said. 'Perhaps I could pick them up sometime?'

'Why don't we meet for a walk?' she said.

'That would be good,' he said quickly. I could tell he wanted to see her again. Even if that meant seeing me, too. Love me, love my dog, pal.

'OK, how about next week?' she said. 'Shall I ring you?'

'Excellent,' he said, and they stood there, looking at each other.

Well, come on, I thought. Do something. I want my walk. I barked and nudged Suki's leg with my nose. She took the hint and leaned forward, gave Luke a peck on the cheek. In return, he gave her a rather awkward hug, but I could sense that she liked it.

She grinned at him. 'Thanks, Luke,' she said, and bent over to clip my lead on. 'Look forward to seeing you next week.' And we walked off. But at the end of the road we looked back and he was standing there, watching us. Gave a little wave.

My ears twitched, then my whiskers, and a funny sensation ran down my spine. Was this man going to be part of our lives, the way Ted had been? Surely not. It was too soon.

But she smelt calm and relaxed, content from being with this man, like I do after I've had a good chew at a bone. She needed that, especially now.

So if he could keep her calm and content, that was fine with me.

That night, watching television, a text came in on her phone. Not an unusual event, so she picked it up and read it, absently stroking my spine. I loved that.

'Ooh, Moll. How lovely.' Pause while she read it again. 'Listen. It's Luke. He says, "I did so enjoy your excellent company over lunch and very useful information. Look forward to a walk soon. Take care. Luke X"

I pricked up my ears. So? He was being polite. Was I missing something?

She read it again then sat back, had a sip of wine. 'Well, he's single and lives on a boat and he said he sometimes needs crew, so we might be able to sail with him!'

I rolled over onto my back, wanting my tummy rubbed. I wasn't sure why she was so excited. I mean boats were OK, but..

She laughed, a lovely sound that I hadn't heard recently. 'I know, Moll. You don't like boats much, do you? But you could stay with Tess or Sheila for the day.'

That sounded better. If Luke was going to make her happy by taking her sailing, that was fine with me. I closed my eyes and concentrated on the blissful tummy rub. Left a bit, down a bit. Aaah, that was it.

21

Luke

Preparations for the operation continued. And though Suki kept busy and sounded cheerful, I could smell the fear and anxiety seeping out of her. Underlying all that was the Missing Ted Smell which made me gag.

She never complained but every now and then her face would crumple and she would lie down on the bed and sob. 'Sorry, Moll,' she said one day. 'I feel as if I've been scraped out inside and there's nothing left. It really, really hurts.'

My poor Suki. I would have done anything to make her feel better, but all I could do was burrow up to her, nudge her with my nose and lick her, tell her how much I loved her. Press the length of my body against hers, feeling her warmth against mine. I tried to send strength and courage from my fur to hers.

Suki and Luke arranged to meet at some woods near Gweek where there was a cafe. It was a cold day, so they decided to have coffee first and shared a flapjack. Luke looked down at me, then at Suki. 'Is Mollie allowed a bit of flapjack?' he asked. He went up in my estimation.

She wrinkled her nose. 'Well, not normally, but these aren't normal times, are they?'

Thank dog for that. I tilted my head to one side and gave Luke my best stare; he obligingly dropped a big chunk of flapjack in my direction. They continued talking, and I wondered if she would tell him about this operation.

'The other day, at lunch, you said something about having to go into hospital,' he said. So he got there first.

She nodded and stirred her coffee thoughtfully. Would she tell him the whole story or play it down a bit? 'Yes, I'm going in ten days' time,' she said, and looked up at him. 'I've got to have a hysterectomy,' she said and her voice wobbled a little.

I moved round to sit by her, nudging her leg with my nose. Automatically she bent down to stroke my ears. 'I've got a lump they're not sure about,' she continued.

'That must be worrying,' he said. Gently.

She looked up, gratefully. 'It is, yes,' she said. 'They think it might be ovarian cancer which is scary.'

'Of course it is,' he said. And even though that's all he said, the smell coming off him was so kind and safe that I breathed out a woof of relief. Whoever this man was, he wouldn't hurt her.

Silence. But it was a comfortable one. He pushed the rest of the flapjack towards her. 'A friend of mine had a hysterectomy a few months ago,' he said. 'It went really well, and the recovery was quick too. It's a very common procedure, so I'm sure there's nothing to worry about.'

She looked up, smiled, and I could smell the relief wafting from her. 'Thanks,' she said. 'That's good to know.' They were both ignoring the fact that she might die because of the lump (I'd heard her crying down the phone to Tess about this) but I was beginning to realise that some things are best left unsaid.

'Would you like another coffee, or shall we walk?' he said.

'Walk, if that's OK with you,' she said. Thank the bone, I thought. Sitting in cafes was all very well but there were squirrels to chase, rabbit poo to eat and who knows what else to explore?

So they finished their drinks, I had a bit more flapjack, and we set off through the fields towards the river. The ground was muddy, but that meant it was kinder to my paws, and there were fantastic smells. We met a greyhound; had a quick chase there, and a spaniel; nose to the ground, not interested in a chat, typical spaniel, and another Jack Russell who was rather rude and had bad breath, and then we walked down through the trees to the river.

It was a happy walk, that one, while they got to know each other a bit. Talk, talk, talk, that's all humans seemed to do. I thought they should use their senses a bit more, like we did, but they didn't. I looked back every now and then to check on their progress, but they were chatting, laughing sometimes, and I was happy that things were going according to plan. None of the heightened emotions that there were with Ted. None of that meshing together of spirits. Just as well, I thought, for that was all too intense, and where did it get us?

As they parted, at the end of the walk, he said, 'I don't know if you'd be interested, but a friend of mine's giving a talk at Flushing Sailing Club next week. He sailed round the world recently, and ...'

'Oh, I heard about him,' she said. 'Yes, I'd love to come and perhaps you could introduce me. I'd really like to interview him.'

'Of course,' he said and his smile was kind and slow. 'Why don't I give you a ring over the weekend and we can arrange where to meet?'

'Perfect,' she said, and stood on tiptoe to give him a kiss on the cheek. But it was a relaxed, safe, friendly kiss.

This Luke could be a good friend, I thought, and that's what she needed right now. No more fraught emotions. Like Petroc: just good friends.

I wasn't invited to the sailor's talk, but she came back smelling calm and cheerful and that was good enough for me. We lay in bed that night and although she tossed and turned for a bit, she went back to sleep, and I sighed with relief. My whiskers relaxed and I had a quick tail wag, relieved that I'd managed to level things out a bit.

The next day was her birthday, a week before her operation. Normally, of course, we would have celebrated with Ted. But her friends brought flowers, cards and presents.

The day went well until the postman arrived with a package that she looked at and tears instantly filled her eyes. I could smell loss overwhelming her like a mouldy duvet. She walked down the hallway into the kitchen and slowly opened a large card. 'From Ted,' she told me, her voice wobbling a little. She didn't tell me what he'd written, but she read it, and read it again, then kissed it and put it down.

Next came the package, in one of those puffy envelopes. She tore it open and pulled out a book. It looked a bit thin, but she opened it as if it were something really precious. 'An anthology of poetry,' she breathed. 'Dorothy Parker,' and started reading.

Dorothy Parker? Who was she? And what made her so special? Judging by the expression on Suki's face, which changed from page to page, she was good at writing poetry. Perhaps I should try it, but then Suki burst into noisy tears and clutched the book to her.

'Oh, Ted,' she wailed. 'Oh God, I miss you.' She sat down at the kitchen table and wept really noisily, so I scampered over and nudged her with my nose. That didn't work, so I jumped on her lap and tried to kiss away her tears.

'Oh, darling,' she said, hugging me tight, and I wasn't sure if she was addressing me or Ted. 'Oh, Moll. What am I doing?'

I barked. It wasn't a question I could answer, but it needed a response. I licked her face again and she gave a watery smile. The sour smell started to go away and I wagged my tail. That was better. After all, this was her birthday. She shouldn't be sad. Why on earth had he sent this book, when he must have known it would upset her?

Later, Luke rang so she invited him to the pub, and I sat underneath the table, by the birthday girl, while Luke bought drinks and some bone-shaped biscuits for me; there was a glass jar of them on the bar. I've tasted better, but you can't be fussy in a pub.

Sipping her wine, Suki opened a big card with dogs on the front. 'Look, Moll, it's you!' she said, putting it down to nose level. I sniffed. It smelt of cardboard and a slight musty smell. Nothing edible or interesting. 'What a lovely card, thanks so much!'

He drank his beer, a slow smile spreading over his face. Cautiously, I sidled closer to him, to give him my thanks. And the curious thing was, the frightened smell had nearly gone. He reached down, and patted my head a bit awkwardly. I could tell he hadn't done that before, and it filled me with a warm glow. Breakthrough!

The evening got a bit noisy once her other friends arrived. Still, they enjoyed themselves, and by that time I'd had a bit of Luke's steak and kidney pie (never had kidney before, definitely worth repeating. Tangy meat, not chewy but delicious) and some of Suki's garlic bread for a real birthday treat.

Once the food had all gone, I was warm and dozy, so I curled up on the seat beside her and listened to the sounds of laughter around me, the wafting smells of different meals going past, and the clink of glasses. We were surrounded by people who loved us and that was a wonderful feeling.

She woke me up a while later, to whisper, 'Going home now, Moll.' I looked up, stretched and yawned. Gave myself a good shake. I jumped off the bench and was ready to go, out into the dark. Back home, to a goodnight biscuit or two and our nice warm bed.

'Shall I walk you up the hill?' asked Luke.

'That would be lovely, thank you,' she said. 'Anne comes a bit of the way and then she turns left and we go right.' And so we headed up the hill, into a spattering of rain in the dark night. They all linked arms and giggled as they went up the hill, then we said goodnight to Anne and continued up the final part of the climb.

Suki yawned and said to Luke, 'That was a lovely meal, thank you so much. And you didn't have to buy so many people drinks.'

'My pleasure,' he said.

'Coffee?' she said, but yawned again and they both laughed.

'I think it's time you went to bed,' he said.

'Thanks again, Luke.' She paused. 'See you for a walk at the weekend?'

I could sense his smile, broadening. 'Great,' he said. 'And Suki...'

She turned, opening the front door. 'Yes?'

'You said you've got to be at the hospital early for your operation. If you need a lift, I'd be glad to take you.'

My whiskers twitched. That would have been Ted's job. She stared at him, and we waited. 'Thank you, Luke,' she said. 'That's really kind, but I've got to be there for six thirty in the morning. I was going to order a taxi.'

'You don't want to go to hospital on your own,' he said. 'Consider me your taxi.'

I could smell her relief and gratitude. Sweetness and peace. 'Thanks, Luke,' she said. 'That's really kind. I'll see you at the weekend.'

We turned and went into the house, while I speculated just what a good friend he was.

22

Post op

While Suki went off for her operation, Emma took me to her house for several days. It smelt of different biscuits, strange meat, a man/boy smell from her son. Her Joey was grey round the muzzle and a bit deaf, but Emma was kind and played with me, and we snuggled up to watch TV at night which was cosy.

We had some great new walks, and Emma took pictures of me running around and sent them to Suki, and told me that she was doing really well and would be home soon. I really missed her particular smell and the musical sound of her voice as she talked to me, or to Tess on the phone. I missed her sudden laughter, the way her voice dropped when she was being serious, or sad. I missed sleeping on our bed at night, with the soft warmth of Suki's body next to mine. I missed our daily routine; the getting up and breakfast, brushing teeth which always meant a walk soon.

I missed the daily snoozes on our bed, or by the fire, dreaming of fox poo and chasing squirrels. Barking at the postie, Fiona, who had sturdy legs and always gave me biscuits. I barked anyway, just to say hello. And of course, as always, I missed my Titch. But I wrapped myself in my happy memories and enjoyed learning new walks, new smells and making a new friend out of Emma and, to a lesser extent, Joey.

Finally, after several days, Emma brought me home, and I was so excited.

But Suki was a different person. She was in bed. In the daytime! She smelt weird and full of chemicals. A bit like Pip when he'd been poorly. Uh oh. When she got up, she walked as if she was about to fall over: she was bent over and smelt really fragile. I tried to bounce on the bed, to welcome her back, and tell her how much I missed her, but I could tell that really frightened her.

What had they done to her?

Still, lovely Av arrived to stay, and she gave me great cuddles and took me for walks and made fish pie and things (I got some of the mashed potato which Suki didn't usually make. It was hot and spicy and buttery and a bit cheesy and absolutely scrummy).

I forgot and bounced on the bed again (only once, because I saw Suki's terrified face). She cuddled me, carefully, as if I might hurt her at any minute, and said, 'It's so lovely to see you, darling Moll, but I hurt all over so we've got to be really careful. OK?'

Well of course I was going to be careful. I could smell how off she was. She needed me to look after her more than ever.

Av gently took me next door for a cuddle on the sofa. Av was great to cuddle; she always wore soft jumpers that you wanted to snuggle into, and she smelt really nice, like jam and cream, and she had this lovely gentle melodic voice that was like having a massage. She said something about Suki being poorly but she'd be better very soon. Well, I knew it was my job to look after her, so whatever she needed I would do. Though I did wonder about my walks after Av went home.

We had a lovely time and Suki seemed to get a bit better every day, though she still spent a long time in bed. She'd have breakfast, then at the time of my walk (thank you, Av) she would go back to bed and was still there till late morning. Then she'd get up for lunch and go back to bed again while Av and I had a long afternoon walk. Then Suki would get up when we came back and had a cup of tea and they opened the wine a bit later, and Av cooked lovely things and they chatted and we all watched telly together.

Suki said she wasn't up to seeing many people, but she wanted to see Luke, so Av got a chance to meet him. He came for supper and despite smelling really worried when he arrived, he soon relaxed, though I noticed he hardly took his eyes off Suki, making sure she was all right. Just what she needed.

One night they were talking about Av having to go home. 'I wish I could stay, but I must get back to Roger,' she said. 'Are you sure you'll be all right?'

'Yes, I'm sure we will,' Suki said. 'Emma's going to walk Moll in the afternoons.'

Av looked worried. 'What about cooking? And cleaning? And walking Moll in the mornings?'

'I think I'll be able to cook now,' she said with a smile. 'You've stocked up the freezer with enough food to last me for weeks. And a friend is going to clean once a week.'

'And Moll?'

'Emma's going to walk her every afternoon.'

'But what about the morning walk?' Av said.

Exactly. What about my Reading Messages Walk?

'I can help,' Luke said.

We all stared at him. I'd told Av that he was frightened of dogs.

'Are you sure?' Suki asked. 'I'm sure I can find someone...'

'No, that's fine,' he said. 'I'd enjoy it. I can walk Moll on my way to work. It'll mean I get some exercise for the day.'

As he'd told us he was outside all day, building boats, this was an odd thing to say, but no one commented, except, 'Well, if you're sure...' from Suki. 'That would be amazing. I'd better give you a key. In case I'm in bed when you get back.'

'Of course.' He looked pleased. 'I'll be very quiet. I mean, I won't wake you up.'

'Oh, don't worry. As long as you don't mind?'

He grinned. 'I'd be happy to, honest. And you're sure Emma's OK walking Moll in the afternoons?'

She nodded. 'Yes, for a month at least, and we'll see how I feel then.'

Luke left soon after that as she got tired easily, and having waved him goodbye, Suki and Av came back into the room and sat down on the sofa. I hopped up in between the two of them. They smelt so different, but both familiar. Such a shame Av had to go home. She smelt like family now.

'Well,' she said, stroking my ears and then my tummy.

'Well what?'

Av gave Suki a gentle prod. 'Well, Luke,' she said. 'He's lovely, isn't he?'

Suki smiled. 'Yes. He is.'

Av grinned. 'And he offered to walk Moll. Are you sure he's frightened of dogs?'

'Well, he was. I think Moll's been working her charm,' Suki smiled. I waited – there was more to come, I was sure. 'Luke's lovely and kind and generous, but.'

'You're still in love with Ted.' It was a statement.

She nodded. 'I do wish I wasn't, and I know how complicated Ted's life is and all that but you can't just stop loving someone, can you?'

Av shook her head, leaned forward and wrapped her arms around Suki. 'No, you can't,' she said. 'But you don't have to get involved with Luke. Just have him as a nice male friend, while your broken heart mends.'

'Is that fair on Luke though?'

Av sipped her wine. 'Have you told him about Ted?'

'I told him I'd just finished a relationship with someone, but I didn't go into details.'

'That's OK then,' Av said. 'Stop looking so serious; just enjoy it. You need to get over Ted, and Luke seems just the right person to help you do that. Make it clear you just want to be friends, and where's the problem?'

From then on, Luke called round every morning after we'd had breakfast and took me for my morning walk. He didn't let me off the lead, but I was happy doing our normal round the block as there were loads of sniffing places, which was where I picked up all my messages. I hated being rushed while I did that, and much though I loved Suki, she was often in a hurry in the mornings, or thinking about other things. But Luke ambled along, whistling sometimes. He never hurried me which was perfect.

He would then take me back, call hello to Suki and sometimes he'd make her a cup of tea, sit on the bed and chat.

'Tell me what boat you're working on this week,' she would say. Not that she knew much about boats, but it kept her in touch with the outside world, which I think she missed a lot.

It was always a sad little moment when he went, but he started saying things like, 'I can call in on the way back if you like.'

And very often, if she didn't have other friends calling in, he did.

For the first few weeks, she dozed a lot, so I lay next to her, to keep watch. It was a slow recovery, but gradually I noticed little improvements. At night she often lay awake in bed, so I would snuggle up extra close. I could smell her grief, and sense that huge hole left by Ted. Sometimes I could tell it overwhelmed her, and that's when I licked her face, or lay on her feet to keep the pain at bay. Nothing could really help with missing Ted. I missed him too, and I remembered how much I missed my Titch, when he was away, so I knew how she felt. But at least we had Luke as our Safe Friend.

Sometimes he stayed for a cup of coffee. Or a glass of wine. As she started feeling better, he offered to take us out to the pub for a drink. 'Oh, how lovely,' she said. 'I feel as if I haven't been out for years!'

He held her hand carefully as we walked out to the car, as if she were very fragile. I could smell his nervousness and his care, and it made me feel sad and happy at once, for I knew she was too vulnerable to get involved with anyone else right now. Ted was hard wired into her. But there was also something about Luke that I couldn't quite put my paw on.

He helped her into the car, as she laughed and said, 'I'm fine, Luke, honestly. I'm much better, you know.'

He drove to a pub in Flushing the opposite end of the village to where Ted lived. Luke parked nearby and escorted us into the pub, found a quiet seat next to the log fire, which was lit, even though it wasn't very cold. I looked round. No sign of Ted. That was a relief.

'Glass of white?' he said.

'Yes please, but I'd like to buy this one. Please, let me.'

'Certainly not.' His smile was like a flash of sunlight that made her smile back.

He came back with a pint for himself, a glass of wine for her and some crisps. Hoorah! Not cheese and onion; salt and vinegar which stung my mouth, but who cared? They were crisps, and I hadn't had any for weeks.

A man came over who knew Luke and they talked about boats, so I didn't really listen. She smiled and seemed happy just to sit. Finally the friend squeezed Luke's shoulder and said, 'Well, I must go. We're eating here tonight. I recommend the pies by the way; they're excellent.' And with a wave of his hand, he was gone.

'Sorry about that,' Luke said. Strange smells wafted off him. Like Cheddar, but not quite. Strong and tasty. That was strange. 'An old friend of mine.'

'Not at all, it's always good to meet new people,' she said. 'Where does he live?'

'In Sailor's Creek; the next creek round to me. He's got a lovely old wooden ketch...' and he was off, talking boat stuff. I tuned out, but tuned back in again when he said, 'Listen, how about some food here? I haven't eaten, and it means neither of us will have to cook.'

'No, that's really kind but,' and then her stomach rumbled and they both laughed. 'Well, OK, she said. 'But only if I can pay. Please.'

'Certainly not,' he said. 'This is my treat.'

'Well, only if I can repay the compliment,' she said. 'Why not come for supper next week? You've helped me so much with walking Moll. I don't know how I can repay you.'

'It's nothing,' he said but he smiled. 'But supper would be lovely one night.'

'Good,' she said. 'How about Tuesday?'

He clinked his glass against hers. 'Tuesday it is. Now, what would you like to eat?'

As ever, my ears pricked up at the mention of food. I sat between them, then realised that the food would take a while to arrive. But it was pleasant to lie on the cushioned seat, feeling her warmth nearby. I liked listening to the pub sounds of glasses clinking in the background. That glug- glug sound when wine was being poured. A yank of the pump to pour beer. The horrific hiss of the machine making hot drinks. Footsteps going to the bar. Cutlery clanking.

A cry from the kitchen announced that food was ready. Hot, piping platefuls were carried across the room and my nose went crazy at the smells. Meat and gravy and pastry and curried lamb and poppadoms and mashed potato with creamy fish sauce and chips with a sizzling steak. Oh, my, I felt quite dizzy.

Then their food arrived. Fish pie for her and a steak pie for him. I sat to attention, glancing from one to another, to make sure I didn't miss anything. Head on one side, ears cocked. They were talking about family: his sister and nephews. Oh, a tiny bit of pastry fell past my nose. Bad manners not to grab that. Flaky loveliness.

Then, just as I was preparing for another mouthful, I heard a familiar clip clop of boots. The smell of salt and surfing, and I looked up and smelt Ted coming in the door.

Had Suki seen? I looked at her, whiskers twitching. I knew her hearing wasn't nearly as good as mine but she usually had a sixth sense where Ted was involved. She glanced towards the door and it was as if time stood still. She stared, as if drinking him in.

Emotions exploded off Suki like fireworks. Love, despair, longing, embarrassment, joy and terror all at once, firing into the ceiling. She literally froze, like I do when I'm hunting, every sense attuned to the man walking towards the bar.

And then I saw Luke looking at her and he read everything there and another strange smell came off him. Like Brie. What did that mean? But my priority was her. Though of course I was delighted to see Ted.

He turned, as if he could feel all our eyes trained on him. He looked at her, and me, and his face lit up. I could almost hear his heartbeat revving up. Then he saw Luke, and his face paled. He hesitated, then came over. 'Hello, Suki,' he said and that lovely deep voice made my whiskers twitch and my tail wagged frantically. It was so good to see him! We'd both missed him so much!

'Hello,' she said faintly. 'Er, Luke, this is Ted.'

'Pleased to meet you,' said Luke, holding out his hand.

Ted shook Luke's hand and looked down at me, for I was scrabbling against his legs by this time. Me! Me! Me! He gave a sad smile and bent down, tickled me under the chin. 'I miss you, Moll,' he whispered.

I barked in reply, just so that he knew I did too. Oh, poor man. It was so unfair. He reeked of loneliness and longing. It was so strong I almost choked.

But he stood up now, looked at her again. 'Glad to see you looking so well,' he said. His voice was gravelly. 'I've been wondering how you were getting on.'

'Doing OK, thanks,' she said, in a voice that sounded faint and watery. Flushed with longing.

He looked down at their food. 'Sorry to interrupt your meal. I'll leave you to it.' He hesitated. 'I'm going to be away for a month or so. Trouble with, you know.' He cleared his throat. 'All the best,' and he hurried back to the bar.

'Bye,' she croaked, and watched him greet a friend who handed him a pint.

There was silence between Luke and Suki. I don't think either of them knew what to say.

'So, that was...?'

'Yes,' she said. 'That was Ted. My ex.' And I had a feeling that she was about to burst into tears. 'Sorry,' she said. 'It's all a bit raw. We only split up a month ago. What with my operation and everything...' She gulped and blew her nose. I put my paws on her chair, rested my chin on her lap while she stroked my ears.

'Of course.' He put a hand out to cover hers. I could smell it wasn't a sex gesture, like when Ted did it, but one of comfort. 'It takes time to get over that sort of thing.'

She stared down at his hand and flushed. 'Thanks,' she croaked. She prodded her fish pie, as if wishing it would disappear. It could have. I would have. But I turned my attention back to her. Longing leaked out of her and I knew she wanted to be sitting next to Ted, laughing and drinking her wine. Holding him. Planning our next adventure for when she was better.

And here she was, with Luke. And, lovely though he was, he wasn't Ted.

Then she took a deep breath. Ted and his friend had moved around the corner so we couldn't see them anymore. 'So,' she said, and I could sense she was trying really hard to ignore the feelings rampaging inside her. 'Did you see how those French sailors are doing in the Vendee Globe? And the British woman is in fifth place. That's amazing, isn't it?'

I had no idea what she was talking about, but I knew a red herring when I smelt one.

Luke attempted a smile. 'Yes,' he said. 'And she's only in her twenties. She's from Lostwithiel, I think and learned to sail at Restronguet.' He ate a forkful of pie and a few crumbs dropped to the floor. They were cold but tasty. I knew I would appreciate the food more than them.

I settled back to stare them out for scraps. But, like her, most of my senses were attuned to our Ted, sitting miserably round the corner.

What a bone.

23

Misreading the situation

The nights after we met Ted in the pub, Suki thrashed around in bed, put the light on and tried to read. Turned the light off. Cried. Read some more. Got up and made a drink. I could understand her turmoil, but it smelt of rotten chicken which was disgusting.

Tess rang and they had a long talk. 'I know it must be really hard for you,' she said. 'But you've finished with Ted, and you have to draw a line underneath it, don't you? You'll just tear yourself apart otherwise.'

Suki blew her nose. 'Yes, you're right,' she said and her voice was so quiet and so sad that I nudged her with my nose. My poor girl. I hated seeing her suffer. 'How's your mum?'

'She's doing OK, though I've got to nip up and see her this weekend.' Her voice dropped. 'I'm afraid to say that when we go up there, Titch has been playing with another terrier he met in the park. Called Daisy.'

I sat bolt upright. Daisy? How dare he? I'd give him a piece of my mind. What about me? About us? I growled, gently, to get the message across.

'I think Moll heard,' Suki said, and laughed.

It was a welcome sound, but really, laughing about Daisy? How could she be so insensitive? Did she not realise how much I missed Titch? And now he was being unfaithful...

'I'll come over after work next Tuesday if that's OK,' Tess said. 'It seems ages since we've had a proper gossip.'

'Come for supper,' Suki said. 'I'm sorry I'm not up to walks yet, but I will be soon.'

'Supper would be great,' Tess said. 'Now, try and put Ted out of your mind for the moment. Concentrate on getting better, and enjoying Luke's company.'

She smiled. 'OK, boss,' she said, and she sounded a bit stronger. I decided to overlook her insensitivity. For the moment.

Suki continued to improve, and Luke was often around. He continued to take me for my morning walk and I think we both enjoyed these times. Luke never rushed me, so the walk took rather longer but was more relaxing. Plenty of time for vital sniffing and reading messages. Luke and I developed a kind of silent kinship and I like to think I showed him that that dogs weren't frightening, or worrying, but a source of comfort, love and joy.

He was a much calmer person than Ted. I'm sure he had problems; all people seemed to make life unnecessarily difficult for themselves, but he was a much calmer personality.

After the meeting in the pub, Suki didn't mention Ted, until a week later, when she stared at her phone suddenly, as if she'd dropped it in a cow pat. From the way she started smelling sour again, I thought, uh oh. The sharp Ted Smell simmered in the background all the time, but every now and then, when she got really upset, it leaked out really strongly.

It made my nose run and my whiskers twitched even more than usual.

She was silent for a moment, evidently reading something, then sank onto the sofa, holding me close. 'It's Ted,' she said. As if I was stupid. 'He says,' and her voice wobbled, 'he says, "It was lovely to see both of you, and in particular, knowing that you are recovering well. I think of you so much but didn't like to intrude. I will be away for a month or so, sorting out my dad's care home, and visiting Jane. All I want is for you to be happy. All my love, Ted."

Her face crumpled and she started heaving, terrible dry sobs that wracked her whole body. 'Ow, that hurts,' she cried, clutching her stomach. 'Damn, my stitches.'

I was really worried, but the pain seemed to jerk her into sense. She held me still, and the sobbing eased a little, and she said, 'Oh, Moll. What am I going to do? I wish I'd never fallen in love with him. It hurts too much. I can't bear it.'

I snuggled up close to her, feeling the warmth of her jumper against my back. It was reassuring, and while I knew just how she felt; I'd missed Titch just as much; I wished that emotions could be less painful.

Later, she said, 'It's kind of a relief, Moll.' We were lying on her bed for her afternoon nap. 'It gave me such a jolt when we saw him in the pub. I don't think I could bear that again. Tess is right. I really must just forget about him. He is no part of our life anymore. We had a good time but that was that. He has too many complications and it hurts too much. It's better this way.'

And though she sounded firm, I could hear the desperation and longing in her voice. She loved him as much as ever, but she knew she was doing the brave thing. The right thing. And I think Luke gave her strength, too.

He came over for supper quite a lot as the weeks passed. 'Honestly, I owe you for looking after Moll, and me,' she said. 'The least I can do is feed you every now and then.'

So we got used to his footsteps coming up the path, the knock on the door, even though he had his own key. She didn't ask for it back, and he didn't offer it, I noticed.

Luke's tread was lighter than Ted's, and he wore different boots, with rubber soles that made less noise. But I could always tell when he walked round the corner of the street, towards us.

I would sit in the window and wait for him. Suki's head would jerk up when she heard the knock at the door, and she would smile, and get up. It wasn't the wide grin that she reserved for Ted, but it was a quiet, steady smile.

Several weeks later, by which time she was definitely feeling a lot better, Luke stayed to watch a film. It was cosy on the sofa, the three of us. It was late and she yawned, and so did he. 'I must be going,' he said.

She sat up, her hair all mussed. She stared at the floor, then looked up. 'If you'd like to stay, you'd be very welcome.'

He looked at her. My whiskers twitched. 'Er, no. I'd better not, thanks,' he said.

'I mean,' she said, her face glowing pink. 'You know I can't do anything. Physically, I mean. 'Because of my operation.' She was so hot now I thought she might catch fire. 'But if you wanted to, you know, cuddle... I would like that.'

'I know,' he said. 'All the same, I'd better not. See you both in the morning.' And he kissed her on the forehead, stroked me, and let himself out.

There was a thick silence after he left, like velvet. 'Well, that was weird,' she said, getting up slowly. 'I thought, well, I thought he might say yes.' She sounded upset. 'But because he's used to boats, perhaps he doesn't like sleeping in houses. Pip didn't at first.'

She got up and started turning the lights out, ready for us to go to bed, went into the kitchen to get my evening biscuits. I scrunched them up, quickly, and jumped onto the bed, waiting for her to come and join me. She took her time, brushing her teeth, getting a glass of water.

As I waited, lying on the bed, nose on paws, I had a feeling that something wasn't quite right with Luke. I couldn't put my paw on it, but there was something off kilter, as Suki would say. The question was, what?

The next morning, Suki was reading in bed when Tess rang.

'Guess what? Suki said.

'You mean Luke? You didn't...? Oh no of course, you can't,' said Tess, and she laughed.

'No, we didn't,' Suki said, and told her what happened.

'Well, there could be all sorts of reasons why he didn't want to stay,' Tess said. 'I think it's good. There's no need to jump into bed, is there?'

'No,' Suki said slowly. 'I mean, I don't want another relationship now. I need to get over Ted.'

'But Luke's there, and you need looking after, so why not?'

'He sent me a text saying he'd be over to walk Moll soon and see me later.'

'Well, that's good isn't it?'

'Yes,' Suki said slowly. 'I mean, I know I need to move on and all that. But, I know this is stupid, part of me gets angry with Luke because he's not Ted. And I get really confused, you know?'

'I do. But remember, you and Ted only broke up a few weeks ago. Then you had major surgery. That's a hell of a lot to deal with physically, as well as emotionally. You're still very vulnerable.'

'I guess so.' She sighed. 'But it would have been nice to have a cuddle.'

'Much better than sex in my opinion,' Tess said. 'But don't rush it. You don't want to take advantage of the poor man. You could always ask him for supper again. That way you've both got time to think about it and can decide if you want to have another go. Perhaps he just doesn't like sleeping in a strange bed. There could be all sorts of reasons.'

Luke turned up every morning to walk me, but he didn't often come over in the evening again. He said he was busy at work. However, I noticed that his smell had changed. He had a faint acrid smell to him at first, when he was frightened of me. But as time went on, that changed to a sweeter pong, like cheese. Stronger and happier.

His footsteps changed, too, and became more confident as they came round the corner. He stood up straighter, and seemed to fit better in his body. Was this because of us? At first I thought so, but then I wondered – was he hiding something?

Still, Suki was more relaxed. I got a rank whiff of longing every now and then, but it was more manageable. She wasn't happy, exactly, but she was more content, and smelled of primroses: that elusive lemony scent.

Gradually life became a little more normal. Suki could walk a little further each day, and she started working, just a few hours at a time, for she got tired very easily.

Sometimes we would drive to the beach to meet friends and walk along the sand. She had to sit down a lot, but I was

happy playing on the beach, and went to join them while
they had a coffee. Sometimes we met Anne for a drink in the
pub, or occasionally Luke would suggest a drink. He never
took us back to the Flushing pub, though. I don't think any
of us wanted to risk upsetting the balance.

Knowing that Ted was away made life easier. He was
further removed, literally, and although we both missed
him, life was safer. She wouldn't get hurt again.

We hadn't seen much of Tess and Titch because Tess was
very busy catching up at work, and Suki couldn't do proper
walks yet. But one Friday Tess rang.

'Shall I come over to you, tomorrow afternoon?' she said.
'We could go to the cemetery so the dogs can chase squirrels
and you can sit down on a bench when you need to.'

'Lovely,' said Suki. 'Can't wait.' And she laughed as I
barked and jumped up and down – I was going to see my
Titch again! All at once I could smell his special scent –
an earthy one behind his ears, that special bum smell that
summed up his bounce and enthusiasm. I could almost hear
his paws pattering along the ground towards me. Roll on
tomorrow!

The following day we had such a wonderful meeting. Tess
and Titch came to our flat and stood in the doorway, and
Titch came running in, like he owned the place (he always
did that), sniffed around and then our noses touched and we
sniffed each other's bums and I read everything there.

Yes, he'd missed me, too. No, he hadn't had many exciting
walks. Yes, he'd been talking to this other Daisy bitch. No,
she wasn't anything like me, and of course it wasn't serious.
That was OK then.

Looking up, I saw Tess and Suki having a long, silent hug.
They stayed like that for what seemed like ages, and they
both looked a bit wet eyed afterwards.

'Come on, I'll make us a cuppa before we go out,' said Suki, and we sat in the kitchen like old times, while Titch explored the back yard, weeing on everything, before coming back to join us.

'You're looking better than when I saw you last,' Tess said, sitting comfortably at the kitchen table. 'You've got more colour in your face.'

She smiled. 'I feel much better. And it's such a relief being able to go on short walks now.'

'How are things with Luke?'

'Good, I think,' she said, pouring hot water into her mug. 'I don't know what I would have done without him.'

'Is there a but?'

'I've been thinking.' Suki sat down. 'At first, when I came out of hospital, it wasn't long after I'd split up with Ted, and I was terribly needy.'

'Well of course you were,' said Tess. 'You'd been through so much. You needed someone to look after you. And there he was.' She blew on her tea before taking a sip. 'You mean, now that you're feeling a lot better, you don't need him so much?'

'No.' She looked down at the table. 'And I feel guilty about that. I mean, it's great feeling so much better, but I need to carry on with my life again.'

'Of course. I'm sure he realises that.'

'I hope so.' Another pause. 'I really value him as a friend.'

'You were the one who wanted him to stay the night.'

'Well,' Suki said, going a bit pink, 'I wanted a cuddle. That's all.'

'Why not just say that, then the air's clear and you can carry on enjoying your friendship?'

Suki nodded slowly, as if there was something she wasn't saying. 'Yes. Yes, of course.'

And I knew, from the way she pushed the hair back from her face, she wasn't lying to Tess, she was just sitting hard on her feelings for Ted. Maybe time would level those out. I certainly hoped so. Luke was like a steady, powerful light, that wasn't affected by wind or rain. Ted, on the other hand, was a candle flame that burned so bright you forgot everything else. But when a gust of wind came, it spluttered and you feared it would go out.

24

A surprise opportunity

As Suki got back into her stride, so did springtime and there were lots of new buds, fresh new grass, bugs nesting in tree roots. Every walk was a joy of new smells. And the sounds! All the different birds mating and nesting. Blue tits screeched at me from their bird house upstairs that Joe had made. They were guarding their young, I knew, but we had several lively chats while I tried to tell them that I was no threat. It was the cats in the area that were the problem. That and the greedy, bad-mannered magpies.

Seagulls shrieked and squawked from the rooftops as they mated, and the ones opposite us always returned to the same nest, year after year. Bumble bees buzzed lazily on sunny afternoons, the muted tones of a radio came from over the road, and overhead was the drone of an aeroplane.

New life was all around us and it seemed a sunny spell of weather was also affecting Suki. She was itchy; I could feel it. Not quite back to normal, but she was back to work and walking much further. Soon she would be able to drive again. And while all this was good news, I could sense a rumble of discontent, though she said nothing.

Until she went to a Girls' Night. This was held monthly, between four of them. They'd meet in a pub and have a meal and some wine and talk. She hadn't been able to go while she was poorly, of course, but she was finally well enough for this one, and I went too, just to keep an eye on her. That lot weren't too free with their food, but I lay at her feet and dozed, one ear open to see if they were discussing anything interesting.

It was a lot of boring stuff about books and painting, then one of them said, 'And how do you feel about Ted?' and my other ear shot up, and my whiskers quivered.

'Well, it's over,' she said, which didn't really answer the question.

'We know that,' said one of them. 'But how do you feel about him compared to Luke?'

The silence went on. I fixed her with my Paddington Bear stare but she wasn't looking at me. She took a gulp of wine. Finally, she said, 'Well, Luke is caring, kind, thoughtful, ...'

'Yeah, yeah, yeah,' said one of the girls. 'We all know he's a saint, but how do you feel about him physically?'

'He's a really lovely man,' she said, and they all groaned. 'But we're not sleeping together.'

'Why not?'

She blushed; I could tell. 'Well, I did offer, but he said no.'

'Well, not everyone wants to sleep with you, darling!'

'No,' she said with a laugh. 'And I'm quite relieved, because although I'm very fond of him, I don't think I'm the right person for him.' She looked around the table.

'You mean, he's not the right bloke for you,' said one of the others.

'Well, no. I mean, I can't have sex yet anyway, after this operation, but ...'

'I don't know, he's quite good looking.'

'Oh, he IS,' she said. 'He's lovely looking and he has a fabulous smile. It's just ...'

'He's not Ted,' said one of them.

Then one of them said, 'So you still think about Ted?'

She nodded, looked down, went pink. 'I've been trying not to, but he sent me a text the other day. It was only about a programme on Radio Four that he thought I might like, but I felt like someone had jump-started my heart.'

'So what are you going to do?'

They all looked at her. She shrugged. 'Nothing.'

'If Ted walked in here now, what would you do?'

She went bright pink but didn't say anything. One of the others laughed and said, 'Jump into his arms!'

'Well, I'd feel like it, but I wouldn't actually *do* it,' she said. 'And I enjoy Luke's company, but I don't want to take it any further.'

'So why ask him to spend the night?'

'Just for a cuddle,' she said in a small voice. 'I like company in bed.'

'Sex is vastly overrated in my opinion,' said one voice. 'So I'm glad you're going to keep him just as a friend. Much less complicated that way.'

'Exactly. Just enjoy it,' said another. 'Now, are we going to have another bottle of wine?'

And so that conversation ended. It got me thinking, though. I'd grown very fond of Luke, and I knew he was fond of Suki, though I sensed in a different way from Ted. I never understood the way humans had to tie themselves into knots over relationships. Why not just be friendly with everyone?

Life rumbled on after that, but Luke was called away to collect a boat from Wales, so we didn't see him for nearly two weeks. When he returned, he was tanned and cheerful and she gave him a big hug. 'You look amazing!' she said. 'So brown and handsome,' she blushed.

He smiled and his eyes twinkled as he bent down to stroke me. I rolled onto my back so he could tickle my tummy, which he did with gentle fingers that smelt of salt and fresh air. 'The weather was amazing and we had a fabulous sail back.'

'Lucky you,' she said. 'Those pictures you sent me were so good. Who did you go with?'

He finished tickling my tummy and straightened. 'There were six of us on board,' he said. Which didn't quite answer the question. 'I knew most of them, and we had a really good time'

'I'm really pleased for you.' She smiled at him. 'Now, would you like to go for a drink or have one here?'

He smelt slightly nervous and my whiskers twitched. What was going on?

'How about having a drink here?' he said. 'I've brought some wine,' and he handed over a bottle.

'Oh, New Zealand Sauvignon Blanc,' she said and kissed him. 'My favourite! Thanks so much. I'll open it, sit down.'

He sat and looked out of the window and I jumped onto his lap and he smelt different. He was in love, I was sure: I knew that smell well. That was interesting. He stroked me as if he needed to calm himself down, and when she came back she poured the wine and chatted about this and that, and I could smell him getting more and more acidic, and then he said, 'Suki.'

She stopped talking. 'What is it?'

He looked over at her and I could almost see all this kindness oozing out of him. It smelt like badger poo coated in honey. He cleared his throat. 'I've been having a think, while I was away.'

And the way he said it, both she and I froze. It was almost as if he'd heard what they'd said about him in the pub. Had someone told him? A shiver ran down my spine, through my fur, for I couldn't bear the thought of him being upset.

'I've been offered a job restoring an old clipper in Scotland,' he said and looked down at the table. 'It means I'd be away for the best part of the year. But I'd learn a lot and the money's good, and Scotland's beautiful.'

There was a silence that smelt unnerving. 'Good,' she said faintly. 'That's amazing. I mean, what an opportunity. Good for you!' And I knew she was thinking, have you met someone?'

He smiled. 'I've got some work I've got to finish off here, but I felt I couldn't pass up this chance.'

'Of course,' she said. 'Absolutely. I'm really happy for you – and the best of luck!' But underneath, I could smell a certain wistfulness. And sorrow? Like the beginning of an easterly wind, I knew it would grow. 'I'll miss you,' she added. Still, she hesitated. Was this it?

He smiled at her. 'I'll miss you too. Very much. But you're able to stand on your feet now. You don't need me.'

'It was never like that,' she protested. With a faint tinge of guilt that smelt of burnt butter.

'I know,' he said, calmly. 'But I was there when you needed me, which was good timing. You'll be able to drive next week. You're firing on all cylinders.' He stopped. 'You could always come up and stay in Scotland, if you wanted to.'

She smiled, but it was a rather wobbly one. 'It's a lovely idea,' she said. 'I'll bear it in mind.'

'I'll text you my address, and do ring.'

'Thanks,' she said, but I could smell the sadness seeping in like a winter mist. I could tell she was feeling abandoned, so I jumped onto her lap and licked her hands. She stroked me absent-mindedly, and I could almost hear her mind scuttling off in a panic. 'We'll stay friends?' she said, in a wobbly voice.

He leaned over and gave her a kiss. On the cheek, I noticed, not on the lips. 'Of course,' he said. 'And now, I'd better go.'

'Go?' she said, in alarm.

'Yes. I've got quite a lot to sort out.'

'Oh. You're welcome to stay for supper,' she sounded so crestfallen that I licked her again.

'That's very kind,' he said. 'But I'm leaving next week and I've got a lot to do before then.'

'Next week?' she echoed. 'Right.... well. Best get going.' And she got up and gave him a hug. 'I really will miss you,' she said, as if he didn't believe her.

'And I'll miss you too,' he said. 'But we'll keep in touch. I insist.' I looked at him and noticed tears in his eyes as well. They had a long cuddle, then he pulled back. 'Bye, Suki,' he said softly, and he left the room. The front door shut, and we heard his footsteps down the path, then watched as he walked along the road, gave a wave, and gradually disappeared from sight.

'Oh, Moll,' she said, as tears rolled down her face, slowly at first, then in a torrent.

Sometimes you don't know what you've lost until it's too late.

25

'Well, that was a surprise,' Tess said later, when she came over.

'Telling me,' said Suki. She smelt confused and unhappy. 'I feel so awful for saying those things about him to you, and to the girls in the pub...'

'But they were true,' Tess said. 'And this way, you don't have to admit that you still love Ted.'

'I didn't say that,' she said.

'No, but you do.' She chuckled. 'Presumably he's met someone else.'

'He didn't say he had.'

'No, he didn't say he *hadn't* – that's the difference.'

'Mmm,' Suki said. 'I wonder who it is?'

'It doesn't matter, does it? This way you're both quits.'

'What do you mean?' Suki shifted on the sofa and reached for her mug of tea.

'Well, he must have known how you felt about Ted. It's not good being in a relationship with someone who still loves someone else. This way you both leave with your pride intact.'

'I suppose so.' Suki sighed. 'I can't really think straight at the moment.' She sat back and scratched my ears. 'Luke and Ted are so different. My feelings for Ted are so strong and overwhelming I don't know what to do with them. There's so much chemistry there. Not just physically, but we know what the other's thinking. Whereas I don't have that spark with Luke, but's a really good man, and I care very deeply for him.'

'If you put the two of them together, they'd be the perfect man,' said Tess. 'At least you didn't hurt his feelings,' she added.

'He hurt mine,' said a small voice.

'Not irrevocably,' said Tess firmly. 'You're surprised more than anything else.'

'I'll really miss him,' she cried. 'I will. Much more than I thought.'

'I'm sure you will. He's been a brilliant friend, even if you weren't lovers. In fact, he couldn't have been better.'

'No, he couldn't and I'm really grateful,' Suki said. 'When he came back, he seemed more sure of himself and a bit shut off. He'd always seemed very open.'

'The plot thickens,' said Tess. 'I know it's a bit galling when something like this happens, but he deserves to be happy, doesn't he?'

'Oh, absolutely,' Suki cried. 'No one deserves that more. He is a truly good man. I just wish...'

'Wish he'd told you who he's fallen for?'

'Well, yes.'

'I'm sure he will, in good time,' said Tess. 'Anyway, if you miss him that much, you can always go and see him. Moll can come and stay here.'

Suki laughed, a rich gurgle that I hadn't heard for a long time. 'Really? I might take you up on that. Moll and Titch would love that.'

They both laughed then. And while I was a bit taken aback at the idea of her going off without me, if it meant that I could spend more time with my Titch again – well, that would make it all worthwhile.

But my immediate problem was what would Suki do now?

She was very quiet for several weeks after Luke left, and cried over the last text he sent. 'I'm being stupid I know,' she said, in between sniffs. 'I do love him, just differently from the way I love Ted. Ignore me, Moll. My blood sugar's low. I probably need to eat.'

At that point her phone rang. It was Anne, asking her to meet for a drink. I was glad when she said yes, but this time I decided to stay at home for a rest. Much though I loved her, Suki's emotions were all over the place and it was quite exhausting. I loved lying next to her, feeling the smoothness of her skin against my fur, but confusion and discontent had an unsettling smell, like sour cheese.

I wanted time to myself to process what was happening. After all, I had grown fond of Luke too. I loved the outdoors smell of his jacket, flung over a chair in the kitchen. The sea smell of his work bag. The unique denim smell of his jeans which was comforting and reassuring. I loved the quiet rumble of his voice; a bit like Pip's.

I liked the way he looked at me, steadily, with a hint of a smile. Always ready for a game. But now we weren't part of his game anymore. I needed time to come to terms with that, just as she did.

I could smell all the love he had. I'd thought it was for Suki, but now it seemed it was for someone else. It was strong, and flowed out of him like badger poo. As she said, he really deserved to be happy. I really hoped he would be.

After Luke left, we had long, solitary walks. 'I need time on my own, and with you, Moll,' she said. 'Time to lick my wounds a bit. Reassess things.' So we would walk and sometimes she would talk to me. I always liked that.

Her pain this time was very different to losing Pip or Ted. 'I feel I might have made a fool of myself,' she said to Tess one night, in a hushed voice.

'Why? You didn't declare undying love for him, did you?'

'No. But I thought, well, it sounds really arrogant now, but I thought he loved me and – well, I don't think he did.'

A slight pause, and Tess said, 'I think you'll find he did, but not in a romantic way. And that was exactly how you felt about him.'

'Perhaps you're right,' she said, her voice up a notch. 'Though I miss him so much. He'd become part of the fabric of our days. I really miss his ... solidity. Just knowing he was there. And now he's not.'

'He's still around,' said Tess gently. 'He's just not as close. I bet if you needed him, he'd be there.'

Suki wrinkled her nose. 'I'm being selfish. But I do miss him. More than I'd thought I would.'

One sunny afternoon, we were walking down through the woods towards one of my favourite beach walks, when suddenly she stopped. I'd run on ahead, but looked back and saw her standing in the middle of the path, so I scampered back to check what was up.

'I've just realised, Moll,' she said. 'I've been feeling so abandoned and sad. Not as much as after Pip died, but it's still been hurtful.'

I looked up at her and my whiskers twitched. So what was new?

'But now I've had time to sift through that, I've realised I feel free.'

I looked back at her and barked. Had she gone bonkers? Of course she was free.

'I mean, it's the first time I've been without a man in my life for a long while,' she continued, as if I hadn't spoken. 'I'm not a wife, not a carer, not a widow, not someone recovering from major surgery. I'm Suki!' she looked down at me. 'I'm me and I'm free!' And she started laughing.

I wasn't sure what was so funny, but it was good to see her happy, and it was exciting, so I twirled round and round a bit, and then she said, 'Come on, Moll. We need to celebrate! Last one to the beach is a sissy.' And she ran down through the trees. I let her get ahead, as she still couldn't walk as far as she used to, then I caught her up.

Free, eh? I wondered what that would entail...

'So what are you going to do?' asked Tess while they were having a drink one night.

'Well, I don't know,' she replied. 'But I FEEL different. That's the important thing. I've come to the conclusion that I'm better off without a man in my life.'

Tess and I looked at her as if she had gone mad.

'I mean, perhaps I didn't grieve Pip enough,' she said. 'I was all over the place crying my eyes out, missing him, when along came Ted and then, bang! That was that.'

Tess sipped her glass of wine thoughtfully. 'I think you grieved Pip enough,' she said. 'But surely grief isn't a finite thing. I mean, you don't just stop, do you, just because you meet someone else? It carries on, underneath it all.'

Suki stared at her for a moment. 'Yes,' she said. 'You're right. I suppose I'll always miss Pip, though he's here all the time, in a way.'

'That's lovely,' Tess said. 'I hope I'm around for my family after I'm gone.'

'Oh you will be,' she said with a grin. 'I can promise you that, Tess, you'll always be around.'

Tess laughed. 'So, are you taking a vow of celibacy?'

Suki laughed. 'No! But I think I might be better off without any entanglements. For a bit,' she added. 'Just while I get my head straight.'

'OK,' Tess said, but it sounded like she didn't really believe her.

'I don't want to have to worry about anyone else for a while.'

'Sounds sensible. Perhaps you need to get away for a bit?'

'Actually, I've got another review to do. In ten days' time. Would you like to come?'

Tess grinned and I could smell her excitement. 'Of course! Where is it?'

Suki smiled back. 'Good. It's a dog-friendly pub in North Cornwall.'

'Wow. Fabulous!'

'We get two nights there with breakfast and dinner.'

'Sounds perfect,' Tess said. 'Drinks are on me.'

To be honest I wasn't that fussed about going away. But Suki seemed to like it, so I went along with it, but the amount of upheaval involved was incredible. Mind you, most of the packing was for me. My food, my toys, my blanket, my bowls, my treats. Then her clothes and stuff from the bathroom. Sometimes, if we were going for longer, she'd pack half the kitchen into boxes and that was all piled into the van.

The smell of anticipation was nice though; like a summer's evening, all warm and relaxing. And despite not being able to sleep on our bed, I enjoyed the strange smells when we got there, even if the bedding was sometimes washed with a very strong scent that made my eyes water and my whiskers twitch.

This time I was given my own little blanket which was snuggly and warm against my coat, and I also had a little welcome pack with treats in it and poo bags and we had some great walks along the beaches up there. They had dinner in the pub the first night and I had some of their chips which tasted of oil and salt and a bit of sharp vinegar mixed in with the spuds and were just fantastic.

The two of them talked and talked and walked and walked and seemed to be enjoying the fact that they were on their own. Oh yes, I thought. Just wait. But I kept my mouth shut and didn't bark at all. The most important thing was that they relaxed and enjoyed themselves. If Suki was happy, then so was I. OK, Pip?

Even so, I really liked coming home. I missed the familiar smells of our duvet, the soft prickly feel of the hall carpet under my paws. The familiar smell of my bowls and my biscuits. The salty tang of the sea, blown in on a breeze. The noise of Mel laughing upstairs, the slow rumble of Joe's voice in response. The seagulls, the sound of traffic, the streetlight shining in our window. It all made up what was our home, and I was so glad for what we had.

The following evening Suki met some friends to see a film which usually meant she was out for several hours. I didn't mind. I was quite tired after the travelling and all those different smells and food and walks and a different routine. I dozed on the sofa, then decided to move onto our bed and was having a lovely dream about chasing squirrels in the woods when the door opened and in she came.

I jumped off the bed, ran into the hall and gave her my usual bouncy welcome – and that's when I smelt wine; they must have gone to the pub afterwards, but, I sniffed again, just to make sure. Not just wine, but, yes, it was TED! I barked and she laughed and suddenly she smelt fizzy again. That fizz she got when Ted was around. So what had happened?

She patted me, went to the kitchen and got me a few biscuits (I had her well trained) and then we both sat down next door on the sofa. 'Well, Moll,' she said, and her eyes were shining really bright and sparkly. 'You won't believe who I've just met.'

I barked. Silly woman. Did she think I couldn't smell?

She laughed – and I realised I hadn't heard that sound for so long. 'You know we went to see this film at the Poly? Well, I got there early and was looking at the pictures on the wall and suddenly I had this really weird feeling. As if someone was watching me.'

I got that the whole time. It wasn't weird. I nudged her with my nose to hurry up. What happened?

She stroked me absently. 'Well, I was just turning round when this voice said, "Suki!" and I knew it was Ted.' She took a huge breath in, and let it out noisily. 'And I looked at him and, oh, Moll, I couldn't speak, and my legs were so shaky, I felt like I was falling into a hole.'

These humans were so weird. Why did they waste so much time thinking about what to SAY? Why not just bark and get on with things? I snuggled closer, licked her hand.

'And so I said hello but I couldn't think what else to say. I looked into his eyes and I felt as if I was on fire. And I wanted to cry and laugh and jump into his arms all at the same time. But I just stood there, looking stupid, and then Anne and David turned up and we went to see the film, but I couldn't concentrate. I have no idea what happened. All I could think of was Ted sitting two rows behind me. And I'm pretty sure he was looking at me.' She sighed again and stroked my nose.

'After the film, he said would we all like to go for a drink and I was going to say no, but Anne and David said yes let's go for a quick one, so we did, and then Ted walked me up to the top of the High Street, where his car was parked.' She was talking faster and faster. 'He did offer to walk me home but I said no. Though I wished I'd said yes now. And, oh, Moll, I don't think I'm making sense. My head's all in a whirl.'

I knew what this meant. A night of tossing and turning, of the light going on and off, reading, putting the book down, turning the radio on and off. I would lie at the bottom of the bed and let her get on with it.

Maybe I should have groaned at the thought of Ted coming back into our lives. He'd caused so much unhappiness and upheaval. So many sleeplessness nights and days of tearful misery. But seeing her shining like that brought back everything that we loved about him. How could I judge her for loving him when I loved him too?

I felt her fingers comb my fur, and knead out the knots from my shoulders, and I thought – oh, lovely, and my joints went all floppy. I caught another whiff of Ted and I thought, yes, I miss him too. That scent of spontaneity and fun. Of laughter and love. Of confusion and sadness, but I didn't want to dwell on that.

And as she got ready for a night of wakefulness, I jumped onto the bed and snuggled up to her with a feeling of excitement that was catching. It had jumped from her skin onto my fur, and wriggled its way down to my whiskers.

Ted was back!

26

Reunited

No, she didn't sleep much that night. Tossing and turning again, but at least she wasn't miserable. In the morning she looked at her phone, then looked at me and laughed. 'No, I'm not going to text him, Moll,' she said, and gave me a hug. 'We'll go for a walk and celebrate the fact that the sun's shining, shall we?'

That was good enough reason for me, but I could smell the change in her. It was as if all her senses had suddenly come alive again, having been asleep for ages. There was a sparkle in her eyes. Her hair looked curlier, and shone in the sunlight. She smelt different, too: a heavy rich smell like damp earth with overtones of silvery excitement, like the smell of rain. It was a giddy mix.

We walked down to the beach and I played with several other dogs, cantering in and out of the sea, where little waves rushed forward and retreated, playing games with us. I liked these friendly little wavelets that whispered across the sand, not like the big scary ones.

We were walking along the path by the sea, when her phone pinged and we both jumped. She looked at me, then at her phone and we both knew.

'It's from Ted,' she said, somewhat unnecessarily. 'He's, oh!' she looked up, across the car park, and waved.

I looked towards the other cars, then I smelt him, and it hit me how desperately I'd missed him, too. I meant to be standoff, remembering how much he'd hurt her, but I found myself dashing over the road, weaving in and out of people, cars, cyclists and joggers. I wanted to be the first to reach him! I heard his rich laugh, then the salty smell of him and he gave a bellow of joy as I reached him. He bent down to stroke me, to tickle my tummy, and I was barking and he was laughing and it was really joyous.

And then she arrived, and he got up, and they both looked at each other, and slowly, almost in slow motion, they walked towards each other. I barked and twirled round as I do when I'm excited, and his face had the biggest smile ever, and her face lit up like St Anthony's Lighthouse in the dark and they stood there looking at each other, and even though they didn't touch, it was like electricity singing along cables. I'd never forget that.

Then he came forward and gave her a peck on the cheek but I could tell he really wanted to sweep her into his arms. Do it! I barked. Do it, she'd love it! But he didn't.

'How did you know I'd be here?' she said.

He shrugged and smiled at the same time. 'I didn't. But I've got a meeting round the corner at ten and it's such a lovely day I thought I'd come down a bit early, see the sea before I start work.' He bent down and scratched my back, just how I like it. 'Have you got time for a coffee?'

She nodded, and I could smell everything that she wasn't saying. Love poured out her like liquid honey, and it was gushing out of him. We walked back across the car park to the beach, and he bought two takeaway coffees and a doggie biscuit which tasted like burnt toast but I forgave him.

I led the way back along the beach, scampering over the wet sand, chasing bits of seaweed (nice and salty) and the odd bit of pasty (a bit soggy but OK) to the far side where we sat on some rocks and I had my biscuit and she said, 'So how are things?'

He sat and stared at the sea for so long I didn't think he'd ever answer. But eventually he said, 'Much the same as before. But I've got Dad sorted with a carer who comes in every day, so that's an improvement. He likes her and she helps get him up and gives him his breakfast and she reads the paper to him and sometimes they play Scrabble. Then she does his housework and gets his lunch and he has a nap and then another carer comes and gets him his tea and stays for a bit and gets everything ready for when he goes to bed and makes sure he has his tablets and he seems happy with that.'

'That must be a great relief,' she said.

And what about the wife? That's what I wanted to know. I barked, but they didn't seem to understand, so I dug a hole in the sand. They still didn't get the hint, so I ate the rest of my biscuit and went fishing in one of the rock pools and kept one ear open.

'And your wife?' she said. At last.

He shrugged. 'Much the same.' His voice had dropped and I could hear all the hurt and sadness in him. It was like a big heavy stone strapped to his back so he couldn't get rid of it.

'I'm sorry,' she said, and I could smell the sorrow and disappointment that came off her in sharp waves, like an easterly wind.

There was an awkward smelling silence, so I came back and snuffled her with my nose. She patted me as if she was concentrating really hard, but her face was pink and her eyes were wet, as if she was trying not to cry.

Ted looked at her and put down his coffee. 'I'm the one who's sorry,' he said. 'About everything. I've only ever wanted you to be happy.'

She looked up, into his eyes, and they looked wetter. 'Thank you,' she croaked.

His eyes looked wet too. 'Are you happy, you and Luke? He looked a good man.'

'He is.' She hesitated, and I held my breath. Would she tell him? 'But we're not together anymore.' And her voice cracked a little.

'Oh, I'm so sorry, Suki. He seemed just right for you.'

Liar, I thought. I could smell the relief in his voice. He might just as well have shouted, 'So she's not seeing Luke! Hooray!'

She gave a half smile that smelt of regret and sadness and a bit of relief too. 'Well, that's how life goes, isn't it? He's got a job in Scotland, and I'm really glad for him.'

I'd come to realise that a lot of the time humans said one thing and meant another. No wonder they got so confused.

'So, how's life?' He threw a stone along the sand and I chased it. Not too far so I could still listen.

'Oh, the usual. Work's a bit quiet but that's good as I still get tired and have to have a kip.' She smiled. 'I've got more work lined up for next month, though. And a few reviews.'

He looked at her and love poured out of his eyes. 'Good. Still singing?'

She nodded. 'Yes. Thursday evenings, as always.' She looked at him and bit her lip. 'And how's work for you?'

'Busy. It's been a bit too busy actually, what with trying to sort Dad out and everything. But I've got a few projects that I can put off till later in the year, so that's a relief.'

'Still boating?'

He breathed out slowly. 'No,' he said, and looked over to where I was digging in the sand. 'It's not the same on your own.'

She picked up a pebble and threw it into a rock pool. 'No, it isn't,' she said softly. 'It's not the same at all.'

He looked over at her. 'If ever you felt like a walk, or a trip out in the boat, just let me know,' he said hesitantly. As if he was expecting her to say no.

She looked at him and smiled and it smelt warm and full of joy. 'What about a surf?'

He caught her smile as if it was something precious, and smiled it back. 'Or a surf,' he said and it seemed like he couldn't stop staring at her.

She looked at him, the way I look at a really nice bone. Like I can't wait to taste it. 'Sounds good,' she said, and looked away quickly.

'Would you mind if I text you? See if you'd like to go out one afternoon?'

She looked over at him and then back at me. 'No,' she said, her voice like a whisper. 'No, that would be good.'

He smiled, and it stretched across his face and wiped out all those tired, sad lines. I could smell that he just longed to gather her into his arms and hug her, so tight, but he didn't. 'Good,' he said. And with that one word I knew he was back in our lives. What was it they said in films? For better or for worse. I only hoped it wouldn't be for worse.

We went our separate ways after that. They both had to work, but I could sense how different she was. So much for being happy without a man! Every fibre in her body was attuned to him, even though he wasn't actually with us. As if he'd taken up residence inside her again. She was bubbling, waiting for a text, or a phone call. And she didn't have to wait long.

He rang that night. Asked if we'd like to go for a walk after work the following evening as the forecast was good. She said yes, put down the phone and danced around the room.

'Oh, I know I should say no, Moll,' she said. 'But he makes me feel so alive!' She sat down heavily on the bed beside me and I bounced upwards. She didn't notice. 'I just want to be with him.' She sighed. 'That sounds crazy, doesn't it after all that unhappiness? But he – I don't know, he gets into my blood stream. I'd rather be with him than with anyone else.' She grinned. 'Apart from you, of course.'

I nudged her hand with my nose. I'd heard all of this before, of course, but it was nice to hear it again. To hear that love for humans was the same as for us dogs.

'The thing is, I feel whole when I'm with him. When I'm not, I feel as if huge chunks of me are missing. And I can't bear that.' And she looked at me with such love in her eyes that I felt as if I were going to drown.

I gave a bark of understanding. After all, I loved him too, and I loved our time together, just the three of us. I was interested to see how long it would be before they got back into each other's beds.

The following evening Ted picked us up and we drove towards Helston, turned right down a maze of tiny roads before parking in the middle of nowhere. We got out and Ted produced a rucksack. 'Provisions,' he said cheerfully, and slung it on his back.

The evening air was warm, and the sun was low in the sky but not too low, and I ran on ahead as there were so many new smells. Strange rabbits, a badger sett, fox poo and all sorts of foreign smells. I liked it here; no other people, bouncy turf that was kind to my paws, and I could run and explore everywhere. No cars or pavements. Bliss.

I hurried back after chasing a rabbit or two, to listen to what Ted and Suki were saying. How nice and warm it was. I hadn't missed anything then.

Then, 'So you've made a good recovery?' Ted asked. He'd already asked that the day before, but he smelt nervous. A bit unsure.

She nodded, but looked at the ground as they walked along. 'Yes. I'm more or less back to normal now. And I can drive again which is a great relief. It was quite nice being chauffeured for a bit. Then I got fed up and wanted my independence back.' She looked up and smiled. 'I'm pretty good now, I just get really tired sometimes.'

He frowned. 'We won't go too far then.'

'Honestly, I'm fine,' she said, still smiling. 'So how are things with you? Really?'

He hesitated. Uncertainty radiated off him like sour milk. 'My wife is no better. In fact, I think she's worse. But there's nothing anyone can do, which is the awful thing.' He stopped. 'I'm sorry. I didn't want to talk about her with you, of all people.'

'I don't suppose you do talk about her, do you?'

He shook his head. 'No. Who to? And what could I say?'

She put her hand out to touch his arm. Then pulled it back, as if she'd been burnt. 'I'm so sorry, Ted.'

He tried a smile but I could smell the sadness and confusion underneath it. 'Well, that's just how it is. I don't know if it's better when she does recognise me, because I feel terrible that I've let her down. Or when she doesn't know who I am and I wonder why I bother going, and then feel guilty for even thinking that when she's my wife.'

Suki flinched.

'I'm so sorry, Suki, I shouldn't have said that, to you of all people. I just...'

'It's OK,' she said, though she looked as if he'd slapped her.

'It's not OK. God, I'm such a fool. I promise I won't ever do that again.'

'Ted. It's OK.'

'I'm so sorry. I haven't been able to get outside recently and it takes its toll.'

It was true, he looked as if he'd been hiding under a stone for the last few months. He smelt stale; as if he was tired from his head to his boots. Tired and sad. That sour milk smell drifted over again. Uncertainty and unhappiness. All the uns.

She glanced at him sideways. 'You must get out more, then,' she said softly. Gently. And the honey smell coming from her banished the sour milk smell. He smiled at her, properly this time. 'Race you to that tree over there,' he said, and they took off, running and shrieking, while I bounded along with them, barking and running as fast as my paws would take me.

I won, of course, and they arrived after me, red-faced and panting. 'That was close,' she said; he'd got there first. 'I don't know who's more unfit, you or me.'

He leaned forward. 'You've got an excuse, you've just had major surgery.'

'And you've been sorting out everyone's problems,' she added. 'As usual.'

He straightened. 'Needs must,' he said, and it was as if that chill wind had blown back in. 'Anyway, I've brought some snacks. Hungry?' He swung the rucksack off his back and we sat down by an old oak tree, whose limbs lowered over the grass, which was long and dry and tasted sweet.

He produced drinks – water for me, and a small bottle of wine for them. Then he gave me a chew which tasted of beef and was wonderful. They had prawn sandwiches and crisps. Crisps!!

'This is fantastic, Ted,' she said, taking one of the sandwiches he handed her. 'Thanks so much. You've gone to a lot of trouble.' And the uncertain, hurt smells vanished.

He poured them both a little glass of wine, clinked glasses. 'I'm so glad to see you,' he said. 'I didn't think we'd ever get to do this again.'

She looked down and flushed. 'I didn't either.' She ruffled my neck, carefully not looking at him.

There was silence, but it was a comfortable one while they ate and drank and I chewed. Lovely treat. Crunchy and rich. Just right to get my teeth into.

'Perhaps we could do this again?' he said. As if he expected her to say no.

She looked at him and smiled. 'Perhaps we could,' she said. And her smile forgave him everything.

He grinned back, as if he'd won the lottery, and then the smile faded, like the sun going down. 'I've thought of you every day,' he said, looking down at his feet. 'I've missed you so much.'

There was a long silence, then she said, 'I've missed you too.'

He looked down at his hands, holding a cardboard cup. 'I so wish things were different,' he breathed. 'I really do.'

She looked at his long fingers, holding that cup. 'Me too.'

'But it wasn't fair on you,' he said, as if to himself.

'No,' she said. but her voice was fainter this time. She edged closer to him and took his hand, held it tightly.

He looked down, as if her hand was a thing of wonder. A precious bone. 'I can't offer you what you deserve,' he said.

'But I truly love you. More than I can say. More than anyone else could.'

'I know,' she said, her voice gruff.

Unsaid, hung the question, what shall we do? Well, it was fairly obvious, but in true human terms they were making the usual hash of coming to a conclusion.

'So. We'll take what we have and make the most of it.' Her voice was strong and true. Smelt of no-nonsense pine wood.

He looked at her and carefully wiped a few stray curls back from her face. 'But it's not fair on you.'

'It's not fair on you, either,' she said.

'You deserve someone you can go on holiday with, make plans with, live with. All that kind of thing.'

She shrugged. 'Maybe. But we don't always get what we deserve. Life *isn't* fair.' She looked out over the fields. 'What we have is this connection. We've always got on so well, not just in bed,' (she blushed) 'but in what we do, and the way we think, and discussing things. We've always been very close, haven't we?'

He nodded, his eyes damp. As if he couldn't speak.

'What we have is rare,' she continued. 'And it seems stupid to waste it. So yes, it might not be fair or what we deserve, or any of that stuff, but it is what it is.'

There was a long silence, while indecision wafted off him like bonfire smoke on a windy afternoon. 'I hate having to lie,' he said. 'Or rather, lie by omission. I so want you to meet my Dad. The rest of my family. But I have to protect Jane, or rather, her parents.'

I saw her stiffen. She didn't like that. But it was part of the package. Or rather, his package.

Then he said, 'I want you to be absolutely sure, Suki. I couldn't bear to lose you again,' and his voice cracked.

She bit her lip and her eyes went very wet, and love poured out of her like a fast dripping tap. 'If we're going to try again, we need to find a way to make it work,' she said, and her voice wobbled, then settled again, like Ted's boat when we hit a wave.

Ted looked up. 'Exactly,' he said, hope flaring in his eyes. 'So what would be best for you? What would help you?'

She wrinkled her nose. 'I need you to tell me that you love me. I mean, I know you do, but I need to hear that. And I know life has thrown things at you that neither of us saw coming, but I need to know that I matter.' She didn't say that she needed to come first. But looking at his face, he knew that.

'You always come first to me,' he said simply. 'And of course, I will always tell you if I need to be somewhere else.'

'What about you?' she said. She sounded as if she was in a business meeting with an editor. I've sat in on those, usually held in cafes. I often got a bit of cake or flapjack. 'What would help you?'

He shrugged. 'Just being with you,' he said simply. Then he took a deep breath. 'But if you should meet somebody else, who can give you more than I can, you must feel free to go. To be happy.' He smiled, but it was a bit wobbly. 'But for God's sake give me warning.'

She smiled. 'Of course,' she said.

He hesitated, and then he held out his arms and she got up and sat on his lap, and wound her arms around his neck and he pulled her to him and they kissed and kissed until they had to come up for air.

I barked and he still held her and the smell coming off them was the best ever. Like fox poo and cheese and cuddles all at once.

I gave another quick yip, just to remind them that I was there, then I left them to it and returned to my chew. All this show of affection was a bit much for me. Still, she was so happy, which meant I had fulfilled my promise.

27

Godrevy

The next few months were very special. If I'd thought they were close before they broke up, now they were like one person. I had never seen either of them so happy. Which rubbed off on me, of course. You couldn't be miserable when the people you loved most in the world were so joyous – and loved you, too.

It wasn't that simpering love that you saw on television. No, this was a strong cable that bound the two of them together. It was the colour of silver, and so strong and so clear, I could almost see it. They disagreed sometimes, like most people, but that usually ended up with one of them laughing, then he would tickle her, and they'd ended up cuddling.

They were careful with each other now, as if their love was so precious it might break. And that made sense to me, given what they'd been through. Dogs knew how valuable love was, so it was about time they learned it too.

He would turn up with presents that he'd obviously spent time thinking about. A pair of earrings that she'd admired. A book she'd been wanting to read by an author she was going to interview. A lightweight rucksack to put all our stuff in when we went on the boat, or walking, with special pockets for a drink for me, treats for me (and her) and a towel and things. One day he gave her a locket which had belonged to his grandmother. She asked for a piece of his hair, which was apparently what they did in Olden Times, whenever that was. She put some of my hair in there as well, in case you're wondering.

Gradually, she got busier at work, and so was he, which meant that they were frequently very tired. One evening, we were round at Ted's house for the night, sitting on his sofa watching television, when he said, 'Sod it. We need a holiday.'

She was lying with her feet in his lap and looked up. 'Holiday? Where?'

'Well, somewhere we can take Moll, of course,' he said. 'A client of mine has a chalet on the Towans near Hayle. What do you think?'

She grinned. 'Sounds lovely. Near Godrevy. Let's have a look.'

He reached for his tablet and soon they were looking at it with squeaks of excitement. 'Perfect,' he said. 'Quiet. Near the beach. Pub nearby.'

'Brilliant!' she said. 'Let's book it. I'll pay you back tomorrow.'

'My treat,' he insisted. 'The only question is, when do we go?'

There was some discussion about their respective work commitments, then Ted typed a bit more, before saying, 'It's done!'

They arranged to go the following month, but a few days before we were due to go, Ted got a phone call while he was with us. His face went white while he answered it, and the smell coming off him was like rancid cheese. His shoulders slumped, then he put the phone down and put his arms around Suki, held her tight.

'That was Dad's carer. Dad's had a fall and is in hospital. I'm going to have to go and see him.' He paused. 'I'm really sorry, I know how much we both need this break, but I have to see how he is.'

She drew back, looked down. 'Of course you do.' She sighed. 'Should we try and postpone it?' A flat resignation underscored her words. She smelt of despair and sadness.

'No. I'm sure we won't need to do that.' But he sounded desperate, and pulled her to him again.

When she spoke her voice was muffled. 'Which hospital is he in? Treliske or West Cornwall?'

He pulled back, looked down at her. 'West Cornwall.' Then he smiled. 'Of course! We won't be far away. We can go ahead as planned!' The foul smell vanished. 'Good thinking, you clever woman.'

She smiled back, but I could smell the nervousness underneath. I knew she was wondering what else would go wrong with his poor dad?

But thankfully nothing did. Ted went to see his father, who was soon let out of hospital and back home with his carers, with a warning to be careful.

And so, a few days later, we all set off in Ted's car. I was intrigued: I'd heard about chalets but didn't know what they were. They sounded like a type of sausage, so I was excited and hopeful.

After a long drive, we turned down a narrow road, past a hut and into a field with lots of little houses. I could smell salt, and ozone, and hear waves in the distance. On one side of the field was a huge mountain of sand: it looked terrifying to me, but Ted and Suki didn't even comment.

We stopped outside one of the square wooden houses, which had a little terrace outside, and they unloaded stuff from the car while I explored inside. The house had one bedroom, with the sun streaming in through big windows. A bathroom and a kitchen and sitting area and that was it – all that we needed.

Ted left us to go and see his father while Suki got things organised and unpacked. Soon it looked cosy, almost like it did at home. Our duvet on the bed, my bowls on the floor. Our stuff in the kitchen and the bathroom. I had my tea and felt settled.

Outside was a grassy area with loads of rabbit droppings. Bunnies! And at the bottom of the the sandy mountain, I smelt lots of dogs, rabbits, a fox, magpies and seagulls – all kinds of delights. We scrambled up the top of the hill, slipping and sliding and laughing, then reached the top and there was a big grassy area, with lots of little hills. Then in the far distance, a tall finger on an island sticking out of the sea. 'That's Godrevy lighthouse,' she told me. 'It's very famous and this beach is where my mum used to come when she was a child.'

We explored the little hills with patches of sand among the bouncy grass, which was more wiry than the usual stuff at home and smelt of salt and sunshine. I loved it here, and chased some of the birds, nearly caught a rabbit, and played with a greyhound. We had a race but I let him win. Greyhounds always got very insecure about losing.

A bit further on we came to a cafe and she bought a coffee and we sat outside. They provided bone-shaped dog biscuits which were tasty, too, then her phone rang and I could hear it was Ted.

'How is he?'

'He's OK, but this fall knocked his confidence. I said I'd stay while he has his tea, then I'll come straight back to the chalet.'

'Or we could meet for a drink? There's a bar overlooking the lighthouse. I could meet you there in about an hour if you like.'

'Even better. We can have drinks overlooking the beach.'

We nipped back to the chalet, then set off on a shorter route to the bar, me scampering over the bouncy turf that made me feel like a puppy again. I was only twelve, and knew I was very fit my age, but sometimes I was aware of slowing down a bit.

When we got to the bar, Ted was already there, ordering drinks and a packet of crisps. Crisps! This was going to be a perfect holiday.

She leaned over and kissed him. 'You look a bit pale, are you OK?'

He smiled and nodded, but I could smell the dry, dusty scent of his father on him. It lingered on his trouser legs and his jacket, settled in his hair. The smell of old person and disinfectant and of giving up. It was a horrible, frightening smell that made my fur stand on end and my whiskers droop. I shrank back and jumped onto Suki's lap as soon as she sat down. I had to absorb the salty outdoor smell of health. That done, I relaxed, jumped off and enjoyed some crisps on the floor.

I was tired after that and sat on the sofa between them, listened to their gentle voices; his low and deep: hers lighter and brighter, as they discussed what to eat that evening, what to do tomorrow. I dozed, thinking with joy of having a whole week ahead of us. No work, just my favourite people around all day to play with.

The days passed in a blur of sun with lots of new walks and visits to cafes and pubs and lots of sleep for us all. They didn't get up till late, made lazy breakfasts and then we'd leave Ted to do some work while we had a gentle stroll.

Later, we'd set off and explore somewhere different and nearly always finished up at a pub and sat in the garden with crisps and drinks. Everything was new and the locals were friendly and I could smell all the stress sliding off my people: they looked younger by the day.

But on the fourth day, Ted woke up and he smelt bad, like very burnt toast. We were all lying in bed, them drinking cups of tea, and Suki looked over at him. 'What's the matter?' she asked. His face had gone grey.

'Nothing,' he said, but you could see he was lying.

'Ted.' Her voice was a warning.

'I feel a bit dizzy,' he said.

'Dizzy?' She sat up in bed. I did too.

'It's my heart,' he said. 'It's beating really fast. It won't slow down.'

She felt his wrist. Then laid her ear on his chest. 'Hmm, that is quite fast,' she said, and quickly got up, went next door. We heard her talking, then her head popped round the door. 'Just rung the NHS number,' she said. 'It would be a good idea to get you checked out.'

Ted shook his head. 'No, honestly, I don't want to spoil our holiday.'

'You'll spoil our holiday if you *don't* go,' she said, and leant over, kissed him. 'Come on, lazy bones. Up you get while I take Moll out.'

A bit later we arrived outside this long low building and Suki took Ted inside. They were gone for ages, so I snoozed in the car, waking with a start when I heard their footsteps coming across the car park.

The doors opened and they got in. He smelt old and frightened. Panic and uncertainty wafted off him in acrid bursts and got stuck in my nostrils, made my whiskers twitch. Fear crept down my back as I waited to hear what they said.

'Well, the good news is that it's not a heart attack,' he said. He didn't fool me. He was terrified.

'Mmm,' she said. 'I've been googling Atrial Fibrillation and like the doctor said, it's very common.' She read aloud from her phone. 'The exact cause is unknown but it's more prevalent with age and affects certain groups of people more than others, for example, those with heart conditions.'

'Well, I'm only 47, and I don't have any heart conditions,' he said.

'Certain situations can trigger AF, including binge drinking alcohol, being overweight, drinking too much caffeine, illegal drugs, especially speed or coke, or smoking.'

'I don't do any of those,' he said, his voice louder now. 'And I'm not overweight.'

'And it can be exacerbated by stress,' she added.

They looked at each other. 'Shit,' he said and laid his head on her shoulder. She stroked his hair, kissed him and stroked me as well. Firmly but gently. I could feel the atmosphere in the car begin to settle. Finally he raised his head and kissed her slowly, thoroughly. I could see his strength seeping back.

'Thank you,' he said.

'My pleasure. Now, we make you an appointment to see your GP as soon as possible,' she said. 'Then you can be referred if necessary.'

'OK.' His head slumped again, but he brought it back up. 'But my heart's back to normal again now. Feel it.'

She felt his pulse and nodded. 'That's good. He said to keep checking it, didn't he?'

He nodded. 'Yes, though I'll know if it's not right. I'd better keep a record, I suppose.'

'That's what he said.' She leaned over and kissed his nose, lightly: a butterfly kiss.

He smiled and I could see him relax more. 'Thank you, my darling. What on earth would I do without you?'

She smiled, said nothing.

He kissed her, then leaned over and tickled my tummy. 'Sorry, Moll, we mustn't forget you.' Already his voice was stronger. 'Now listen, we've got another three days of holiday. So let's make the most of it!'

She smiled and nodded. I barked. They laughed. We drove back to the chalet for a lazy breakfast, and although we did, indeed, make the most of the remaining days, they were tinged with anxiety. Suki took me out for the late-night wee walk on our own and talked to me then. Well, it was more like talking to herself. But I knew she needed to talk, even if I didn't reply.

'Is this really Atrial Fibrillation? Oh, Moll. He won't find out until he's had tests, apparently. Which I hope they can do next week. But he might have a heart attack. Or a stroke. Apparently the chances are much higher. How can he decrease the stress in his life? It's impossible, but we must be able to do something.' On and on she went, and it was always the same sort of thing, every night.

Bless her, she needed to get it out of her system, and with Ted safely inside the chalet, so he couldn't hear, I could sense her worry lessening. What started out as a thick fog of words became a thin stream, until we were able to go back and she could join Ted in bed with a calmer mind.

The strange thing was that, although there was a definite air of apprehension until Ted saw his doctor, it was as if life had come into sharp focus. It made it even more precious. I could almost hear a clock ticking, meaning they had to make the most of every second. And they did. They treated each other even more carefully. With respect and an even deeper love.

This love tasted of blue cheese (my new favourite, courtesy of Ted when Suki wasn't looking). It shone dark like a plum: red and purple: strong, powerful colours. It smelt of earth after a rain shower. Of the bark of an old oak tree. It was smooth to the touch, like a velvet curtain. And it bound us three even closer together.

28

Diagnosis

Over the next few weeks, Ted was very tired, and took to having a nap in the daytime at weekends. Most unlike him, though I did it all the time. I liked lying on his stomach, as I had with Pip, feeling the warmth of his body under the roughness of his jumper. It was my way of passing on hope, and strength.

Suki made him an appointment with a doctor, who referred him to the hospital where he was to have several tests, so I waited in the van while they went inside. They had both been smelling terrible over the past weeks: curdled anxiety and fear which almost put me off my food. Not quite, but I sincerely hoped that someone at the hospital would make them feel better.

However, when they walked back to the van, I could tell it wasn't good news. His head was down, his shoulders slumped, and she seemed to be supporting him across the car park. She looked very pale and small and smelt fearful. Though not as frightened as him.

'Well, they were very thorough,' she said, half to me and half to him. 'It's definitely Atrial Fibrillation. But that's really just a medical term for a fast heart beat.'

'It's a bit more than that,' Ted said. 'It's the heart not shunting the blood round properly. He said that it can get stuck in one of the chambers and that's when you get a stroke or a heart attack.'

'But you're very low risk,' she said firmly. I could tell she was trying to be optimistic. 'You're not overweight, you don't smoke, you don't eat rubbish food and you don't go on benders. You look after yourself, so I'm sure you'll be fine.'

He looked up at her and gave a faint smile. Wafts of sour milk drifted off him. 'I know, you're right. I must be more positive,' he said. 'But I can't tell you how scary it feels when my heart's racing that fast. I feel as if I'm going to die any minute.'

She leaned over and kissed him. 'No, I don't know what it's like and I imagine it's very scary. But loads of people live with AF, he said, and nothing awful happens. You just have to take the tablets. Let's just take it day by day, OK?'

'You're right, of course.' He leaned over and stroked my tummy, as he knows I like it. Though I had the feeling he was comforting himself as much as me.

I didn't really see the fuss, though my heart beat was always very slow. Too slow, the vet said. But I'd had this all my life so it didn't bother me. Surely he could live with his heart going a bit fast?

Ted was given some pills, but he complained they slowed him down too much. 'I feel sluggish and lethargic and I can't think properly,' he said. 'The last job I did was awful, I couldn't think straight.'

'But you said the client was really pleased.'

He nodded. 'Yes. That's the weird thing. Perhaps it made me concentrate more, but the job felt a lot harder.' He sighed. 'I'd feel so much better without these bloody drugs.'

'Yes, but while your heart's going funny, you must take them,' she said decisively. 'Even if they do make you feel awful.' She looked at him with a beady eye. 'You don't want a heart attack, do you?'

He paled. 'No. You're right,' he muttered, and went and took his pill.

He didn't smell right these days: a bit like rusty metal. He was often pale and shivery and seemed exhausted the whole time. It was horrible to see and worse to smell.

He still went to work, but he wasn't as busy as he had been. And while he would still come for walks sometimes, I could see that it was an effort for him to go far. 'Sometimes, my heart goes so fast I worry in case it gives up,' he said, smelling like an old toolbox.

Suki didn't say much in front of him, but she talked to me, as we lay in bed, or walked along on our own. 'It's horrible, Moll,' she said. 'His confidence has shrunk, and he's become a smaller version of himself. He's completely lost his zing. I don't know what I can do.'

The one good thing about all this was that he wasn't expected to rush down and see his father, or up to see Jane while he was feeling so poorly.

'It's about time his brother and sister took their turn looking after his dad,' Suki said to Tess on the phone one day. 'Just because he's nearer, he does all the work. So I'm glad they're doing their bit for once.' She sighed. 'Though it would be so nice to meet them. I feel shoved to one side when they come down. I know they don't stay for long, but normally I'd see them, wouldn't I?'

'Of course,' said Tess. 'But nothing about your relationship with Ted has ever been normal, has it?'

'No, you're right. Anyway, you said you've got some news. What is it?'

Tess sighed. 'Well, I'm about to become a granny.'

'Really? You mean, Steve's girlfriend's pregnant?'

'Yes, but there's a complication.'

Suki laughed. 'There are always complications in your life. What is it?'

'She's expecting twins.'

'TWINS?!' she said. 'My God. When?'

'She's not due till March. But also, Mum is a lot better, so it means I can start set up my own business and give in my notice. At last!'

'Oh that's fantastic news!' Suki cried. 'Oh, Tess, I'm so happy for you. That's amazing. So we can meet up for a walk next week, all being well?'

'Absolutely,' she said. In the background I could hear Titch barking, so I barked back at him and suddenly the world didn't seem such a dark and smelly place, but opened a door into somewhere with sunlight and rabbits and fox poo and treats. And, of course, my Titch.

Titch and I hadn't met for a proper walk for months, because Suki hadn't been well enough, and I noticed that he smelt slightly foreign, and his eyes were a little dimmer. He'd gone a bit deaf too, but he complained that I couldn't hear him properly either. However, he was still my precious Titch.

We met at our favourite spot near Roundwood Quay which involved a walk along a steep potholed lane, a trot through some fields and then a scamper through the woods, with lots of squirrels and rabbits, magpies and crows. Titch and I weren't as fast as we used to be, I realised, but as we ambled along together again, time melted away. We nuzzled up together and it seemed as if nothing had changed.

'Isn't it lovely seeing them walking together again?' said Tess, as if reading my mind. 'They must have missed each other as much as we have.'

Suki laughed. 'I should say so. They look happy now, though, don't they?'

'Absolutely.' Tess pointed to their favourite bench on the quay. 'Shall we sit in the sun?'

'Good idea.' They walked over to the seat while we sniffed around. There were always good quality crumbs as it was a popular place for picnics and barbecues, even in winter.

'So how's Ted now?'

'The AF comes and goes,' Suki said. 'He gets very frightened when he's having an attack, and I'm not surprised. If I put my ear to his chest it's terrifying hearing his poor heart racing. But the drugs that slow his heart down, exhaust him and make him really cold. He's like a clockwork toy with the mechanism running down, but I can't wind him up.'

Tess sighed. 'I am sorry, Suki. Is there nothing anyone can do?'

She shook her head. 'Nope. We went along to a support group the other day but it was incredibly depressing. I don't think we'll go back.' She shrugged. 'Still, he's not had an attack for a week now so maybe they'll get less frequent. I just feel a bit hopeless.'

'Poor love, that's a horrible feeling,' Tess said. 'On a different topic, what are your plans for Christmas?'

'Quiet. Ted's not going anywhere, thank God, so we can have a restful time.'

'Would you two like to come over to us? Steve and his girlfriend aren't coming over until Boxing Day, so Paul's dying to have someone to cook for. It'll make it more Christmassy.'

Suki grinned. 'That would be really lovely, Tess. I'll check with Ted but I think it would do him good. As long as we can bring food.'

'We'll sort that out nearer the time,' Tess said. 'Just get him to say yes first.'

Ted eventually agreed to go to a Christmas meal with Tess and Titch, though it took some doing.

'I'm not very good company,' he said first of all, then, 'It'll be too much work for them, it's not fair.'

Eventually Suki rang Tess in despair. 'Pass me over,' she said, and when Ted was on the phone, she said, 'Listen, Ted. We're going to be on our own and we'll be drowning in food and it won't feel Christmassy unless you share it with us, so please come. Otherwise Paul will be unbearable, and we'll be eating bloody turkey till February.'

At that Ted chuckled. 'OK, if you insist. But let me know what we can bring.'

In fact it was a fabulous day. We had a lazy breakfast (toast and a bit of egg for me, smuggled by Ted), then a walk along the beach which was busy because of the Christmas Day Swim. Lots of people, with flasks of hot drinks and cake and biscuits and mince pies. Everyone was in a good mood, so I got a lot of very tasty treats.

Ted gave me a new collar and matching lead, and gave Suki a framed photograph of the three of us together. He'd asked someone to take the picture of us a few months ago at Godrevy (before he got poorly) and they were both smiling and had their arms around each other, and I was sitting in front of them and I was smiling too.

'That is just so gorgeous,' she said, and her eyes were all wet. 'That's the best present I've ever had. The three of us together.' And she pulled him in for a big kiss and a cuddle and I barked and they gave me a cuddle too. 'Will you hang it up for me? I'd like it on the wall, over there, so it's the first thing I see when I come into the room.'

Ted beamed and looked happier than he had for ages. 'Of course, my darling,' he said, and wandered off to get a hammer. I must say we did look very splendid together.

We went over to see Tess and Paul and Titch later that afternoon and the flat smelt delicious. Hot meat wafted from the kitchen and I could smell so many vegetables and roast potatoes and gravy, my nose and whiskers were all a-quiver.

'Hello, darlings,' said Tess, giving each of us a huge hug; me included, of course. 'Now come and have your presents.'

I had a big bone which I started to chew right away, and I didn't really hear what presents they had because my mouth was full, and I needed all my concentration, but it sounded like they were having a good time.

A bit later, my jaw was tired, and there were even better smells coming from the kitchen, as well as a lot of clanging and banging and steam and heat, and then Paul brought the food in, bowl by bowl.

'I've never seen so much food on one table,' Suki laughed. 'You're amazing!'

'And Moll and Titch have their own bowlfuls, look,' said Paul proudly, carefully putting them on the floor for us.

Well, I'd never had such a meal before. We had turkey and gravy with potatoes and sprouts and stuffing and carrots and cauliflower and little sausages and bacon and Titch and I ate so much we could hardly move and had to have a snooze afterwards.

Ted looked pale when we arrived, but after a glass of wine and a plateful of food he looked pink again and smelt better than he had for ages. He actually laughed several times, and he and Suki relaxed and chatted and played games afterwards and it was lovely to see everyone look so happy. And of course, I had my Titch, so I was delighted.

'I love you so much,' Ted said as he drove home later. 'Whatever happens, you know I'll always love you and I only wish I could change things.'

She snuggled up to him and looked out at the starry night. 'I know,' she said softly. 'I know.'

Wouldn't it be lovely, I thought, picturing me lying down beside Titch, our noses almost touching, if we could be like this forever? *This* is what happiness tastes like.

29

Recession

'Normally I hate January,' Suki said in bed one morning, 'but I'm quite enjoying this one.'

Ted chuckled, a rare sound recently, and turned over, dislodging me for I was lying at his feet. 'Sorry, Moll,' he said, and turned to Suki. 'Why are you enjoying this one?'

She laughed, sleepily. 'Because I can take advantage of your body,' she said and rolled over to face him. 'I quite like being with you.'

He kissed her nose. 'It's not bad being with you, either. Shall I make tea?'

'In a minute.' She snuggled in closer and while I was glad for them, I wished I had Titch to snuggle up against. 'I haven't finished with you yet.'

The bed got quite busy after that so I jumped off and had a sleep on the sofa which was covered in a soft blanket and wasn't liable to move. I had noticed that Ted didn't smell nearly as bad these days. Christmas Day seemed to have been a turning point.

'It's been over a month since he had an AF attack,' Suki told Tess as we walked along one day. Titch and I were so happy to be in each other's company. Of course we still chased squirrels and rabbits, but at a rather more sedate pace than we used to. 'I'm keeping everything crossed that maybe, just maybe, he might be OK.'

'He looked awful when you arrived at Christmas,' Tess said. 'But he soon perked up, didn't he? A glass of wine, some food and good company always helps, doesn't it?'

'It certainly does.' Suki smiled. 'The colour's coming back in his face, and he's not moving around like an old man anymore, which is such a relief.'

'What about those pills he hated?'

Suki wrinkled her nose. 'Well, he's either got used to them or he's stopped taking them, though he denies that.' She sighed. 'He's got to go and see Jane and his Dad, but it's like he's been fading away and it was horrible to see.' She tried to smile. 'It was like losing Pip all over again.

Tess gave her a big hug. 'I know. I do feel for you.'

When they pulled apart, Suki said, 'Meanwhile, guess who I got a long email from?'

'Give us a clue.'

'Scotland.'

'Not Luke?'

She nodded. 'Yes. He's having a brilliant time. Sounds really happy.'

'Good – I'm glad for him,' Tess said.

'Exactly. He's such a lovely fellow. I'd love to see him again. One of these days.'

'I bet.' Tess threw a stick for me and Titch and we ran after it, then I trotted back to hear the reply. 'Didn't he invite you up?'

'Yes, but it's one hell of a journey,' she said. 'I haven't told him that I'm back together with Ted. I feel a bit guilty.'

'No need,' said Tess briskly. 'He's a big boy, I'm sure he can handle it. Did he say anything about a new partner?'

'No, but I'll ask,' she said. 'I was so pleased to hear from him.' She paused. 'I haven't told Ted yet.'

Tess gave her a sharp look. 'No need for him to know everything,' she said. 'You know, you said you were feeling stuck. A change of scene might do you good.'

I barked in agreement, but I could see from Suki's sloping shoulders that she was unlikely to take up the idea. Still, it might get her thinking...

After another month, it seemed that the AF had gone.

'I've been OK for six weeks,' said Ted. 'I just hope this is the end of it, darling.' He enfolded her in his arms and she was quiet, but I could sense she was thinking what I was thinking – yes, we hoped so too.

We were all nervous, but gradually the underlying smell of panic receded, like watching the tide go out. However, all this had taken a toll on all of us. I mean, Titch and I were getting older, so in a way our lives were more precious than our owners, because we had less of them.

Titch complained I was getting grumpy in my old age. I was 13 and he was 14, but he was just as bad. One thing I hated was being woken up when I was asleep. Suki frequently got up in the early hours of the morning to pee and took ages to get back to sleep which in turn disturbed me and Ted. Have you heard the expression, "Let sleeping dogs lie"? Well, there's a good reason for it.

One day, Suki was at work when I noticed a stillness in the way she was sitting. She usually fidgets a lot, but this time, she was so rigid I could smell something was up.

I wriggled forwards from where I was lying on the bed behind her, and nudged her with my nose. She looked down, as if surprised I was there, and I caught a whiff of something sharp and unhappy, like stale sweat. What on earth was it?

'It's another email from Luke,' she said.

Ah! I'd thought it might be.

'He sounds happy and settled, which is great.'

I waited. There was a BUT ...

'He says he'd like to ring because he's got something to tell me,' she said. 'But if it was good news, he'd email, or text, wouldn't he? I do hope he's OK.' She stroked me gently. 'Perhaps I'll ring him. I don't think I can stand waiting.' And she pressed a button on her phone, waited while it rang and rang.

She was just about to end the call when Luke answered. 'Hey, Suki!' His voice came over the phone loud and clear. 'I was just about to ring you. How are you?'

'We're fine. Are you OK? I was a bit worried by your email.'

He laughed, but sounded a bit nervous. 'I'm fine. I've got something to tell you.'

'What is it?'

A slight pause. 'I haven't been entirely honest with you,' he said, his voice low and warm. 'I am so fond of you, and hope we can always be good friends, but, well, when we met, I told you that I'd just come out of a relationship, like you had.'

She nodded. 'Yes, I remember.'

'Well, I'd thought that it was over, and I was heartbroken, like you with Ted. And much though I was glad to be there for you, I could tell that you still loved him. So when this Scotland job came up, it seemed good for both of us if I took it. I could never be Ted.'

'Of course not; you're you,' she said, sounding puzzled.

'But I'd only been here a week when Jim rang me. Asked if he could come and see me.'

'Jim?'

'Jim's my ex,' said Luke.

My ears, and I bet hers, caught the word HE. So that was why he'd been holding back.

'Right,' she said slowly. I could smell confusion, tinged with a bit of relief. 'I didn't realise you were ...'

'No, and I should have told you,' Luke said, and he sounded so embarrassed, and so awkward I felt really bad for him. 'But you had enough to think about, I knew neither of us were ready for another relationship, and you needed looking after.'

'Right.'

'I didn't want to mislead you, and to be honest I thought you'd realised anyway, when I said I didn't want to stay the night.'

'I was a bit unsure,' Suki said.

'I really thought Jim and I were over,' Luke said. 'But we talked a lot, and I told him about you, of course, and, to cut a long story short, he lives about half an hour away, so we're going to try again.'

'Wow,' said Suki. I could smell she wanted to shout with relief. Though part of her felt confused. 'I'm really glad for you.'

'And he'd like to meet you.'

'Good. I'd like to meet him, too.'

'So I do hope you'll come up soon.'

'Love to,' she said, but I could smell her head was buzzing too much to think about a trip to Scotland. 'Well, thanks for letting me know, Luke. I really hope you and Jim will be happy. You deserve it.'

'Thank you, Suki,' he said. 'You, too.'

She finished the call and sat staring out of the window, though I don't suppose she registered what was out there.

I could hear seagulls crying. Joe sawing some wood. A blackbird's insistent call. The duvet was soft against my fur. My whiskers brushed against her, to give her comfort.

She gave a huge sigh and turned to me. 'Bloody hell, Moll, that was a bit of a bombshell.' She sighed. 'Why didn't I realise he was gay? And why didn't he tell me? It's nothing to be ashamed of.'

I yipped. Looking back, there was that bloke in the pub, and that funny smell coming off Luke. His refusal to stay the night. The fact that he never kissed her like Ted did...

'I just want him to be happy. And don't look at me like that.' She got up and flounced off to make a cup of coffee. Hmmm, I thought. It's touched a nerve, which is no bad thing. She needs to find a way to feel Unstuck.

It was a joy to see Ted return to his old self, smelling of sunshine and sea and outside, mixed with the office smells from his work. He wasn't cold all the time and his face had lost that awful pinched look.

'I feel myself again!' he said, jumping out of bed one morning. 'And I hardly dare say this, but I don't feel frightened any more. I can't tell you the relief!'

She smiled and smelt of grass on a sunny day. 'I'm so glad, darling,' she said. 'But just because you're better, don't overdo things, will you?'

He bent to kiss her. 'No, I'll be careful. Though I might overdo you.' Which meant another session of the bed going crazy. I sloped off to the sofa again.

But of course getting better meant he had to go and see his Dad, then Jane.

He was gone for most of a week to see his Dad. 'Sorry, darling, but I feel I owe him some time.'

'No, I understand,' she said, and she smelt as if she did. No nasty sourness to her.

But then of course, there was the visit to Jane, and her parents, and the family up there.

'I'll have to go for a couple of weeks,' he said. He smelt sour again, but a stressed sour, not a poorly one. It was still a vile smell though. 'I haven't seen Jane or the family for months now.'

She didn't reply, but a horrible smell started seeping out of her. And not saying anything was actually worse than her getting angry.

He stopped suddenly: I think he realised it sounded as if he was trying to explain, or make excuses, and it was still such a bone of contention between them. Me, I like my bones to be edible, but humans evidently don't.

So Ted was gone for the best part of a month, though he came back in between visits. I was glad she was busy with work, but I could smell how rootless she felt.

One day we were at home when she got a text from Petroc asking us over for supper and Scrabble. I liked it there; the kitchen was warm from an old Raeburn, and there were comfy armchairs and a good sample of crumbs on the floor. Just my sort of place. Petroc was good for Suki – he smelt of old biscuits which was soothing, and they could talk about anything; I knew she could trust him. When we arrived, he gave me a very tasty bit of mature Cheddar, and Suki a glass of wine. 'How are you, my dear?' He said, pouring himself a glass of wine while he stirred something on the cooker. 'I understand Ted is off doing his duties.'

'He is,' she said warily, as if unsure how much to say.

'It must be even more difficult, when you've got used to him being around so much,' he ventured.

'It is,' she said, sounding grateful that he'd opened up the topic. 'For a while now, he's always been around to talk to, and know that I'll see him later, or tomorrow.' She sighed. 'And of course he's lovely to share a bed with.' She went a bit pink. I was surprised the bed was still in one piece, they used it so much. Bounce, bounce, bounce. Creak, creak, creak. Nothing like what I got up to that long ago time, but the smells coming off them were like sweet fresh cowpats, so despite the groaning, they evidently enjoyed it.

'Well, he won't be gone for long, will he?' said Petroc. He added a pinch of salt and pepper to his concoction. 'In the meantime, maybe you could take advantage of being able to do what you want, when you want.' He smiled at her. 'Not having to cook for anyone...'

'He does most of the cooking.'

'Really? You have got him well trained. Anyway, eating what you want....'

'To be fair he always asks me what I want to eat first.' She paused. 'Though he doesn't like salads. Or stir fries much.'

He smiled. 'There you are you then. And at least this way you don't get tired of each other.' He looked at her. 'What is it, my dear?'

Suki tried to smile, but she was still smelling like rotten meat. 'It's as if part of me's missing,' she said, her voice fading to a whisper. 'And I hate feeling dependent on anyone.'

'That's not being dependent,' Petroc said. 'That's loving someone.'

Suki gave a wobbly smile. 'Maybe. I guess so.'

I looked at her, thinking of Pip. I barked: just a little yip.

'I mean, it was different with Pip,' she continued. At last, she was beginning to understand me. 'That was a different sort of love.' She stopped, as if she'd said the wrong thing. 'I mean, it was more...' she stopped, obviously trying to find the right word... 'Steady. Certain. I mean, we were included. In family stuff. We WERE family.' She sighed. 'Now we're not. And that's OK. Except that...'

'It's not,' Petroc finished for her. 'I know just how you feel, Suki. It's very hard and opens up a real Pandora's Box of emotions, doesn't it? You feel angry, you hate them and love them at the same time. You feel jealous of the other person, then hate yourself for your feelings. I do sympathise.'

'But that's what I signed up for,' she blurted. 'I mean, not signed up for, but, you know, that's just how it is. For now.'

Petroc looked at her steadily. 'For now,' he repeated, as if he knew something we didn't. Then he looked away and said, 'Right, this is ready now. Let's eat,' and the topic was closed.

They played Scrabble after their meal, but we didn't stay too long because Suki was tired. But I knew Petroc had given her food for thought.

That night she lay down on the bed next to me and laid her head against my belly. I don't usually like that sort of thing as her hair tickles, but there are times when you have to put up with it. I knew she was thinking of what Petroc had said. She was going to have to think her own way out of this one.

30

Something must change

Ted came back from his travels looking pale and smelling terrible. Sour milk, gone-off chicken, you name it, just disgusting. He came into the flat, gathered her up in his arms and they stood there for a long time, rocking, not saying anything.

Then we all sat on the sofa together. They both had a glass of wine and held hands and she turned the television on, but I don't think they watched it. The air was thick with unhappiness, like a winter fog that seeps into your bones.

The only thing he said was, 'I'm so sorry.'

Usually she would say something to make him feel better, but this time she just said,

'So am I.'

I waited for one of them to say something else, but they didn't. So I sat beside them, smelling the mixture of anguish and sourness and so many levels of pain and love that are difficult to explain to you humans who don't smell like us. And I felt really sad, for I could see this going on for years and years. And I had a feeling that the misery would eat away at them until it gnawed their love into nothingness.

Something had to change. But what? And how?

I talked to Titch about Suki's problem. He listened, with his head on one side, and was silent for a moment. Then he barked, 'Why doesn't she leave him?'

'Because she loves him. We both do.'

'I think you could do better. You don't need someone with that many problems.' He looked at me, head on one side. 'I know it's not that simple, and yet it is. Sort of.'

I twizzled my nose. 'I know. You're right. I just wish I could get Suki to see that.'

'You'll have to wait till she sees the light, won't you?' He sneezed. 'Oh, look, a squirrel!' And he was off.

Titch and I did have a few discussions about ageing. We didn't exactly call it that, but I'd noticed that his hearing wasn't as good as it had been. Having barked, very loudly, several times, during which time he got quite tetchy, he retorted that I was as deaf as a tree, too.

That quite upset me.

Then we both calmed down and chased a rabbit. Well, if you can chase a rabbit slowly. It got away and we came back, panting, and I said, 'you know, I can't see like I used to.'

'I know,' he barked. 'It's frustrating, isn't it? I would have got that pesky bunny last year and now I just didn't see it.' He sighed. 'We're slower, Moll. We can't run like we used to.'

I yipped in reply. 'I hate getting older. Most of the time I'm fine. I mean, we can both still do long walks...'

'But it takes longer to recover,' he finished, and looked at me. 'Though you'll always be the same to me, Moll.'

My whiskers quivered. I loved it when he was romantic. 'You don't look a day older than when we first met,' I replied, and that warm sweet smell of love came wafting over like a summer breeze.

We lay on the ground, side by side, nose to nose, warming our bones in the sunshine, and I thought, when you're with the one you love, who cares about getting older?

The next morning we met Ruth, who lived round the corner with Ernie. He was a Border Terrier and a bit younger than me but rather a wuss, bless him. This time they had this very nervy dog with them who barked weirdly.

'This is Lainy,' said Ruth. 'She's a rescue from Romania.' She had to shout because Lainy was barking so frantically. Her ears were flat on her head and her tail was down. She was one unhappy dog.

Ernie looked at me and his whiskers shook. I could see Lainy was driving him barking and I wasn't surprised.

'I'm trying to find a foster home for her,' Ruth said. 'She had one but it didn't work out. If you hear of anyone, do let me know, won't you?'

'Of course,' said Suki.

'Poor girl,' Ruth said, looking down at her. 'I hope she finds a good home. She was rescued from the streets of Romania.'

Streets? I looked around me. I knew these streets like the back of my paws but I wouldn't want to live on them.

'She was found wandering around with no mother or father, and she'd lost her siblings, too,' Ruth continued.

No family? A shiver ran down my spine. I don't often think of my family, but at least I had one. Just imagine losing them so young. No wonder she barked funny and was in such a state. I'd thought she was a jumped-up young girl, but this brought another side to it all.

'She was taken to a kill shelter,' Ruth said, and her voice shook.

A kill shelter? My whiskers shook. Kill? As in...

'Yes, she would have been put to sleep, Moll,' Ruth said. 'Can you imagine it? But a charity brought her over here and she went to live with a family in Redruth.' She sighed. 'But they didn't know how to treat her and she got really scared, so it didn't work out, poor thing.'

I growled.

'That's just terrible,' said Suki, and sympathy shook out of every pore. 'The things some people put dogs through. Poor defenceless girl.'

'And because she was so frightened, she started nipping them, apparently.'

Hah! Good girl. Just what I would have done. I began to warm to her.

'And they said they didn't want her.'

Didn't want her? Ernie and I looked at each other, scandalised. I mean, Suki had her faults, but she would never not want me. Would she? I looked up at her, and shook from the tips of my ears, right down my spine.

'Poor darling girl,' said Suki. Lainy had, thankfully, stopped barking, though she was pulling and tugging at her lead, clearly desperate to run away. We couldn't understand her though; she barked funny.

'So that's why it's so important she gets the right home,' Ruth said. 'She's been through so much, poor girl.'

'I'll put the word out,' said Suki. Sensibly she didn't try to approach Lainy. I think she might have barked herself horse. 'Best of luck, Lainy.'

We watched Ruth and the others trot down the street, Lainy a bit quieter, but with her tail whirring around as if she were about to take off. It made me realise just how lucky I was to have a loving owner who would, I knew, do anything for me.

For the rest of the day, Lainy's plight stayed with me and almost put me off my food. I resolved I would bark to whoever I met to help her find a good home.

A few weeks later, we got back from a walk to find Ted sitting in his car outside the house.

'What are you doing there?' she said, opening the driver door. 'Why didn't you go in?' She stopped, at the same time as I smelt him. Oh no. 'Is it, have you...?'

He nodded, and the smell was overpoweringly acrid. Layer upon layer of illness and fear and misery. 'It's back,' he said, his head tilting forwards till it touched the steering wheel.

She bit her lip and I could almost hear the despair whizzing round in her head. But she was always calm in these situations, so she put her arm around his shoulders. 'Come in,' she said.

We all went into the house and he sat down while she made them tea and sat on the sofa with him. She smelt of smothered dread: like a decaying rat I came across one day. I can't begin to tell you the mixture of smells but none of them were good. This was dismay mixed with fear and I sensed she was looking into the future and seeing a black hole. Come on, I thought. We've got to do something!

As they sat there, she said, 'I think it would be a good idea for you to see a specialist. Not the consultant at Truro, but someone who specialises in heart problems.'

He nodded. Already he had shrunk to a smaller man. I know most humans can't see spirits, but we can, and his was diminishing before us. It's the sort of thing to give you bad dreams for a very long time.

'I heard a piece on Radio Four about someone the other day. Hang on.' She got out her phone and started pressing buttons. 'Ah, here he is. He's in London.'

'London?' he raised his head. 'That's a long way.'

Oh for god's sake, Ted, I thought. Just get on the bloody train and go and see this guy.

'You can get the sleeper,' she said; she really could understand me now. 'Or you could stay with that friend you were talking to the other day. He'd said he'd always put you up. Here,' she handed her phone over. 'Have a look. He's the guy to see. You just have to get a referral from your GP.'

There was silence while he read, his lips moving slightly as he did so. Then he handed the phone back and kissed her. 'What would I do without you?' he asked. 'You're quite right. He's the expert. Thank you, darling. At last I feel there's hope.'

She smiled and kissed him back and they cuddled for a while. But despite their togetherness, I had a sense that something was changing.

The next morning she woke up early. She crept out of bed to go to the bathroom and instead of getting back into bed, she made some tea and got a blanket and we sat on the sofa and watched the sun come up. She smelt different. As if she'd had a drink with honey in. Honey is the stuff of hope, and brings about strength and change. I did hope it was honey.

'I had the strangest dream, Moll,' she said. 'It was about you and me and Pip and how much we loved each other.' She sighed and gave me a hug. 'And it made me think how much easier our life was without all these problems. You know, wives who are ill and me not being acknowledged, and all that stuff. Anyway, at the end of the dream, Pip gave us a big cuddle and said, "Remember, darling, you have to fight your own corner."' She sighed. 'Remember how he always said that? "Fight your own corner, Suki."' She gave a wobbly laugh, and I could smell the acidity of sadness, but also the love that we shared which was as strong and sweet and solid as an oak tree.

I nudged her with my nose. Go on.

'It was so lovely to be surrounded by his love. It was so *sturdy*. So different to how things are with Ted. And it got me thinking that I want more than what we have now. I really do.' She sipped her tea and sat back. 'So, I know what to do, Moll. I'm just not quite sure how to do it.'

Well, this was encouraging. I licked her hand, just to remind her I was on her side.

'I don't doubt how much Ted loves us, but all this is starting to gnaw away at me,' she whispered. 'I need to think about how to do it. The best way. You know.'

I nudged her again. Of course I knew. I could smell her fear and wonder and trepidation, sitting there like the ingredients of a casserole. 'But I'm going to do it,' she whispered. 'I am, I promise.'

31

Referral

After that, things happened very quickly. First of all, on the morning that Ted went off to his GP to get a referral (whatever that was), we bumped into Ruth and Ernie again.

'Hello, Ernie,' Suki said. 'How's Lainy?'

'She's found a lovely new home near St Austell,' Ruth said. I could smell sadness, relief and love coming from her. It smelt like the stir fry Suki had eaten last night. She threw a lot of strange things together that smelt weird, but she said it worked out all right. 'I would have adopted her myself, but Lainy's rather too high energy for Ernie, and she chases my elderly cat.' She smiled lopsidedly. 'I do miss her though. She's a really lovely dog. So affectionate.'

'Oh well, it's great that she's got a new home,' Suki said. 'It's so sad when you meet these dogs who've had such a rough start, and then people are too ignorant to treat them the way they need. I'm really pleased for Lainy. I do hope it works out for her.'

They chatted a bit more, but I wasn't really listening. In the back of my mind I registered a faint disappointment. A plan that I didn't know I'd been forming had just fallen through.

A few days later, we had a walk with Tess and Titch.

'You look terrible, Suki,' she said and wrapped her in a huge, Tess-type hug.

'Thanks,' said Suki, a muffled voice from the depths of Tess's arms. She came up for air and smiled. 'I can always rely on you to make me feel better!'

'Come on, what's happened?'

As we walked along, me and Titch having a leisurely sniff and wee, Suki told Tess the latest news. 'Ted's got an appointment next week with this guy in London who specialises in heart stuff, and he's going to stay with a friend up there. See if he can get some other help.'

'Like what?'

'They can do this thing where they jump start your heart.'

Tess looked even paler than Suki. 'My God,' she breathed. 'Poor Ted. Doing that to your *heart*! What if he doesn't wake up?'

Suki shivered. 'I did look into that, but it's never happened. It's all very carefully controlled.'

Tess paused and I could smell her indecision. Like black peppercorns. Sour and sweet together. 'Do I get the feeling that you might be moving on?'

Suki bit her lip. Nodded. She told Tess about the dream, about Pip. 'I feel that Ted and I have run our course,' she said sadly. 'I still love him, so much, but – oh, Tess, I can't do this any longer. It's tearing me apart. And it was hearing Pip saying I must fight my corner..'

'Oh, dear of him. Such good advice.'

'Yes! And I've been feeling so lost and helpless and frightened and *stuck*. And I hate feeling stuck. So I think I need some time on my own. Because after Pip died I got involved with Ted, and then with Luke, and now I feel I need to be me. Or at least discover who me is.'

Tess gave her another big hug. 'That is the best news I've heard for ages.' She smiled. 'Don't get me wrong. I really like Ted and you two are so good together. You know, when you two are in a room full of people, it's as if no one else exists. You're so in tune. But he's got so much baggage. And it's not going to go away, and it drags you down, and I hate that.' She paused. 'Have you told him?'

Suki looked down. 'Er, no. That's what I'm working on.'

That evening Ted came to our house on the way home: he was getting the train up to London to see this special doctor, stay a few days with his old friend and he would then go and see Jane and her parents.

'Let me know how you get on,' Suki said, giving him a kiss on the cheek.

'Of course I will.' He looked down at her, opened his mouth and shut it again. 'This isn't fair on you,' he said.

She shook her head. 'No, Ted, it's not. But also, it's not fair on you or Jane or Jane's family.' She looked down and I could smell distress pouring off her like a polluted river.

There was a long silence, then Ted said, 'So this is it?' His voice shook.

She looked up at him and nodded. 'We've said it all before, haven't we? It's not because I don't love you, you know that. I love you so, so much. But I just can't do it any more.' By this time tears were pouring down her cheeks, splashing onto the floor.

Ted didn't say anything. I don't think he could. Gently he wiped her tears away, then held her tight, for a long time. Finally he pulled back. 'Any time you want me to ring, just text me and I'll ring you straight back. OK?' His voice was like an old frog.

She nodded and wiped her eyes. 'Of course. And let me know how you get on.'

'I will.' He looked away, as if he could hardly bear to look at her. He knelt down and stroked me, massaging my spine the way I loved it.

In that moment I forgave him everything. The hurt that he'd caused, albeit unintentionally, and all the unfortunate circumstances of his life which meant that we couldn't be together as we deserved to be. 'We'll always be friends, won't we, Moll?' he whispered, in a voice that sounded as if he was being strangled. I could smell so much love and confusion, sandwiched in between layers of ice-cold fear. I'm guessing it was fear of the doctor, fear about his heart, fear of losing us, fear of Jane's condition. He had so many things to be frightened of, and the worst thing was, they were all out of his control.

I licked his hand as hard as I could, tasting all that bitter fear and trying to take it from him. Give him courage. Make him realise that he could get through this. And I think he knew, for although his tears splashed onto my fur, he whispered, 'Thanks, Moll. You're one in a million. You and your missis.'

Very slowly he got up, as if he'd aged a hundred years, and all his bones ached, and he looked at Suki. 'I'm going now,' he said. 'Best of luck with everything, my darling. Keep in touch, won't you?'

She nodded. I could smell how choked up she was; the smell was overpowering. But suddenly there was this barrier between them, as if neither could bear to touch the other.

He turned, opened the front door and disappeared. We heard his footsteps going down the path, then down the street, clip clop, clip clop, and then she cried, 'Oh, Moll. What have I DONE?'

32

Joe

As I expected, Suki was in shock after that. She cried and cried, curling herself up on our bed like a snail. I lay beside her, and after a few days the crying lessened, though she still smelt like rancid cheese.

Gradually she talked to Tess, so Titch and I were able to meet up, and Petroc, and after a while she started working on another book. Though that brought about another burst of crying. 'We've always done walks with him,' she said, as tears splashed onto her keyboard. 'I mean, other friends as well, but it was always more of an adventure with *him*. Oh, Moll...'

But over the next weeks and months, it was interesting to see how she changed. It was like watching someone try and walk on icy ground (something I'd never managed). They slipped and slid, lost their balance and fell over. If they were lucky, they got up again and finally reached a bit of dry ground. There they could start walking again, placing one paw in front of the other in a more confident way.

She went through the slippy-slidey phase and it was a great relief when she reached higher ground.

S L ROSEWARNE

Months later, when she had her feet more firmly on dry ground, she said to me, 'I still miss Ted with every bit of my body, but I'm starting to feel whole again.' She sighed. 'It's like having had a really bad illness, and beginning to recover.'

My whiskers twitched; I think she'd forgotten her hysterectomy.

'I'm so glad for everything we had, but it had begun to go really wrong. And it's always better to finish things before they get any worse. Don't you think, Moll?'

I barked and licked her hand. I hadn't had that experience, of course: I'd been lucky with Pip and her. But I could smell where she was coming from.

'Are you and Ted in touch?' asked Tess one day.

Suki shook her head. 'No. He asked if we could, but I thought it'd be too upsetting. He did send a few texts just to say what had happened with the consultant. He had a cardioversion which worked, so he was feeling a lot better. But I didn't want to get into a dialogue or it would stir things up again. It's better just to keep him sort of, out there.'

Tess nodded. 'Quite right. Well done Suki. You're a brave woman.'

I snuggled closer, licking her hand to reassure her. She still tasted of herself, just a bit saltier.

A few weeks later, she was working at home when there was a ping from her computer as a message came in. She peered at it. 'Oh, a request via my website for some books.' She read it through and leaned back, a smile breaking through. 'Well, that's cheering. Somebody wants to buy a set of signed books for his mother for her birthday. He's in Penzance.' She typed a reply and sat back. 'He said he could have got some from the Edge of the World bookshop in Penzance, but he wants them signed specially for her. Anyway, it's nice knowing that people still want to buy them.' She turned round and smiled at me and I felt a warm glow. 'That's made me feel much better!'

There was another ping and she sat back. 'That was quick.' She giggled. What a lovely sound. Like cold water running over sun-baked stones. 'He's got a good sense of humour, Moll.' She laughed again as she read his message. 'Oh, OK. He said he would come and pick them up, but he's got to go and see his sister who's in hospital so he won't be here for a week. Can I post them if he sends me the money first? Of course I can.'

She sent off another email at high speed. 'Right, better wrap those books up, Moll, and get them in the post.' She turned round. 'And then we'll go for a walk, eh?'

The next day something happened that got me thinking. Ever since Pip died, my mission had been to look after Suki. I'd never been one to plan ahead much. Our ethos was always to live in the moment, but occasionally something threw you off your walk.

Suki and I were out having a good sniff, as per normal, when suddenly a pain seared through my belly. It quite put me off my stride which, admittedly, had decreased in recent years. (I was 105 now.) I had to limp home and take it easy for a few days which, at my age, might be expected.

I'd never worried about my health. Admittedly my sight had worsened over the last few years, as had my hearing, and I had what was known as a heart murmur, but daily pills sorted that out. But this pain was so sudden that it quite took my breath away. I heard Suki ringing the vet in a panic, who advised rest.

Luckily the pain didn't return, but it made me realise I should plan for the future. Not mine. I knew that lay in the hands of the Great Provider, and I knew She would look after me. But Suki's. Humans were so bad at planning. I needed someone to Carry The Bone.

A few days later, when I was able to resume normal activity, I stopped at a popular wall near my street which is like a noticeboard. All urgent or exciting messages are noted here.

There was one from Ernie, Ruth's brindled terrier round the corner. "Lainy's back," it read. "Foreigner. Rescued. Needs a home urgently."

I balanced carefully on one leg, sprayed a message in reply. *Poor girl. Another home gone wrong? Get in touch asap I have an idea.*

And as we walked back, who should we meet but Ernie and Ruth, with Lainy, her extraordinary tail curled over her back like a banner. This time she was barking at a seagull.

"You remember Lainy," said Ernie, with a twitch of his upper lip.

Lainy was getting on his whiskers again, I could see. She was still panting, rolling her eyes, demanding attention. Her ears were flat against her head, her tail down one minute, up the next. Poor Ernie.

'Sadly her last home didn't work out,' Ruth said and her voice dropped. 'The lady who adopted Lainy has got terminal cancer, so she can't look after Lainy any more.'

'I'm so sorry, how terrible,' Suki said. 'If I hear of anyone I'll let you know.'

'I'd really hoped this would be the right home for Lainy,' Ruth said, and she smelt almost as upset as Lainy was. 'She's had such bad luck, poor girl, and she's such a lovely dog, she deserves a really good home.'

Ernie sneezed and we went our separate ways. But it reminded me of my previous idea. I'd have to suss Lainy out, but she was around three or four, I would say. Fine nose, beautiful dark eyes with black liner around them. And that weird puffy tail. But for all her good looks and neurotic behaviour, I guessed there was more to Lainy than met the snout.

I sensed a fine intelligence. A willingness to trust, despite her bad luck in life so far. A deep affection. She would bond easily. By the way she was pawing Bridget, she was a dog who needed reassurance. But I suppose if she'd had a rough start in life, that made sense. Personally, I didn't go along with all that touchy feely nonsense. Pick me up and I'd nip you. Stroke me when I wasn't in the mood and I'd growl. Or bite. I mean, people have to know their boundaries.

But Lainy looked soft. She had huge dark eyes that looked directly at you. She would smother Suki in licks, I bet (which Suki would love). She would be easy to train. It gave me food for thought – and hope too. I trotted home and lay under the bed thinking how I might make this happen.

Life settled down as before, except that I became tired more easily. I had a few twinges in my gut, like before, though not as bad. My sight deteriorated a bit more and my hearing wasn't brilliant. I told Titch, but he said, 'What?' and sniffed me so that our whiskers tickled. Then he said, 'I love you anyway, Moll, never doubt that'. So I stopped worrying.

We dogs rely on our senses so much more than humans. Losing a bit of sight is neither here nor there when you've got your nose, your whiskers and ears and so on. No, my philosophy was to enjoy life while I could. Why humans didn't do the same thing was beyond me; they were always worrying about stuff that was never going to happen.

Suki was busy with work, seeing her friends and singing, going to the pub, cinema; all the stuff that she usually did. She smelt much calmer; like honeysuckle in a warm breeze. She had begun to smell of strength again, and optimism. And part of this, I think, was due to a flicker of interest that came through her computer.

The fellow who had asked to buy some of her books for his mother emailed most days. She didn't read them out to me any more, but she laughed, and her eyes sparkled when she read them. That was enough for me.

It was obvious that she was better able to cope with life now. She didn't need a man to be happy: she was too independent for that. But ideally I wanted her to have someone to add joy to her life, not complications. This fellow might not be the answer, but if he could be a friend and make her feel good, that was enough.

Next time we bumped into Ernie, Lainy wasn't there. 'She's gone to someone in Mylor,' Ruth told Suki. 'They wanted to adopt her but she chased their cat, she's frightened of their son and not too keen on the husband. She nipped their ankles. So she's still looking for a home.'

I snorted. So this girl had attitude! I liked it! We all needed a bit of feistiness. She would do well as The Bone Carrier. I peed on the wall, slowly and at length, so Ernie could take in what I was saying. *I've got just the right home for Lainy.*

Ernie sniffed hard, looked at me and raised his eyebrows. I nodded. His whiskers twitched, but he didn't reply. But tears filled his eyes, bless him. *No, it's all right* I barked, *but I'll need your help.*

Just tell me what to do. Thank god Ernie barked in English. These foreigners were tricky to understand.

One day, Suki smelt nervous, like rust. She couldn't sit still, and anxiety wafted over in sour gusts. She flicked through her wardrobe, pulled out a purple hoodie and held it up to her face. 'This will do.' She bent and patted me. 'What do you think, Moll? Shall we go and have a walk with Joe?'

Ah; the email man! I roused myself. She knew I couldn't walk very far these days, but I was interested to meet this man. I'd know by his smell whether he was any good for her.

Tess rang just before we left. 'How do you know this bloke isn't a Nigerian scamster?'

'Joe Lambert doesn't sound very Nigerian.'

'No. Well, that's a relief. Have you looked him up online?'

She nodded. 'Yes. He took part in a marathon a few years ago in aid of some charity, and he's part of the gig rowing team in Newlyn.'

'Good. So he must be fit. Now, take your phone with you – make sure it's charged, won't you? Where are you meeting?'

'At Trelissick, in the car park. He's given me his registration number.'

'Good. OK, well, drive round and have a peek. Then, if you don't like the look of him, you can just drive away.'

'I couldn't do that! It's rude.'

'Well, you could send him a message, say you'd had a fatal accident or something.'

Suki laughed. 'I don't think so. Look, I'm sure I'll be absolutely fine. But I promise I'll text you if there's a problem.'

'You'll need a code word. How about Titch?'

I could see Suki smiling. 'OK. Any problems, I'll text you Titch and you can ring me. Happy?'

'Yes.' Big sigh. 'Well, have a good time. Just be careful.'

'Will do. Now, we've got to go, or I'll be late.' She blew a kiss down the phone and I jumped off the bed. An adventure always made me feel better.

As we drove, Suki talked to me, in between singing along to the radio. 'Yes, I am a bit nervous, Moll, but his emails make me laugh so why not meet up? I just want a friend, nothing more. Someone to go walking with. Have a laugh with, that sort of thing. Nothing heavy.'

She looked round anxiously as we drove into the car park. 'Oh well, here we are. Now, we're looking for a red van. Oh, there it is, and he, well, he looks OK.' She drove past, parked and looked at me. 'Ready, Moll?'

I barked yes, she put my lead on and I stuck my nose out, sniffed hard. Too many smells, all coinciding. And then, a strong, calm smell. Like pine wood.

'Suki?' said a deep voice.

She looked round. 'Oh, Joe?'

A tall man with dark hair laughed and held out his hand, which she shook. 'That's me.' He looked down at me and I sniffed again – he wore jeans that smelt of metal and fresh air. I could smell the remains of a cheese sandwich. Washing powder. So far so good.

'And this is Moll? Would she like a treat?'

'Yes,' Suki paused. She didn't usually let strangers give me a treat, but this was slightly different. 'She'd love a treat. Do you have a dog, Joe?'

'I lost her six months ago.' He paused and bent down to give me some gravy bone biscuits. I could see his dark eyes, framed by creases. I could hear the love for his dog in his cracked voice, could smell his deep loss. 'I'll have another one but I'm just, in between.' His voice was slightly higher than Pip's, or Ted's. It was almost musical. Pleasant to listen to. I liked his smell. And his treats.

'I'm so sorry,' she said. 'Shall we go this way?'

As they walked along I kept close. I wanted to listen to the conversation, work out how I felt about this man. Part of me was thinking, third-time lucky? Yet at the same time I felt she needed time to be on her own for a while.

They talked about what they did. He had his own business as a plumber, so he travelled round Cornwall a lot. His mum was a keen walker, and so was he when he had time, but work was really busy at the moment.

They stopped for coffee at the end of the walk, which he insisted on buying. They shared a piece of flapjack and he asked if he could give me a bit too; good man. I dozed at her feet, listening to their voices, which was like a piece of music – his lower tones mingling with her higher ones. Her soprano laugh. His tenor one. It was pleasant, and I must have drifted off, as I woke to Suki saying, 'Well, thanks so much, Joe. I've really enjoyed meeting you.'

'My pleasure.' He paused. 'Shall we do this again?' He sounded a bit unsure.

'Yes, I'd love to. When are you free?'

'As I said, work's pretty busy but I can usually fit a walk in after about 5pm.'

'OK. I'll remember that.' She looked up. 'It would be good to have you as a friend, but I'm not in the right space for anything else at the moment.'

'That suits me perfectly,' he said. 'Friends make the world do round, don't they?' And he glanced at his watch. 'Sorry, got to go. I've got another job at 5. Bye, Suki! Bye, Moll!' And, giving a cheery wave, he hurried out of the cafe with long strides, towards the car park.

'Well,' she said, looking down at me. 'What do you think, Moll?'

I barked. He was OK. Too early for anything else, but a steady male friend was just what she needed. He smelt trustworthy, that was the main thing. No Other Woman smells, no cat smells, no Angst or Poorly smells. So far, so good.

She smiled. 'I think so too. A decent male friend, with no complications. That's what we need.' She stood up. 'Come on darling, let's go home and get your tea.' She glanced down as her phone buzzed. 'Oh it's Petroc. Do you mind if we stop off there quickly on the way home?'

I didn't mind. Although it was time for my tea, I always enjoyed visits to Petroc: the treats were good and he had a soul full of wisdom. We had a lot in common.

Petroc's kitchen was warm, as usual, and full of glass bottles which burbled and burped along long, snaky tubes. 'I'm making rice and raisin wine!' he said with a smile as we came in. Usually wine smelt sour, but this just smelt yeasty.

'Good for you,' said Suki, as we looked at the cloudy liquid belching in its containers. 'When will it be ready to drink?'

'Not for several months,' he said. 'But I have a nice elderflower wine that will be ready very soon if you'd like to sample that one evening?'

'I'd be delighted, Petroc, thank you.' Suki smiled and sat down while she watched him with his bottles. 'Everything all right with you?'

'Very well, thank you,' he said. 'How about you?'

'OK, thanks,' she said. 'In fact, I've just been for a non-date.'

'And what is that?'

'I had a walk with a man just as a friend. I've decided I don't want any involvements at the moment, but male friends are a very good thing.'

'I'm delighted, my dear. Is this the fellow who contacted you about books for his mother?'

'That's him. You have got a good memory!' Suki smiled and stretched her legs out towards the Raeburn. 'We've been emailing most days and he really cheers me up. Neither of us wants a relationship just now, but it's really good to be friends, don't you think? Men have a different perspective on things, I find. That's one of the things I really missed after Pip died. Male company.'

Petroc nodded. 'That's how I felt when my wife died; except of course it was female company I missed. So I quite understand. What was this fellow like in the flesh?'

Suki smiled. 'He's about five ten I would think, with black hair and dark crinkly eyes. He has a nice smile and we both like walking and dogs. He's a very busy plumber, but he's up for another walk, and so am I.'

'Good,' Petroc said, nodding thoughtfully. 'Suki, remember that when you do have another relationship, it's unlikely you'll have the same rapport you had with Ted.'

Suki bit her lip. 'No, I suppose not.'

What a shame, we were thinking. What a waste. But none of us said anything.

'But that's no bad thing,' Petroc continued. 'That level of intensity can be quite draining.'

She smiled, rather weakly. I nudged her with my nose, for comfort. 'It certainly can. The thought of having a less intense relationship sounds a lot more restful.'

'And also, that there is no compulsion to live together. After all, my partner and I are very happy living apart. In fact, I think it's healthier. We both have our space, so we don't get on top of each other. Except when we want to,' he added with a twinkle in his eye that made Suki blush.

'No, you're right,' she said.

'You will never replace Pip, or Ted. Their strong memories will live on, and be part of your life. But you will have new experiences, with new men. And they will be just as important; just different.'

She nodded. 'Thank you, Petroc.' She got up and kissed him on the cheek. 'That was good to hear. I feel better for that, and I think you're quite right. Now excuse me, but I think we'd better go as this one needs her tea. Shall we meet next week for supper and Scrabble?'

'Certainly. How about Tuesday?'

'Perfect.' She gave him another kiss and we departed. But on the way home, and lying beside her in bed that night, I wondered – had I got things wrong?

I'd promised Pip that I'd look after Suki, make sure she was happy. I'd done my best, but I'd assumed that he meant find her another man. Well, I'd done that, but neither of them were quite right, for varying reasons.

Suki seemed happy enough at the moment. She had me, of course, her books were coming along, and her research work was picking up. She was surrounded by people who loved her – me, of course, Tess and my darling Titch, Anne, Petroc and all her other friends, and now, maybe, Joe. Did she really need anyone else?

I had a feeling she didn't.

33

The rescue

The following day we spent a lovely afternoon on the beach, swimming, lying on the sand and I cadged delicious treats off Suki's friends. We were walking back up through the woods afterwards when suddenly I felt that pain again. It slowed me right down.

The next morning I knew I had to leave a message for Ernie, so I peed on all the walls between our houses, on the postbox by the shop, on the walls near the Beacon – all our regular spots. *Need help with plan please contact ASAP.*

I went out every morning after that, but there was still no sign of Ernie. I'd felt so confident that he could help and without him there was nothing I could do. I cursed, barked and growled. Quietly, because Suki was worried enough.

And then, just when I was about to give up hope, I read a message from Ernie on the adjacent wall. *Sorry for delay we were camping. Of course will help. Please send instructions.*

With a burst of energy I sprayed his instructions onto the wall and headed home. I needed a rest but at least Ernie knew what to do. I could relax a little, knowing that he would help carry out my plan.

Sure enough, later that day, Suki came in and said, 'I've just had a phone call from Ruth about that dog, Lainy. She asked if I'd have a walk with them and see if we might take her on. What do you think, Moll?'

I nudged her with my nose. Yes, go for it.

She stroked me, ever so gently, and said, 'Poor darling, you're not yourself, are you? But you think it's a good idea to walk Lainy, do you?' I yipped and she smiled, gently pulled my ears. 'In that case, I'll go and see what she's like. Report back. Have a good sleep, darling.'

The relief! From what I had gathered about Lainy, she had a certain innate charm. I didn't think she'd be easy – she was too insecure for that – but I had a feeling that she and Suki would get on. Would my matchmaking be third time lucky?

Over the next few weeks, Suki met Lainy for several walks and brought her back to the flat to have a sniff around. She was so nervy I had severe doubts at first. But I calmed her down a bit, then told her my plan, and Lainy's dark brown eyes grew wider and wider.

'You mean, a real home?' she yipped in awed tones.

I nodded. 'You won't get a better home, or a better owner.' Lainy looked doubtful, so I continued, 'Suki's kind and loving and you'll get plenty of walks and food. And cuddles,' I added.

'Cuddles? Really?' Lainy's ears shot straight up, like a cartoon dog.

I nodded. 'Yes. Suki is very special. So she needs looking after.'

'Looking after...' I could see the idea was alien to Lainy. 'You mean, live here, and look after her... forever?'

My whiskers twitched yes.

She sat, head on one side while she pondered this. 'You mean, rescue her?'

I suppressed a smile. I'd heard humans talking about dogs who'd been rescued, but we all knew that in fact we rescued them. 'Yes, that's it.'

Lainy's ears shot up again. 'But I not know what to do. You tell me?' She said in her Romanian accent.

'Of course. I'm not going anywhere just yet.'

Lainy looked at me with her head on one side. Intelligence shone from her dark eyes. 'How long will you be here for?'

She was quick that one; she'd evidently seen souls departing. 'I'm not sure,' I said. It was always best to be honest. 'But hopefully a while yet. I don't plan on going anywhere till you're well settled in, don't worry. And Ernie will always help you. Even after I've gone, you can talk to me every night from under the bed. I'll always be here.'

'Yes!' Lainy bounced round the room, snickering, 'a real home!'

Watching her made me tired, but at least now we'd barked, I had a strong sense that this could work out.

I started improving; no more signs of that horrible pain, and got my strength back, and gradually relaxed, knowing that my time wasn't being cut short as I'd feared. I'd planned a few more years with my Titch, to say nothing of my lovely Suki. We had so much to do! Books to write, walks to do, people to meet, food to eat. OK, she wrote the books and articles and gave the talks, but I led the way. Her lack of any sense of direction was astounding.

I'd seen her through many upheavals, including death, major surgery, breakups and near redundancy. I didn't want to go just yet! But at least if my plans for Lainy went ahead, whatever happened, Suki would be looked after and loved for many years to come.

And talking of love, there was my Titch. He and Tess came round, and he looked downcast, his tail and whiskers drooping. 'You not well, my darling?' he whimpered.

I gave him a lick in which I tried to express all my love and longing for him. 'I'm getting better by the moment,' I replied. 'Never be downhearted. We have plenty more joyous times to come. But always remember, when this world is over we've got the next one to look forward to. We will meet there, and have even better times, my Titch.'

'You really believe that?' His eyes filled up, dear of him.

'Of course I do,' I yipped. 'In the rainbow place there are no aches or pains, only endless rabbits and squirrels, Pip and Ted and lovely treats.'

'Really?' He cheered a little. 'In that case, I can't wait.' His ears drooped again. 'But you won't leave me just yet, will you, Moll?'

'Of course not,' I said. 'Now take your Tess home, because I'm feeling rather tired. I'll see you in a few days. And promise me you'll keep an eye on Lainy.'

'Lainy? Who's she?'

'She's going to come and live with me and Suki. You might like her. Get to know her a bit, anyway. She's a pretty girl.'

How easily men are distracted! Sure enough, I could see he was already curious about this new woman. But for now we touched noses and arranged to meet soon, when I was sure I'd be a lot better.

Later that day, Suki came back and lay down on the bed next to me. 'Would you mind if Lainy came for another visit, darling?' she asked. 'I'm not sure if she's right to live with us, but if we see a bit more of her, we can make our minds up. Would that be OK?'

I barked and nudged her with my nose. Of course it was; I'd already decided!

So the next day Lainy arrived for another visit, all twirling tail, flattened ears and high pitched yipping. I barked firmly to put her in her place, and after a few minutes she calmed, lay down beside me and listened. She took in everything I said, looked around and went and jumped on Suki's lap, just as I'd instructed.

Suki was delighted, laughed and hugged her and said, 'Did you see that, Moll?' Lainy gazed at her adoringly, licked her face, then, on seeing my expression, jumped down again. She came across to me, lay down and raised one eyebrow. I nodded, fractionally. My plan was working out.

That evening, as I dozed fitfully, I thought back over my life so far. Of coming to live with Pip and Suki, and what a joyous time we'd had. He always smelt so kind and gentle, for such a big man. The beery smell was part of him: strong but loving. I could tell by the way he stroked me that he loved us both with every ounce of his soul.

He was a real pushover of course. 'Hopeless about discipline,' Suki would moan with a grin. But that was part of his beery charm. I loved lying on his knitted cardigan for a kip after lunch: it was like lying in a patch of autumn sunlight. Like a dog, he understood stillness and patience. And I loved his bursts of laughter, like the rattle of a biscuit tin.

But his decline took a long time and smelt horrible. When I saw his spirit leave, I felt the sharpness of Suki's pain and sorrow, mixed with the warm relief on her skin. I remembered walking down to Greenbank beach at dusk, when she said, "Weren't we lucky to have him?"

We were lucky. And at least I still had her.

Then there was Ted. Another kind and clever man but not without his troubles. We had such games, such adventures. Holidays, reviews, so many walks for so many books. Visits to the pub and lots of cheese and onion crisps. Sometimes he lost his bark, and smelt of anxiety and despair: rank and sharp. But most of the time, we helped him get it back.

They said goodbye so many times. Long days, weeks, months, blotted by tears. There was such a strong current between those two: it was clear how much they truly loved each other. I only hoped it wouldn't get in the way of her becoming happy with someone else.

Then there was kind Luke. I remembered smelling that sour fear on him when he first saw me. But gradually I taught him that dogs weren't dangerous. We were kind and loving and loyal. I would have let him sleep in our bed if he'd wanted. I hoped he would be happy with Jim, whom I would very much like to meet.

And my Titch. What more could I say? My bouncy, irrepressible, Peter Pan of a Titch. My only dog love. If I happened to go before him, I knew that he'd be fine – he had his Tess and Paul and he was well loved in human terms. A bit spoilt but much loved.

Then I thought of Suki's work, which had become more important now she was a Proper Author. I remembered the very first walk we did for the magazine, that hot July day. Suki kept writing notes and it took forever, when I just wanted a good run and lots of sniffs. But after a few more walks, she got the hang of it, and then, the articles! The books! I'm not being boastful in saying I must be the most famous dog in Cornwall.

I was so pleased that my plan for Lainy was working out. I suspected this would be a complex ride; after all, the poor girl had had a fearful start in life. I heard she'd nipped lots of ankles and bitten the postman. It would be a steep learning curve, but I sensed it would be worth it in the long run. There was a loyal, loving dog underneath all the insecurities, and I sensed she would bond quickly with Suki.

I knew, now, that I had nothing to be afraid of. My plans were working out (crossed paws), and when my time finally came, I would see my darling Pip. I would jump around and lie on his tummy again for a snooze. There would be endless cheese and onion crisps, and badger poo, and all kinds of new, and old people and dogs to catch up with.

Suki stroked me and her soft, gentle voice was just what I needed. 'I'm going to have another walk with Joe next week, darling,' she said, stroking my ears. 'I'll introduce him to Lainy. I think it's about time, don't you?'

I inhaled Suki's familiar scent; her sweet kindness and generosity. I could still smell Lainy's sharper, unsure scent, from earlier. She'd lain beside me, perfectly still, but I saw she was taking everything in. She'd blinked, slowly, to say, 'It's OK. I've got her,' so I knew I could relax now, confident that I had done my best. Suki had a full and active life, with more books to come, and a good male friend in the form of Joe, of that I was sure. What happened in the future was up to them.

I had my own plans, of course, for as long as I had left of this life; seeing more of Titch, enjoying our walks and more books. And now, knowing that Lainy and I were going to rescue Suki together gave me great joy and satisfaction. My whiskers twitched, my tail gave a wag and my ears softened. What a plan! How clever I was! And most important of all, I had fulfilled my promise to Pip.

Acknowledgements

To Kerry Barrett, editor extraordinaire, for her enthusiasm and utter belief in this novel. Tammy Barrett, for her labour of love in finding such a good match to Moll, and being so patient explaining the many aspects of cover design. Alexa Whitten of The Book Refinery for her patience, typesetting and doing everything necessary to turn my manuscript into a real book.

Many thanks to everyone who accompanied me on the Moll and Pip journey: you know who you are. And to my readers – Shelagh Smith, Pauline Causey, Christina Lake, David and Jenny Dearlove, for their helpful feedback.

To Pauline, who said, with a glint in her eye, 'Moll should write this story.'

To Sheila Smith, who straight away said, 'Go for it, Girl!' – this book is for you and my other Shelagh Smith in Vermont, sister-in-law supreme.

Special thanks to my mum, Penny Rosewarne, who sadly died on 14th March 2022. She would have been so pleased and proud.

Of course, my special love and thanks to Moll – I miss you every day, darling girl. And to Lainy, the star of the sequel to this tale. Also to Ruth Collett, Bridget Woodman and Lynn Stonehouse, all part of my Dog Support Group. Lainy would not be in my life without them.

More thanks to Nicola Smith for her incredibly generous help and support – without your advice and help, this would never have got off the ground.

And last, but very definitely not least, my love and thanks to Malcolm, for your unwavering support, brilliant ideas, and for making me laugh when I least expect it.

About the author

S L Rosewarne lives in Cornwall with her rescue dog Lainy (who features at the end of The Rescue) and will have her own story in Lainy's Tail, which she is writing now.

Sue spends part of the week on the Lizard with her partner and his rescue dog, where they walk, cycle, swim and grow vegetables. When forced indoors he is addicted to shouting at politicians on the news, giving her the perfect excuse to sneak off and write.

When not writing, walking or training Lainy, Sue sings with The Suitcase Singers, and regularly gives talks to anyone who want to listen to her talking about her work. To her surprise, many have. She appeared on horseback in Fern Britton's My Cornwall in August 2021 talking about Cornish literary influences. The tricky bit was riding for the first time in forty years, but she managed to hang on, and talk at the same time.

Sue is also a freelance journalist, researcher and author of five Cornish literary themed walking books – Discover Cornwall, Walks in the Footsteps of Cornish Writers, Walks in the Footsteps of Poldark, Walks in the Footsteps of Daphne du Maurier and Walks in the Footsteps of Rosamunde Pilcher, all published by Sigma Press and available through her website www.suekittow.com.

Sue Kittow Author – Facebook @suekittow2016

Instagram @walks_cornish_author

Twitter – @floweringpot

Further info

Rescuing dogs

There are many charities who rescue dogs, especially in Cornwall, one of them being the National Animal Welfare Trust – www.nawt.org.uk/centres/cornwall. If you are considering giving a home to a dog, please make sure your circumstances and home are suitable. Young children, other dogs and cats may not be right for a dog who is distressed. Do plenty of research, ask advice and find a good animal behaviourist, like Ruth's Pet Behaviour Services.

Atrial Fibrillation

This is a very common heart condition, but left untreated can lead to stroke, heart failure and other heart-related problems. For more advice see the British Heart Foundation website – www.bhf.org.uk/informationsupport/conditions/atrial-fibrillation.

0300 330 3311 Monday to Friday, 9am to 5pm.

Printed in Great Britain
by Amazon